OUT OF THE AGES

OUT OF THE AGES

DEVEREUX PRYCE

Edited and with an introduction by
Gina R. Collia

Published by Nezu Press
Queensgate House,
48 Queen Street,
Exeter, Devon,
EX4 3SR,
United Kingdom.

This edition published 2025

Out of the Ages first published by Leonard Parsons, 1923.

ISBN-13: 978-1-917113-06-9

Cover: *Grand Portico of the Temple of Philæ*
by David Roberts RA, June 1856.

In the interest of preservation, the punctuation and spelling of the original first edition text have been maintained, and the original formatting has been used wherever possible. Only minor publisher errors and spelling inconsistencies have been silently corrected.

Sir Gerard Albert Muntz, 2nd Bt.

Gerard Albert Muntz: The Renowned Metallurgist Who Had Never Been to Egypt

by Gina R. Collia

Devereux Pryce was the pseudonym of Sir Gerard Albert Muntz, second Baronet Muntz, of Dunsmore, in the parish of Clifton-on-Dunsmore, co. Warwick. Gerard was born on 27 November 1864 in Leamington Spa, Warwickshire.[1] The fourth of eight children, he was the eldest son of Philip Albert Muntz (1839-1908) and Rosalie Muntz (1838-1919).[2] Gerard's parents were first cousins: his paternal grandfather, George Frederick Muntz (1794-1857), was the elder brother of his maternal grandfather, Philip Henry Muntz (1811-1888).

—The First Philip: Gerard's Great-Grandfather—

Gerard's great-grandfather, Philip Frederick Muntz (1752- 1811), was of Polish descent.[3] Born in Alsace, he relocated to England and settled in Birmingham in 1792.[4] On the advice of Matthew Bolton, Philip bought shares in Mynors & Robert Purden, merchants, and the firm became known as Muntz & Purden from that point on.[5] In March 1793, he married Robert Purden's daughter, Catherine (c. 1775-1861), and in November the following year the couple's first child, George Frederick—Gerard's paternal grandfather—was born.[6] At the time of George's birth, Philip and Catherine lived in a house situated at the corner of Newhall Street and Great Charles Street in Birmingham.[7] By the time their youngest child, Philip Henry—Gerard's maternal grandfather—was born, on 21 January 1811, they were residing at Selly Hall in Worcestershire,[8] and, in addition to the mercantile business in Great Charles Street,

Philip had set up P. F. Muntz and Co., 'rollers of copper and all sorts of metals', in Water Street.[9]

—George Frederick: Gerard's Paternal Grandfather—

Philip Frederick Muntz died in the summer of 1811, and George, at the young age of eighteen, took over management of both of the family businesses.[10] He dedicated a great deal of time and energy to the metal works, and in 1832 he patented 'Muntz's Metal', a metal alloy used in place of pure copper to sheath the hulls of ships, the manufacture of which made him a large fortune;[11] it was later used in the construction of the famous clipper ship *Cutty Sark*. From that point on, George left the running of the rolling mills and mercantile establishment to his younger brother, Philip Henry, and focused on the promotion and production of Muntz's Metal.[12]

In October 1818, George married Eliza Pryce (c. 1799-1873), the daughter of a clergyman.[13] They had nine children, the youngest of whom, Philip Albert—Gerard's father—was born on 5 January 1839.[14] George and Eliza lived first at Hockley Abbey, moving to Ley Hall (now Lea Hall) in Handsworth Wood in the 1840s.[15] In 1850, George took the lease of Umberslade Hall, near Tamworth-in-Arden in Warwickshire; the estate was later purchased by his son, also George Frederick, and the property remained in the family until it was sold in the 1960s.[16]

George was one of the founding members of the Birmingham Political Union 'of the Lower and Middle Classes of the People', which called for the extension of suffrage rights to all men who contributed to local and national taxation, and he was elected Liberal MP for Birmingham in 1840, retaining his seat until his death in 1857.[17] Apparently, George was 'the first civilian who wore a beard in the House of Commons', and most likely he would have been insulted for doing so.[18] But the Muntz men were keen on beards… beards, large families, and the name Philip—which did make researching their family history somewhat interesting.

—The Second Philip: Gerard's Maternal Grandfather—

Like his elder brother, George, Philip Henry wore a beard. He was active in local politics from a young age, and he was only twenty-six years old when he was appointed one of the committee which petitioned Queen Victoria for granting Birmingham a charter of incorporation in 1837. The petition was granted, and the charter of incorporation was received the following year. Philip was elected alderman on the city's first town council in 1838, and then mayor and magistrate in 1839, and he represented Birmingham as Liberal MP between 1868 and 1885.[19]

'Statesman No. 210: Mr. Philip Henry Muntz, M.P.' by Carlo Pellegrini, published in *Vanity Fair*, 7 August 1875.

As a young man, Philip Henry spent several years in Germany, where he met and married Wilhelmine Dolhofen (1810-1891); their wedding took place in June 1831, and they travelled to England together two years later.[20] Between the years 1832 and

Prince Albert's Visit to Birmingham, Muntz's Rolling Mills.
Illustrated London News, 9 December 1843.

1856 they had fourteen children—six sons and eight daughters—one of whom was Rosalie, Gerard's mother, who was born in 1838.[21]

On 29 November 1843, Prince Albert made a tour of several of Birmingham's manufacturing firms, and the Muntz rolling mills at Water Street received a royal visit. George being away at the time, Philip conducted the prince and his attendants around the premises. Prince Albert was shown the manufacturing process of Muntz's Metal, and, instead of carpeting, 'a quantity of the patent yellow metal, used for the sheathing of ships' bottoms… was laid down for his Royal Highness to walk over.'[22]

George Frederick Muntz died at Umberslade Hall on 30 July 1857.[23] When his will was published, it inspired a certain amount of strong criticism; some thought it unfair that it did not divide his property equally amongst family members, and it was noted that 'he did not leave a farthing to the Charities of the town of his birth—the town which had done so much for him, and for which he had always professed so much attachment.'[24] He had grown more egotistical during the last years of his life and was described as 'one of the vainest of men'; he 'thought himself *somebody*', and he would rage and fume 'if any newspaper dared to doubt the wisdom of any remark of his'.[25] Two years prior to his death, during a meeting of the Administrative Reform Association at Bingley Hall, the politician George Dawson remarked that the newspapers would not be able to print George Muntz's speech verbatim as 'no printing office in the world would have capital I's enough.'[26]

'Metal' (Philip Albert Muntz) by Sir Leslie Ward, published in *Vanity Fair*, 23 July 1892.

—The Third Philip: Gerard's Father—

Two years after George's death, on 8 June 1859, his son Philip Albert, then twenty years of age, married Philip Henry's daughter Rosalie, who was twenty-one years old.[27] By this time, the latter's family had settled at Edstone Hall, near Stratford-upon-Avon in

Warwickshire. Philip and Rosalie made their home at Thickthorn House, near Kenilworth in Warwickshire, and their first child, Frances Ethel, was born there in May the following year, followed by Vera Gertrude in 1862 and Nora Violet in 1863.[28] By the time their first son, Gerard Albert, was born in 1864 the family had moved to New House in Keresley.[29] After Gerard came Duncan Albert in 1867, Cecil Albert in 1870, Mildred Rosalie in 1872, and Norman Albert in 1876.[30] For the Muntz family, the name Albert had become almost as appealing as Philip by this time. Big beards, however, had already gone out of fashion.

—Gerard Albert Muntz—

Gerard was educated at Harrow, Neuwied-am-Rhein in Germany, and King's College London.[31] In 1883, at the age of eighteen, he began working in the family business, and he devoted himself to the metal industry from that point on. In the same year, his father, who had always been a Liberal, declared himself a Conservative.

Dunsmore House, c. 1905.

He was returned as one for North Warwickshire in 1884, then elected MP for Tamworth in 1885, a seat he held until his death in 1908.[32] Philip was a typical 'country gentleman', devoted to hunting, shooting, and all outdoor sports, all of which he enjoyed within the grounds surrounding recently-built Dunsmore House, the new family home situated in the village of Clifton-Upon-Dunsmore, near Rugby.[33]

Sir Philip Albert Muntz, 1st Bt. *Leamington Spa Courier*, 25 December1908.

Gerard's engagement to Katie Blanche Prinsep (1866-1951), eldest daughter of James Hunter Prinsep, late of the Bengal Civil Service, was announced in March 1893.[34] They married three months later, on 28 June, at St. Paul's Church in Knightsbridge.[35] Gerard's sister, Mildred, was one of four bridesmaids; she was his only surviving sister at that time, Frances, Vera, and Nora having died before the spring of 1890.[36] Gerard and Katie settled at Summerfield House in Sutton Coldfield, and their first child, Enid Avril, was born on 7 April 1894.[37] Kate Audrey followed on 31 May 1895.[38]

Muntz's Metal Company was reconstructed in 1890 and re-registered in the June of that year.[39] Philip Albert was a director of the new company, and in 1896 Gerard became managing director; he remained so until 1921, and he was consultant director right up to the time of his death.[40] He devoted most of his time to research, making an exhaustive study of the properties of copper, copper alloys, and other non-ferrous metals, and he wrote a number of scientific papers.[41] Gerard was 'a tall man, of fine presence'. He had a very cheerful disposition, and 'his bluff and hearty manner and kindly and wise counsel' made him popular amongst his fellow metallurgists and engineers. He was encouraging and supportive of newcomers to the field and generous with advice.[42]

Gerard and Katie's third daughter, Mavis Christian Phyllis, was born on 3 November 1896.[43] Joan Frances Cecil was born on 14 December 1899, and Mary Vivian arrived on 13 May 1903.[44] In the autumn of 1906, Gerard moved to Walmley House, in Walmley, Warwickshire, and on 28 February the following year he filed for divorce and petitioned for custody of four of his five daughters.[45]

Gerard and Katie had lived together happily, or so it had seemed to the former, until the summer of 1906.[46] But rumours had begun to circulate, and it was often remarked by 'the servants and others' that young Joan, who was then six years old, looked a lot like the family doctor.[47] As a consequence, on 20 August Gerard questioned Katie as to whether or not she had been entirely faithful to him, and she admitted to having committed adultery with the family doctor, James Fraser, who had been a personal friend of Gerard's for years.[48] Gerard was so upset, he paced about the house and garden all night long, and the following day he confronted Fraser. Much to his surprise, the doctor did not attempt to deny the affair; two days later, Fraser was dead.[49]

According to Mr. Bayford, who acted on behalf of Fraser's family, he had died of heart failure 'following the shock of the petitioner's accusation'; the doctor who certified the death—a friend of Fraser's for many years—recorded the cause as 'angina pectoris'.[50] At the time of his death, on 23 August 1906, James Fraser was thirty-nine years old. Having hailed from Inverness, he had moved to Warwickshire seventeen years earlier, and he was considered 'one of the most respected members of the medical profession in the borough'.[51] He had been married just over two years when he died, and he had an infant daughter.[52]

The judge, Mr Justice Bargrave Deane, agreed that, as he was deceased, Fraser need not be named during the divorce proceedings, which took place on 31 July 1907. Fraser was only ever referred to as 'Dr. X.' in newspaper reports at the time.[53] During the hearing, servants confirmed that Fraser had visited Katie when she was not unwell and had spent hours alone with her in her bedroom. Katie, who by that time was living on Jersey in the Channel Islands, did not appear in court to defend herself, and she did not dispute the charge that Joan was the child of James Fraser.[54] Gerard was awarded his divorce and custody of his daughters.[55]

Philip Albert received a baronetcy in the 1902 Coronation Honours list, becoming 1st Baronet Muntz, of Dunsmore, in the parish of Clifton-on-Dunsmore, co. Warwick.[56] Upon his death, on 21 December 1908, following a stroke earlier in that year, his son Gerard succeeded to the baronetcy.[57] The following year, on 19 March 1909, he married Henrietta Winifred Graves (1883-1969), third daughter of Lieutenant Colonel Francis Lowry Graves, at St. Clement Danes Church, Westminster, and the couple made their home at Tiddington House, in Stratford-upon-Avon in Warwickshire.[58] Gerard and Henrietta's first child, Ora Henrietta, was born on 10 May 1911, followed by another daughter, Désirée Violet, five years later on 19 February 1916.[59] Gerard's only son, Gerard Philip Graves, was born on 13 June 1917.[60]

Gerard was an original member and instrumental in the formation of the Institute of Metals in 1908, of which he was vice-president in 1909 and president in 1910-1911.[61] He became a

Tiddington House, c. 1910.

member of the Institution of Mechanical Engineers in 1910 and was vice-president from 1919 to 1925.[62] He was chairman of the Associated Manufacturers of Brass and Copper Tube of Great Britain, a member of the council of the Birmingham Chamber of Commerce, and a fellow of the Royal Society of Arts.[63] And during the First World War he was chairman of the Non-Ferrous Metals Committee of the Board of Trade in 1916 and 1917, his 'profound knowledge of metallurgy' being of great use to the government.[64] He was one of the founders of the British Non-Ferrous Metals Research Association, an original member of its council, and eventually its chairman.[65] In May 1926, at a gathering at Birmingham University, he was awarded the Thomas Turner Gold Metal in recognition of 'conspicuous service to metallurgy and metallurgical science'.[66]

You are possibly wondering at this point, as I did when I first began researching his life, why Gerard, a man of business and science who had devoted so much of his life to researching copper and other non-ferrous metals, chose, at the age of fifty-eight, to publish a novel—his only work of fiction—about a cursed Egyptian scarab beetle, containing a vivid description of travel within a region of the globe he had never visited.[67] There are a few things that shed light on the matter.

Gerard's brother, Cecil Albert Muntz, was an engineer. He began his career as an apprentice at the London and North Western Railway Company and went on to become one of its divisional mechanical engineers.[68] In 1902, he moved to Egypt, where he worked as deputy traffic manager on the Egyptian State Railways, becoming chief mechanical engineer in 1922.[69] He would, no doubt, have included details of his various adventures in Egypt when writing home. Gerard's only surviving sister, Mildred Rosalie, visited Cecil in Cairo in November 1903—wintering in Egypt was popular at the time—and no doubt she would have had tales to tell of her own experiences when she returned to England.[70] Gerard expressed the nature of his own interest in ancient Egypt when he gave a presidential address at the annual meeting of the Institute of Metals in London in January 1910, pointing out that:

> 'Those who lived in the twentieth century sometimes flattered themselves that they were a wonderful people, and that their science surpassed immeasurably the knowledge possessed by their forebears. But which of them to-day knew the secrets of the ancients of Egypt and Babylonia, which enabled them to harden bronzes to a cutting edge, and so face the stones of those marvels in architecture, the pyramids and temples of Egypt?'[71]

In November 1922, the tomb of the boy king Tutankhamun in the Valley of Kings, on the west bank of the Nile at Thebes, was discovered by archaeologist Howard Carter and his patron,

George Herbert, 5th Earl of Carnarvon. The media frenzy that followed the discovery inspired a huge amount of interest in Egypt and more specifically in the boy king himself; the world was seized by 'Tutmania', as it came to be known. When Lord Carnarvon fell ill and died in Egypt the following April, from blood poisoning complicated by pneumonia, the papers were full of stories of evil forces and Egyptian curses; Sir Arthur Conan Doyle suggested, when interviewed on the *Olympic* as it arrived in New York, that 'An evil elemental may have caused Lord Carnarvon's fatal illness. One does not know what elementals existed in those days, nor what their form might be.'[72] There were reports of a mummy in the British Museum which, according to Conan Doyle, was guarded by an evil elemental, and 'everyone who came in contact with it came to grief'.[73] And the novelist Marie Corelli claimed to have warned Lord Carnarvon of the dangers of excavating the tomb, of 'divers secret poisons enclosed in boxes in such wise that they who touch them shall not know how they come to suffer'.[74] The press went wild with stories of death coming on swift wings to those who dared to enter a pharaoh's tomb and disturb his rest, and, though not new in itself, the idea of the 'mummy's curse' sprouted wings and took flight in such a way as to render it immune to all sensible, logical argument, despite the fact that Carter, the one most likely to be targeted by a vengeful elemental or mysterious poison, remained alive until 1939.

Interestingly, the Muntz family knew Marie Corelli, who also lived in Stratford-upon-Avon. Marie attended political meetings and various social gatherings, including weddings, with members of the Muntz family—her name often appearing alongside theirs in the social pages of the newspapers—and Gerard's second wife, Henrietta, attended Marie's funeral in April 1924.[75]

So, Gerard had an interest in the use of metals in ancient Egypt, and he moved in the same social circles as the lady who had apparently warned Lord Carnarvon of the dangers of disturbing the rest of ancient Egyptian pharaohs. His brother had lived in Egypt for a number of years and would have been a ready source of valuable information about the country and travel within it. And there was such an interest in all things Egyptian at that time that any novel set in Egypt—especially one about a cursed artefact—would have had an instantly enthusiastic readership.

In July 1923, less than a year after the discovery of the tomb of Tutankhamun, *Out of the Ages* was published by Leonard Parsons; a 'popular edition' was issued by the same publisher in April the following year.[76] Gerard's nom de plume, Devereux Pryce, was created by combining the maiden name of his grandmother Eliza Pryce with that of his great-grandmother Mary Devereux. Though the fact that Gerard was the author of *Out of the Ages* was mentioned in his obituary in the *Journal of the Institute of Metals*, it appears that it was not common knowledge.

The first several chapters of *Out of the Ages* concern the relationship between three 'friends' during an extended holiday in Ireland: Thira Colquhoun is a rich, beautiful, married woman who is very used to having her way; Jack Winthrop is the man she wants to have her way with; and Janet Baxter is the woman unfortunate enough to stand in her way. Janet is innocent, Thira is manipulative, and Jack is often uncomfortable. It is interesting, considering his own history, that Gerard chose to make one of his main characters a manipulative, reckless, and utterly selfish married woman who thinks nothing of destroying her marriage; for that matter, she is willing to cause pain to Jack Winthrop too, the man she claims to love, if doing so takes her a step closer to her goal.

For reasons I won't go into, because it would give away too much of the plot, Jack ends up overseas, and Thira's health declines as a result. Her doctors advise a change of climate, so Thira, her husband, and a group of friends set off for distant shores. During their travels, the Colquhouns and their companions sail up the Nile, where a French archaeologist invites them to visit a recently excavated tomb. It contains the remains of King Amenhotep's favourite, a priestess who was 'put to death by suffocation with the wax cloth'. And one of the Colquhoun party does exactly what you should never do when you visit the final resting place of a murdered Egyptian… she removes an ancient ivory cylinder as a keepsake. The description of the oppressive atmosphere within the airless, lightless excavated tomb is excellent; it is hard to believe that Gerard himself had never set foot inside such a place.

The main characters of the Egyptian part of the story are King Amenhotep and the priestess Ohora, the former being based on the eighteenth-dynasty pharaoh Amenhotep IV, who changed his name to Akhenaten in the fifth year of his reign. Akhenaten abandoned traditional Egyptian polytheism in favour of Atenism and introduced sweeping religious reforms. He initiated a programme to erase the name and image of the god Amun from all monuments, and he closed many of the existing temples, putting their priests out of a job. Akhenaten is also thought to have been the father of Tutankhamun.

Though described as 'cleverly woven' by one critic, reviews for *Out of the Ages* were generally rather lukewarm.[77] While the general public couldn't get enough of all things Egyptian, the critics seem to have been sick to death of hearing about the place by the time Gerard's novel was released. One suggested that there should be a 'close season for all Egyptian relics with a supernatural influence'.[78]

Gerard suffered a serious heart attack in April 1924, and he was confined to his bed for several months afterwards.[79] He recovered enough to return to his usual activities, but he was never quite himself again.[80] He grew increasingly deaf towards the end of his life, making it impossible for him to take part in much discussion, but he remained cheerful and supportive.[81] He died suddenly at his home on the evening of 22 October 1927; he was sixty-two years old.[82] His funeral was of 'simple yet impressive character', and he was buried in St. James' Churchyard, in the village of Alveston, about a mile from Tiddington House, on 27 October.[83]

Notes

1 *UK and Ireland, Find a Grave Index, 1300s-Current.*

2 Philip Albert Muntz was born on 5 January 1839 and died on 21 December 1908. Rosalie Muntz was born in 1838 and died in November 1919. See *UK and Ireland, Find a Grave Index, 1300s-Current.*

3 Bernard Burke, *A Genealogical and Heraldic History of the Landed Gentry of Great Britain & Ireland*, Vol. 2. London: Harrison, 1871, p. 962.

4 Birthplace, see *UK and Ireland, Find a Grave Index, 1300s-Current.* Move to Birmingham, see *The Biograph and Review*, Vol. 3. London: E. W. Allen, 1880, p. 47.

5 Matthew Bolton was an English businessman, mechanical engineer, inventor, etc., and the business partner of James Watt.

6 John Alfred Langford, *Modern Birmingham an its Institutions: A Chronicle of Local Events*, Vol. 1. London: Simpkin, Marshall & Co., 1873, p. 439, and Sidney Lee (ed.), *Dictionary of National Biography*, Vol 39. London: Macmillan and Co., 1894, p. 313.

7 E. Edwards, *Personal Recollections of Birmingham and Birmingham Men.* Birmingham: Midland Educational Trading Co. Ltd., 1877, p. 82.

8 *The Biograph*, op. cit., p. 47.

9 Edwards, op. cit., p. 83, and *Wrington's New Triennial Directory of Birmingham*, 1818, p. 92.

10 Edwards, op. cit., p. 83.

11 Sidney Lee (ed.), *Dictionary of National Biography*, Vol 39. London: Macmillan and Co., 1894, p. 314.

12 *Leamington Spa Courier*, 29 December 1888, p. 4.

13 *UK and Ireland, Find a Grave Index, 1300s-Current.*

14 *England, Select Marriages, 1538-1973*, and *UK and Ireland, Find a Grave Index, 1300s-Current.*

15 George Muntz is listed as living at Hockley Abbey in W. M. West's *The*

History, Topography and Directory of Warwickshire, 1830, p. 367, and at Ley Hall in the *Gentleman's Magazine*, Volume 19, 1843, p. 644.

16 Edwards, op. cit., p. 83.

17 John Alfred Langford, *Modern Birmingham an its Institutions: A Chronicle of Local Events*, Vol. 1. London: Simpkin, Marshall & Co., 1873, p. 439.

18 George Jacob Holyoake, *Sixty Years of an Agitator's Life*, Vol. 1. London: T. Fisher Unwin, 1893, p. 28.

19 *The Biograph*, op. cit., p. 49, and *Leamington Spa Courier*, 29 December 1888, p. 4.

20 Time in Germany: *Illustrated Midland News*, 19 February 1870, p. 6. Wilhelmine's dates: *UK and Ireland, Find a Grave Index, 1300s-Current.*

21 Rosalie was baptised on 21 June 1838, see *England, Select Births and Christenings, 1538-1975.*

22 *Aris's Birmingham Gazette*, 4 December 1843, p. 2.

23 *Birmingham Journal*, 1 August 1857, p. 6.

24 Edwards, op. cit., p. 88.

25 Ibid., p. 87.

26 Ibid.

27 *Banbury Guardian*, 31 March 1859, p. 3.

28 *Morning Post*, 11 May 1860, p. 7, and *Warwickshire, England, Church of England Baptisms, 1813-1910.*

29 *Warwickshire, England, Church of England Baptisms, 1813-1910.*

30 *England, Select Births and Christenings, 1538-1975*, and *Warwickshire, England, Church of England Burials, 1813-1910.*

31 Education details: obituary in the *Journal of the Institute of Metals*, Vol. 38. Institute of Metals, 1927, p. 344. Neuwied-am-Rhein: For more than a hundred years, British business class families sent their children to the Moravian boarding schools set up in Neuwied-am-Rhein. See Dr Marianne Doerfel, 'British Pupils in a German Boarding School: Neuwied/Rhine 1820-1913' in *British Journal of Educational Studies*, Vol. 34, No. 1, February 1986, p. 79.

32 *Country Life*, 26 December 1908.

33 Ibid. Philip Albert Muntz built Dunsmore House in 1881.

34 *Morning Post*, 24 March 1893, p. 5.

35 *Westminster, London, England, Church of England Marriages and Banns, 1754-1935.*

36 Frances died at the age of twelve in 1872, Nora was two when she died in the summer of 1865, and Vera died at the age of twenty-eight at the beginning of 1890. See *Birmingham, England, Church of England Burials, 1813-1964*, and *Warwickshire, England, Church of England Burials, 1813-1910.*

37 *Birmingham Daily Gazette*, 10 April 1894, p. 8.

38 *Leamington Spa Courier*, 8 June 1895, p. 5.

39 *Birmingham Daily Post*, 20 May 1890, p. 6. Company reconstruction is a process whereby a company's business and assets are transferred to another company, new or existing, that consists of substantially the same shareholders.

40 Obit. in Institute of Metals, op. cit., p. 344.

41 Ibid.

42 Ibid.

43 *Morning Post*, 7 November 1896, p. 1. Joan: 1*939 England and Wales Register.*

44 Joan: 1*939 England and Wales Register.* Mary: *England & Wales, Civil Registration Death Index, 1916-2007.*

45 E*ngland & Wales, Civil Divorce Records, 1858-1918.*

46 *Coleshill Chronicle*, 3 August 1907, p. 5.

47 Ibid.

48 Ibid.

49 Ibid.

50 *Birmingham Daily Gazette*, 1 August 1907, p. 6, and the death certificate of James Fraser. The judge in the divorce case did ask if Fraser had committed suicide; he was told that the deceased had been attended by four doctors and the cause of death had been heart failure. Two of the doctors had been partners with Fraser in the same medical practice. The men were all members of the same football club and appear to have been good friends, so they knew him well.

51 *Walsall Observer*, 25 August 1906, p. 7.

52 *Sutton Coldfield News*, 25 August 1906, p. 10.

53 *England & Wales, Civil Divorce Records, 1858-1918*, and *Coleshill Chronicle*, 3 August 1907, p. 5.

54 *England & Wales, Civil Divorce Records, 1858-1918*, and *Birmingham Daily Gazette*, 1 August 1907, p. 6.

55 *England & Wales, Civil Divorce Records, 1858-1918.*

56 *London Gazette*, 25 July 1902, p. 4738.

57 *Lichfield Mercury*, 25 December 1908, p. 5.

58 *Westminster Gazette*, 22 March 1909, p. 8, *Stratford-upon-Avon Herald*, 19 February 1909, p. 5, and *1911 England Census.*

59 *England & Wales, Civil Registration Death Index, 1916-2007*, and *Rugby Advertiser*, 26 February 1916, p. 5.

60 *UK and Ireland, Find a Grave Index, 1300s-Current.*

61 Obit. in Institute of Metals, op. cit., p. 344.

62 Ibid.

63 Ibid.

64 Ibid. and *Stratford-upon-Avon Herald*, 22 June 1917, p. 3.

65 Obit. in Institute of Metals, op. cit., p. 344.

66 *Birmingham Daily Post*, 14 May 1926, p. 1.

67 Obit. in Institute of Metals, op. cit., p. 345.

68 *The Sphinx*, Vol 32, No. 591, 15 November 1924, p. 14.

69 Ibid.

70 *Warwick and Warwickshire Advertiser*, 31 October 1902, p. 5.

71 *Globe*, 19 January 1910, p. 5.

72 *Daily Herald*, 6 April 1923, p. 1.

73 *Birmingham Daily Gazette*, 7 April 1923, p. 1.

74 *Western Daily Press*, 26 March 1923, p. 11.

75 See: *Birmingham Daily Post*, 26 May 1900, p. 8; *Stratford-upon-Avon Herald*, 2 June 1900, p. 7, and 3 August 1900, p. 8; *Leamington Spa Courier*, 11 December 1903, p. 5; funeral, *Stratford-upon-Avon Herald*, 2 May 1924, p. 8.

76 *The English Catalogue of Books*. London: The Publishers' Circular, Limited.

1923 (1924), p. 280, and 1924 (1925), p. 285. Also, *The Bookseller*, 12 June 1924, p. 101.

77 *Birmingham Daily Gazette*, 30 August 1923, p. 4.

78 *Daily News*, 28 August 1923, p. 7.

79 *Engineering*, 28 October 1927, Vol. 124, p. 560.

80 Ibid.

81 Obit. in Institute of Metals, op. cit., p. 344.

82 *Stratford-upon-Avon Herald*, 28 October 1927, p. 2, and *England & Wales, National Probate Calendar (Index of Wills and Administrations), 1858-1995.*

83 *Stratford-upon-Avon Herald*, 28 October 1927, p. 2.

OUT OF THE AGES

CHAPTER I

"I CAN'T think why you are so horribly rude to that girl, Jack; you have behaved simply disgracefully to her ever since we came here. Why can't you treat her decently? If you don't like her, you might at least leave her alone."

"My dear Thira, what a fuss about nothing! The girl is quite capable of taking care of herself, and if I am rude to her she is quite as rude to me. I don't like her. She annoys me; she has such an infernally good opinion of herself."

"Well, you might at least remember that she is my guest as much as you are. The way you behaved to-night, while she was singing to please me, was simply abominable; instead of sitting quiet you were chatting away with Mary in that corner, quite loudly."

"Really! I'm awfully sorry, Thira, if I have annoyed you. Why didn't you tell me sooner? It's the first time *you* have ever complained that I didn't behave nicely enough to a girl; it's generally been the other way round."

"Oh, don't be silly! This is quite another thing. Other girls may run after you and make a fuss with you because they think you are somebody, but Janet is quite different; she knows her place and was thankful enough to me for bringing her over here to give her a rest. I don't mean you to be nice to her in that way; but you might treat her decently to please me, that's all."

"Oh, of course if you put it like that, I must do what I can. I promise to reform; but she will wonder what on earth has happened to me to make me so different."

The speakers were Mrs. Colquhoun and her guest, Jack

Winthrop; they were old friends and very good pals, in fact some people thought too good. She was about twenty-five years of age, and he a little older. Her husband, many years her senior, simply worshipped her, thought she could do no wrong, and let her do just what she chose in everything. He was a wealthy man, well-born, but spent most of his time in the City, where he was much occupied in matters of finance.

Richard Colquhoun had taken a great fancy to Jack Winthrop some years before, when they had met frequently during the course of business. The acquaintance soon ripened into friendship; Jack in due course was asked to Colquhoun's house, and found the young wife a charming companion with whom to pass his spare time. Colquhoun, to his surprise, seemed to have no objection to a young and good-looking man acting so frequently as her escort—in fact seemed rather to encourage it than otherwise, for as time went on he would often suggest that Thira should take Jack with her on various excursions.

It was, perhaps, a rather risky experiment; but having once thrown the two together, he could not have done a wiser thing. Jack, although by no means immaculate, and no better than most other men of his years and upbringing, was a "sport"; and this action of Colquhoun's and the confidence reposed in him put him on his honour not to abuse it as nothing else could have done.

Jack had always taken the good things of life pretty freely, as they came to him, up to now, but he was not lacking in what is called "grit." Born to fair prospects, of a very good family, but with no immediate hopes of anything more than an income of a few hundreds a year, he had had the good sense to see that to live an idle life, waiting for dead men's shoes, was a poor game, and had taken up engineering seriously as a profession. So far he had been fairly successful in making a position for himself, and was earning an income sufficient to ensure him a comfortable independence. He worked hard, but was able to find time for enough pleasure to temper the monotony of it; he found Thira pleasant as a companion, and, having become a *persona grata* in the Colquhoun household, without thought of the future, he made the most of this opportunity of obtaining plenty of amusement at small expense.

For a considerable time the danger of the situation had not struck him. He liked Colquhoun very much, and, in spite of the difference in their ages, the two had become close friends. The elder man was rather lonely in his private life, having always been too immersed in business to find time for social recreations—those lighter pursuits and hobbies which go so far to help a man forget his anxieties; then, a few years before the beginning of this story, he had married Thira. An unsophisticated girl, she was flattered and pleased that a man of the world should set so huge a value upon her, and when he asked her to marry him, after a very slight hesitation she accepted him, imagining that she loved him; whereas it was the novelty, the idea of being independent of her people, which appealed to her, and the fascination of wider horizons.

At first everything had seemed so new and wonderful that serious thoughts were crowded out. She was duly presented at Court, and had been the sensation of the season. With her big blue eyes and her glorious golden hair she was bound to attract attention, and her husband's wealth emphasised it.

For the opening months of their married life, Colquhoun had taken things more easily, travelled with her, shown her the world; and although she soon discovered that she did not love him, she respected him and was grateful for her improved position, for all the good things it brought her, and was happy enough. Presently, however, the long weeks of leisure wearied him; he heard the city calling; and he left her for a few hours each day. As time went on, these absences grew longer; business once more claimed most of his thoughts and time. His wife, having no children to give her a centre of interest, finding her new life after all rather dull, sought her amusements in society, becoming a butterfly, aimless and wandering. Then one day her husband brought Jack Winthrop home, and almost immediately a blank was filled. From the first Jack appealed strongly to her, and she was only too glad to take her cue from her husband, and make use of him.

The situation was quaint and piquant, almost more so to him than to her; for to her, in her ignorance, there seemed nothing very strange in the arrangement, especially as Colquhoun, quite content, appeared even to encourage it.

So things had gone on until now, about two years from their first acquaintance, and she had discovered that she could not get on without Jack.

She did not know what was the matter with her, but somehow this year's London season had, to a great extent, lost its charm; and when the time came for their customary round of visits after the season was over she was not inclined to accept any of the various invitations from friends which she received, nor did she want to go abroad.

After much discussion, it occurred to Colquhoun that a place he had on the west coast of Ireland might suit her. It was in a wild, inaccessible part of the country, surrounded by moors and mountains, the house standing close to the sea, looking out across the Atlantic, with only a few rugged islands between it and America. Good rough shooting and excellent fishing was to be had on the estate, and if a man knew how to handle a boat there might be a little sailing along the coast and among the islands; but it was no place for a novice. Thira jumped at the idea as a complete change, and it was decided that a party bound for the far west would solve the problem pleasantly.

Jack was included as a matter of course, for "Jack knew everything about sport and was always so useful." Eventually it was he who arranged the details of the journey, and who provided (at Colquhoun's expense) the outfit of dogs, guns, fishing tackle, carts, harness, and all the trifles that go to make a holiday complete. Horses and ponies and the usual conveyances of the country could be obtained on the spot; Jack was commissioned to run over and see about these also. In his company Thira purchased the numberless little accessories without which, she was sure, the expedition would not be a success. It was Jack, too, who selected the members of the party, except for a few special friends and protégés of Thira's, whom she asked without consulting anyone.

When the hour of departure arrived, Colquhoun was detained by pressure of business, so it fell to Thira to act as pioneer. The indispensable Jack had been sent on a couple of days before to make general preparations, so she was left to her own devices on the journey. However, everything had been so fully mapped out that she had no anxiety as to safe arrival, especially as Jack had promised to meet them at the other end. She looked forward to the prospect of acting the part of a hostless hostess with him as her major-domo, so that just she and he should have the arranging of the whole programme in their own hands.[1]

Everything had fallen out as she hoped, with one important

[1] Major-domo: an individual who makes arrangements or takes charge on behalf of another.

exception—Jack himself. Somehow, she thought, his manner to her seemed, when they met, a little different, though she could not make up her mind where the difference lay, or be certain that it was not merely her imagination. She had noticed it almost at once. He appeared quite jolly and bright when they arrived; then, when she told him that Richard would not be able to come for some days, he seemed not only surprised, but annoyed, and not at all pleased, as she had expected.

The truth was that Jack felt vexed with Colquhoun for letting him down in this way. It was all very well to be free of his house, and he had no objection to taking Thira about in town; but to have her thrown on his hands like this, for possibly several days, might prove embarrassing, especially as he had noticed of late a change in her attitude towards himself, which was not quite in harmony with the footing of "pals" which they had enjoyed for some time past. However, as there was nothing else to do at the moment, he decided to make the best of it.

One of the party was a Captain Seymour of the Royal Navy, a man of the world at present occupying one of those snug home billets which the Navy reserves for its pets. With him, however, it was a well-earned sinecure, for in all parts of the globe, notably in South America, China, and West Africa, he had seen much active service in the many exciting and sometimes dangerous disturbances which this country expects her handymen to deal with on the spot.

A sprinkling of young sportsmen, all good fellows, formed a section of the company, and several women, most of whom hardly enter into this story, though an exception must be made in favour of Mary Macintyre, Thira's cousin. A girl, she would have liked to call herself; but she was already over thirty, and no man brave enough to undertake her guidance had yet appeared; she was, however, a very good sort and by no means to be ignored—in fact there was little to know about sport and games which she did not know. Also there was Janet Baxter, the cause of the dispute between Thira and Jack.

The only daughter of a country parson, with musical and histrionic tastes, she had been sent to Dresden to develop those talents which her parents hoped she possessed. There she had studied hard, and had returned with a magnificent voice and a craving for a career in grand opera; her father, however, strongly opposed this, and for a time there was some bitterness on the subject. Unluckily, or perhaps luckily for Janet, he did not stay long on this earth to interfere with her desires, for his death occurred within a year of her return. If he ever revisited this world in spirit, he may have wished that he had not repressed his daughter's musical aspirations.

With a very limited income, Janet and her mother were left to shift for themselves, and gravitated naturally to London as the cheapest place to live in. There Janet insisted upon adding to the funds by taking pupils for singing. This step brought her in touch with people of some importance, among others with a professor through whom she obtained minor engagements in opera. Acquitting herself well, she soon attracted attention, and before long achieved her desire, finding herself behind the footlights in operetta—in small parts, it is true, but with good prospects. Although well on the way to earning a considerable income, she continued to train a few select pupils for singing, Thira being one of them. She had taken a great fancy to the girl, and, having made a friend of her, often invited her for other occasions than instruction in music. At Thira's house she had more than once met Jack Winthrop, but the situation had been rather strained. Jack knew nothing about her except that she gave Thira music lessons and did something on the stage, and her association with the theatre caused him at once to class her as beyond consideration in the matter of real friendship. She, on her part, showed him pretty plainly that she did not mean to be treated as anything but an equal; so it had been with some dismay that Jack, on the arrival of the house party, perceived Janet Baxter as one of the guests, and likely to remain so for some time.

Thira, in the kindness of her heart, knowing that the girl had practically nothing to do during the dead season, asked her to join the party, and Janet, who had never seen Ireland, consented happily. She did not know that Jack Winthrop was one of the company, and even if she had it would probably have made no difference to her acceptance of the invitation, since she had no particular feelings about him, considering him merely as a rather conceited young man who needed to be taught his proper place. She had not the remotest idea of his footing in the Colquhoun household, or that he would be acting practically as her host. As it happened, he actually was acting as host, for that was the position he occupied from the first.

Thira was much concerned when she realised the growing animosity of these two. Jack, in her eyes, was perfection itself, so, womanlike, she at last attributed the trouble to Janet, and had some rather warm arguments with her on the subject. Janet naturally defended herself, saying that Mr. Winthrop was rude to her, but if it annoyed Thira to hear her snub him she would ignore him. This she did bravely for a time, but her new line of conduct only made Jack think her more priggish than ever, and he almost deliberately made things unpleasant for her.

It was just after a more than usually flagrant instance of this antagonism that Thira took him to task. He was annoyed that she, of all people, should side with Janet against him; usually she came to him for advice and help in all things, and looked up to him as a paragon of wisdom; therefore it jarred upon him that she should take Janet's part. However, if she really meant it, and it seemed that she did, she should have her way; he would bury his feelings and change his tone to this girl, who was only a music mistress, but who evidently expected to be treated like a duchess.

He felt sure that, if he chose, he could easily make her like him. He had only to accept the rôle she evidently wished to play, assume his most courteous manner, lay himself out to be specially nice to her, and no doubt she would at once drop her supercilious attitude. Fair ladies in the past had been inclined to spoil Jack, and though not really conceited, he knew well enough that he was good-looking and when he chose to exert himself could be attractive.

* * * * * *

It was already late when he went down with Thira to the smoking-room, where there was generally a pleasant gathering of the various members of the party before bedtime. They had lingered upstairs after the others had left the drawing-room, which, curiously enough for a country house, was on the first floor, and on entering the smoking-room they drifted apart. Suddenly Thira called him. He turned, and saw her sitting with Janet and two of the younger men of the party: Charlie Payne and Bertie Wilson.

'Jack, do you think it's safe? Charlie wants to take Janet across to the Black Isle in a boat to-morrow. I tell him it is madness, and that not even the local fishermen will go there if they can help it."

Charlie Payne laughed. "They are not a very brave race, these local fishermen. To my mind they know uncommonly little about a boat, anyhow."

"But the tides are awful round these islands; I really don't think you ought to go, or to take Janet."

Jack waited for a lead from the girl. There was a certain element of danger in the trip, though not so much as Thira seemed to think.

"If Thira considers it so risky, perhaps we had better not try it," remarked Janet at last.

"That is quite a nice way of putting it, Miss Baxter; it hurts no one's feelings and leaves everyone happy," said Jack.

"I don't know what you mean by making everyone happy; nor do I see whose feelings want saving."

"Oh, I only meant that you let Payne down gently, and saved yourself rather a risky trip."

"Do you think I am afraid, then?" she flared up.

"Not a bit of it! I should never associate fear with you; but it would be a risky journey with only one man in the boat, unless you are a sailor yourself. You may be, for all I know; but if not, it would be safer to have a second man with you."

"Does that mean you are offering us the pleasure of your company? Of course we all know that with you on board we might safely sail across the Atlantic; but I couldn't think of accepting such a sacrifice of your valuable time."

It was a nasty speech, and spitefully meant. Jack would have liked to retaliate, but remembered his promise to Thira, and refrained. Thira, however, objected to seeing her favourite treated like this.

"Don't be such a little spitfire, Janet; you ought to be much obliged to Mr. Winthrop."

"Oh, don't mind me, Thira," said Jack. "I know what Miss Baxter means, and it serves me quite right for always trying to run the show; but really I must plead not guilty this time. I was only thinking that if she would take the larger boat, and could persuade Wilson here to join the party with another lady to make the quartette, it would be a good idea; besides, Wilson has sailed all round the British Isles in a ten-ton yacht, so knows a good bit about the game. No doubt Payne knows a lot, too, but this coasting business among islands needs practice, and two heads are better than one."

"What's that you people are discussing?" asked Mary Macintyre, joining the group.

"Janet and Charlie are talking of going to the Black Isle to-morrow in the little boat, and I tell them it is dangerous. Jack has just suggested that they should take the larger one and get Bertie to go with them, but I don't know yet if he will. Will you, Bertie?"

"Of course I will if I can be of any use," replied Wilson; "but I must have another lady. I wonder who would come."

"Would you take me?" asked Mary.

"Take you! I should jolly well think I would; but if you come I can stay behind, for you know as much about the business as I do."

"Do you think I am going as one of three? Not likely! If you go I will, if not I won't."

After more discussion matters were settled satisfactorily, and a little later the lades went off to bed.

CHAPTER II

THE next morning opened fair and sunny with a light breeze; just enough to break the long even swell of the Atlantic rollers which rode so majestically in, one after the other, to crash in green curling waves on the iron-bound coast.

Shortly after breakfast the contingent sailing for the Black Isle was ready to start. A hamper for lunch had been carried down to the little sheltered cove which served as a harbour, where Wilton and Payne had been overhauling the boat and tackle to see that all was sound. Jack and Bertie, mapping out the trip, had agreed that if when the boat approached the island there was much sea on, no attempt should be made to land, but that she should be put about and run back to one of the coves on the mainland for lunch. Charlie Payne made light of possible danger. It was a poor look out, he said, if he and Wilson couldn't manage a boat for a run of a few miles out and home, and he scoffed at the idea of any difficulties in landing.

The ladies, looking very workman-like in blue serge frocks and coats, anticipated their trip with keen pleasure. Janet was inclined to be witty at Jack's expense, asking him whether he thought they might possibly be just able to manage the boat without his assistance; but he merely laughed, wished them a successful sail, and expressed a hope they would not be sea-sick—an aspersion which was greeted with derision. Captain Seymour, who was booked for shooting with Jack, strolled down to the shore just before they put off, and added a word of caution, which evidently carried more weight with the uninitiated than all that Jack had said.

They were off at last. Payne held the tiller while Wilson set the sails, Payne admitting that he did not understand that part of the business, though he said he could steer.[2] The two left on shore stood for a few moments to watch them fairly under way, and at once had the opportunity of judging Payne's capabilities. The boat was cutter-rigged; Wilson had the mainsail up, and was busy with the jib, which he had just set as they slipped out of the cove, while Mary held the main-sheet which was rove through a block.[3] The sail, not completely set, was scarcely drawing at all, but as they ran out from under the shelter of the cliffs the wind caught it full, and the boat began to heel over sharply. Wilson shouted to Payne to ease her off, but he, not comprehending what was meant, let her fall away. The gunwale was almost under water before Mary had time to let go the sheet and send the sail flapping idly in the wind.[4] The boat, thus freed, came up on an even keel. Wilson scrambled aft as fast as he could, and although it was already too far for the on-lookers to hear exactly what he said to Payne, they could tell from his expression that his words were not exactly complimentary. He took the tiller himself, and a moment later had the sail sheeted home and the boat pointing well up into the wind.

"Ah, that's better!" said Seymour. "I thought they were over. If that girl hadn't had the sense to let go the sheet they would have been. That fellow Payne's a lubber."

Jack laughed. "Oh, Mary has her head screwed on right; she

---

[2] Tiller: used to steer the boat, a handle attached to the rudder.

[3] Cutter-rigged: fore-and-aft-rigged on one mast in the manner of a cutter. Jib: the sail at the front of a boat. Main-sheet: a line or rope used to control the angle of a sail.

[4] Gunwale: the upper edge of the side of a boat.

knows pretty well all there is to know about sailing; but I doubt if Wilson will think it good enough to try to land on the Black Isle with such a lieutenant as Payne."

The boat was evidently in good hands now, so after watching it for a minute or two longer, Seymour and Jack turned away, and a few minutes later went off after snipe. There was plenty of sport; by lunch they had a couple of dozen of the little brown, white-waistcoated birds in the bag. They took their meal—a cold snack and a drop of whisky—under the shelter of a stone wall, following it by a pipe and a quarter of an hour's rest. Seymour had seen so much and done so much that if in the mood for talk he was better than any book of adventures. To-day he was in his best vain, for he liked Jack and found in him an intelligent listener who could understand and appreciate the points of a story. The two spent a very pleasant morning. Their excursion took them out of sight of the sea, and by half-past four they had run short of cartridges and turned homewards. Their shortest way back, instead of crossing the marshy lands, was to climb the hill and make straight for the shore. Arrived at the top, they had a fine view of the ocean and the long range of coast.

"By Jove! I wonder where that boat is?" exclaimed Seymour, as they stood facing the sea.

"Well, they are not to be seen; but Wilson's safe and Mary's a host in herself, so probably they're all right," said Jack; but he did not feel quite happy about them, and he had a vague suspicion that Seymour also felt uneasy.

When they reached the house there were no tidings of the mariners, nor was there any sign of the boat in the harbour. Thira had not returned from her drive, but after a little discussion among the others it was decided to scout along the coast in both directions for traces of the missing ones. Six of the party set out for this purpose, but had not gone far before they saw four people coming towards them along the cliffs.

They all hurried on, shouting and waving welcomes which they were puzzled to notice were not so cordially returned; on meeting, it was at once evident that things had not gone quite smoothly. Wilson frowned, black as thunder, Janet looked perturbed, while Mary seemed to be highly amused. Payne was wringing wet, and the others were not in much better plight.

"Oh dear!" laughed Mary. "It's a mercy that we are any of us here at all! I really thought I should get a paragraph in the papers, and hoped that a few of you would shed tears over the sad fate of one so young, cast away among the rocks of the Irish coast."

"Why? What happened?" asked Jack.

"Oh, don't ask me! Ask Janet! Ask Mr. Wilson or Charlie Payne! He knows most about it, poor dear."

But no one else seemed willing to volunteer any information until, in response to a question from Seymour as to how on earth he had got so wet, Payne burst out:

"Wet! Naturally I am wet; so would you be if you had fallen into the sea off the Black Isle. It was Wilson's fault."

"My fault!" exclaimed Wilson. "That'a the limit! It was your own silly fault, fooling about with the boat instead of staying quiet as I told you."

"Why on earth should I do as you told me, I should like to know?"

"Because you don't know enough to be allowed to do anything by yourself."

"Oh, dry up, you two," interposed Jack, "or we shall never get to the bottom of the story; let Mary tell us, if she can stop laughing."

"I absolutely decline to tell anybody anything until I have changed into dry clothes and had some tea, so good-bye for the present. Don't let those two boys get near each other, or there will be bloodshed; I've had trouble enough as it is for the last three hours keeping them apart. Come along, Janet; you are about wet through too."

Mary and Janet vanished, leaving the two men still grumbling.

"She's right," said Seymour. "You two fellows go and change your togs before you spin us the yarn."

Wilson protested that he wasn't so wet that he needed to make a fuss about it; but it was no use, he had to go. Payne seemed glad enough to retire. The others adjourned to the smoking-room, where tea and hot whisky and water were available. In about half an hour Mary appeared and reported that Janet intended to lie down until dinner-time, as she was rather upset.

"Now, please tell us what really did happen," said Seymour.

"Well, joking apart, it was very nearly a nasty business. We got to Black Isle all right, and there was no sea on worth mentioning when we arrived, so we found a little cove and ran the boat in. We took the hamper out, and started to climb the cliffs to find a good place for lunch. We had a good meal and then loafed round for a bit before thinking of starting back. It was rather jolly up there, and we didn't bother ourselves about the time or tide. Presently Charlie suggested to Janet that they should go farther along the cliffs to get another view, and as Bertie and I weren't inclined to move or go scrambling about rocks, we stayed where we were. We thought they would only be away a few minutes; but as time went on Bertie began to get restless and started to talk of tides, and the probable difficulties of getting home with a strong ebb against us. Of course we knew about the dangerous tide-race between the Isles and the mainland, but with the steady wind blowing I didn't think there was any danger from that, so I told

Bertie not to worry; but he was not satisfied and went off to look for the others."

"A nice trick to play," growled Seymour. "That fellow Payne ought to be kicked; these tide-races here are not to be fooled with."

"Oh, well, I suppose it was a case of 'where ignorance is bliss.' He knows nothing about tides or anything else to do with the sea, and never thought of it. After half an hour had passed and there was no sign of any of them, even I began to get fidgety, and I went as well to look for them. I hadn't far to go, for after rounding a point about fifty yards off I saw all three scrambling along the rocks towards me, about a quarter of a mile away; so I sat down and waited. Bertie was in front, the other two behind, Charlie helping Janet along. As they came nearer I could see there had been a row, for the two boys were barely on speaking terms, and Janet was looking furious. When they at last reached me Bertie insisted that there was no time to be wasted, so Janet and I scrambled down to the boat, leaving the others to pack the basket and follow. It seemed, from what Janet said, that Charlie had taken her some way along the cliffs, and that they hadn't thought about the time, but had sat down to watch the sea. There Bertie had found them and had, she said, been very rude to Charlie, and by no means too polite to her about being away so long: she thought the boys would almost have come to blows if she hadn't been there.

"We all got on board as quickly as possible, and Bertie pushed off. It was quite calm inside the cove, but we could see nasty choppy little waves outside. There was no wind under the land—the boat had to be rowed out, but remembering our experience of the morning, Bertie got the sail up before we cleared the cliffs; then he made me steer while he and Charlie took the oars. Janet sat on the bottom of the boat at my feet to keep it steady, she said, laughing, but it turned out less of a laughing matter than she thought; it was a good thing she did, for as we cleared the land the wind came with a gust off the cliffs and I had to hold on tight to keep her from falling away. Bertie shouted something to me, I couldn't quite catch what, and jumped forward to look after the jib. Charlie also shipped his oar and then stood up; Bertie shouted to him to sit down or he would have the boat over, but he took no notice—just turned his back and began to speak to Janet.[5] Bertie's language was more forcible than polite; as you know, he doesn't mince matters when he gets excited.

"The wind was most puzzling under the land—it seemed to come from all points at once. I had the sheet in one hand and was steering with the other, and had all I could do to hold on. I called to Charlie to come and help me, but just as I spoke a gust came suddenly from the opposite direction, and in a second, before I could do anything but shout, the mainsail gybed.[6] I simply yelled to Charlie to sit down—I saw what was coming—but the boom caught him, knocking him clean overboard.[7]

" 'Luff! luff! luff!' shouted Bertie, and I had to do it or we should have been over and all in the water together.[8]

"The tide was running like a mill-race beside the island, and though the wind helped us, it didn't help poor Charlie. When I could spare a moment to look, he had come up, and his head was bobbing about in the waves thirty yards away. I never saw a man

---

[5] Shipped his oars: stopped rowing and pulled the oars inside the boat.

[6] The mainsail crossed from one side of the boat to the other.

[7] Boom: a spar (pole) along the foot of a rigged sail.

[8] Luff: sail nearer to the wind.

look so frightened in my life. Janet went as white as a sheet, but Bertie looked grim.

" 'Good heavens, Bertie! He'll drown!' I shouted.

" 'Drown be blowed! He can swim! It's his own fault if he'd got a ducking! Do him good for being so pig-headed.' However, a moment later he had taken the tiller from me and was handling the boat as though he had lived in one all his life."

"So he has—or at least a good slice of it," Jack put in.

"Well, anyway, almost before I should have thought it possible, we were close to Charlie, who was puffing and spluttering in the short seas, evidently thinking his hour had come.

" 'Chuck him the slack of the sheet—there's nothing else handy!' Bertie called, so I shouted to Charlie and threw it. He understood, and managed to clutch it.

" 'Hold on for all you're worth while I bring her up,' yelled Bertie, but poor Charlie wasn't prepared for that. We were travelling at a good pace and he was simply ripped through the waves like a porpoise. He held on for a couple of seconds and then, with a despairing yell, let go and was adrift again!

"Bertie's language was something fearful, but it didn't stop him acting. I really thought for a moment that Charlie would be drowned from sheer fright, for he had his mouth wide open and his eyes were starting out of his head as we glided away from him. It took us a few moments to go about, but then Bertie managed, very cleverly, to bring her up almost on top of Charlie, and to hold the boat up into the wind so that she lay with flapping sails close beside him. We threw the rope again, and this time he was hauled in, and gripped the side of the boat.

" 'Now then, be quick! Climb in or we shall be swamped!' yelled Bertie. Charlie made a feeble effort, and then gasped, 'Oh, I can't!'

" 'Good Lord, you *must!*'

" 'But I can't! It's too far up! There's nothing to get my foot on.'

" 'Oh, damn the man—haven't you got any arms? Here, Mary; hold on to the tiller, but don't let her fall off if you can help it. Play with her.'

"There was a beautiful simplicity about his instructions, for the mainsail was flapping and the boom was swinging backward and forward over my head, but I did my best and succeeded pretty well, while Bertie, hauling on Charlie's collar, heaved him into the boat like a sack, and let him drop on the floor, where he collapsed.

"Just at that moment the boat got the best of me. She refused to answer her helm and fell away; the mainsail filled and the boom swung over, and I was in terror lest it should knock Bertie out; but before I knew what had happened he had taken the tiller out of my hands and we were slipping easily through the water as if there had never been any trouble at all; and he sat there quite cool and collected, looking as if it were an everyday occurrence to save a man from drowning.

"Janet tried to recover the poor shipwrecked mariner, who was still looking half dead. I suggested neat whisky.

" 'Anything you like,' said Bertie, 'but for goodness' sake let him lie still or he will be falling out again. He makes good ballast where he is.'

"Janet looked as if she could have bitten him, but as for Charlie, I think he really was feeling too bad to take any notice of anything.

"A drenching of cold water down my back made me notice that it was much rougher than it had been. We were running across the stretch between the island and the point out at the north end of the bay. We were about three-quarters of a mile from the straits, but what I saw there made me feel a bit uncomfy, for the whole sea was a mass of tumbling breakers. I had never been out there on the ebbtide before, and although I knew there was a nasty race at such times, I had never before realised what a race could mean; only a lifeboat could have lived a minute among those breakers. I turned to Bertie, who was looking stern, and raised my eyebrows. 'It will be alright if the wind holds, but I daren't ease her; she must just go through it, even if it comes to baling,' he said quietly.

"We were tossing about in high style; the wind, as you know, was rising into almost a gale, and we were ripping through the waves and shipping a lot of water. In spite of the strong wind it was taking us all our time to hold our own against the tide. The bottom boards were already awash when Bertie told me to look in the locker and get a scoop, and as Charlie was now sitting up again and seemed better I suggested that it would help to warm him if he baled a bit. He hadn't the faintest notion how to set about it, so I told him and Janet to shift out of my way, while I pulled out the boards and began to bale from the well.

"More and more water came aboard, and it was a stiff job to keep it down at all, for there was a good three inches swilling about, and Janet had to move on to a thwart to get out of it; however, she found a tin pan in the lunch-hamper and helped me, and we managed to keep it under until Bertie had run us past the point into quieter water.[9]

"There was not so much tide in the little bay, but we daren't venture into the open again, so we ran the boat into a creek and landed. The rest you know, for here we all are, safe and sound."

Charlie had a bad time when he turned up later, but Janet stood

[9] Thwart: part of an undecked boat, going from one side of the hull to the other, that provides seating.

up for him and attacked Jack furiously when he suggested that "Fools rush in where angels fear to tread." She rose on the instant like a trout to a fly.

"I suppose you are posing as the angel?"

"Not much in my line, Miss Baxter."

"Oh, I don't know. You said something about 'fearing,' didn't you? I thought perhaps the cap fitted."

Jack flushed, but said nothing. Thira, however, blazed out.

"Don't be a little fool, Janet! If it hadn't been for Mr. Winthrop you would have been at the bottom of the sea by this time, and as for his being afraid—he knows more about sailing a boat than any man I have ever met, and certainly far more than anyone here, unless perhaps it is Captain Seymour; I forgot he was present."

"Oh, my line in boats has been something bigger," laughed Seymour. "I should be frightened to death in a cockle-shell like that in a sea-way."

"Oh yes, we all know that!" said Jack ironically. "Of course we don't suppose that you ever were really at sea; you were like the H.M.S. *Pinafore* sailors."

After this conversation languished, for both Janet and Charlie were still decidedly sulky. This had a depressing effect on the remainder of the company, till at the conclusion of a somewhat strained evening Thira announced that she was tired.

"Good-night, everyone; I'm sleepy. The rest of you can sit up as long as you choose; but, Jack—don't make any other arrangements, because I want you to take me fishing to-morrow on the lake. William says the water is in fine fettle and we ought to have a good catch."

"All right, I'll arrange things; but you must be ready to start by not later than nine o'clock."

The others had all gone to bed, and Jack was left to put out the lights. He sat for a few moments thinking over the events of the last few days: of Thira's attack on him for his treatment of Janet, his attempt to be nicer, and the manner in which it had been repaid. Afraid, indeed! What a little spitfire the girl was! It really would be worth while to make her climb down. It would be a good thing too in another way, for Thira was beginning to expect too much of him. By way of a beginning, to show he was not altogether a fool, why not start now and fetch home the boat alone? A great idea! And fifteen minutes later he was out of the house on his way to the boat.

It was not the best sort of weather for sailing a boat single-handed, but Jack had a strong grain of obstinacy in his character, and having once set out to do a thing was not likely to be deterred by any ordinary difficulty. He had some trouble in picking his way along the coast path, but presently he reached the spot where the boat had been run ashore. The first thing he did was to bale the water out of her; then, leaving the mainsail as it was, he hoisted the jib and was soon running before the wind towards Kilmona.

It was rather weird out there alone on the ocean in that little boat. There was a cold, grey half-light, which made the cliffs look black and forbidding, and the boom of the waves among the rocks did not sound inviting. He kept well out, to avoid possible hidden reefs near the shore, for there was still a sea on though the tide had turned.

He had plenty of time for thought on his way, and mused upon the state of affairs at Kilmona, which he did not like. If it had not been that by taking himself off he would leave Thira in rather a nasty hole as to running the show single-handed, he might have been tempted to choose discretion as the better part of valour and run away from what he instinctively felt was a dangerous situation. However, until Colquhoun came he must just stay on and manage to steer a safe course as best he could. At any rate, there was always this girl, Janet Baxter, to help matters out, for Thira had asked him to be nice to her, and could not complain if he took her at her word; though it was evident that the young lady herself would not be a passive factor. She had taken a very strong dislike to him, which it would be difficult to overcome. To start with, he meant to make her swallow what she said about his being afraid. It made him feel hot all over to remember the way she had said it. He was still meditating vengeance when he arrived at the little harbour, and had to switch his thoughts in a more practical direction.

CHAPTER III

JANET awoke next morning feeling limp and not at all inclined to get up, so she told the maid to bring her breakfast upstairs later on, and then lay back idly considering the events of the previous day.

It certainly had been rather exciting, and she supposed that there had been some danger in it all; at any rate it was no joke for poor Payne; she had really thought he was going to be drowned. The others had been horrid to him about falling overboard, as if he had done it on purpose. He had been so nice to her on the island; in fact, he always was nice; so sympathetic and thoughtful, though possibly a trifle selfish underneath. She fancied that he liked to make a good impression, but a boat did not seem the most suitable place to show off his abilities; he was better on *terra firma*. Now, Mr. Wilson *was* at home in a boat. He had been very cross and sarcastic now and then, bit he knew what he was about—she couldn't help seeing that; yet, taken altogether, she did not feel pleased with the day's doings. Even Thira had taken the other side; and as for that Mr. Winthrop, he was almost insufferable sometimes; he seemed to think he was the only creature on earth who knew anything, or could do anything. For her part, she was not at all sure that there was any foundation for his assumption. At this point she dropped off to sleep again, and only woke when the maid brought breakfast an hour later.

"Will you please ask Mrs. Colquhoun to come up to me if it is convenient?" she said to the girl, who was busy putting the room tidy.

"Mrs. Colquhoun went out more than an hour ago, with Mr. Winthrop."

Janet felt annoyed; she thought it discourteous of Thira to go off with Jack without coming near her or even sending a message, quite forgetting that probably Thira had been told that she wished to take her breakfast in bed and rest awhile. However, it was no use lying there feeling miserable and neglected, so having finished her breakfast, she got up and went downstairs, only to find that everyone had gone out.

For want of a better occupation she decided to look for Jack and Thira, who, she knew, had gone fishing. It did not occur to her that she might not be wanted, nor did she remember that "two's company, three's none."

It was a lovely morning; she enjoyed her walk up the valley in the brilliant sunshine, and it was not very long before she came within sight of the loch, and of the fishers in their boat. Sport, judging by appearances, was not brisk, for the rods were hanging idly over the side and the two were quietly talking.

For the first time Janet began to wonder if she was likely to be welcome. It had never struck her before that there was anything between these two but the most ordinary camaraderie, but now her doubts were aroused. She felt a little annoyed with herself for having been such a fool as to come; but as she was now close to the water's edge, it would look strange to turn back without a word of greeting. The boat drifted about a hundred yards from the shore, and to attract their attention she had to raise her voice to hail them. Only then did they realise her presence. They turned towards her, and Jack waved his hat, but Thira only stared. Janet was rather at a loss what to do, but Jack saved the situation by taking an oar and sculling in.

"Hello, Miss Baxter—how did you get here, and what are you doing all by yourself?"

"Oh, I lay in bed rather late, and when I came down I found that everyone had gone out. You were the only two of whom I could get any news, so I thought I would stroll up and see how you were getting on. What sort of sport have you had?"

"Oh, not so bad," said Jack, holding up a string of fish. "At first we did rather well, but for the last half-hour the fish have stopped talking. I don't think we shall do any more good with this bright sunshine and the water so smooth."

Thira, hitherto quiet, now began to tease Janet for lying in bed all the morning, and asked her what she intended to do with herself until lunch. Janet wished sincerely she had not come, for she had no plans, and, taken unawares, was obliged to confess as much, though she said she meant to take a stroll round before returning. To Thira's annoyance, Jack suggested perversely that Janet should come into the boat and have his rod.

Janet hastened to assure him that she had never fished in her life and knew nothing about the art.

"All the more reason to learn now you have the chance!" retorted Jack.

"Oh, but she can't learn from the boat!" cried Thira.

"No; perhaps that would be difficult. But, after all, why stop in the boat? The fish are evidently not going to oblige, so suppose we go down the burn? We may have better luck there."

Thira did not seem pleased with this idea, but she could hardly do anything but agree, so she landed with her companion, and they all three walked to the burn.

Jack insisted that Janet should take his rod and try her hand for the first time at fly-fishing, which necessitated a good deal of elbow-room, so that Thira thought it desirable to go a little way off and fish on her own account.

Janet was astonished to find how pleasant Jack could be. Over and over again, hopelessly entangled with the line, she caught the hook in her clothes or in the bushes, or wound the cast round a stone, but he took it all quietly; simply disentangled the line patiently and told her it would all come right by and by if she would persevere. She felt stupid, but he showed not the least irritation, but only explained with unfailing smiles the difficult problem of casting a line accurately—which looked so simple until she tried to do it.

Thira soon caught several fish, and then came back and criticised Janet with an air of superiority which was rather galling. She continued to scoff till the genial instructor offered to bet her a pair of gloves that his pupil would land her first fish before lunch. Thira took the bet, and almost immediately something happened which made Janet's heart quicken. She had managed to drop her flies just where Jack had told her this time. There was a swirl and splash, and the line stretched taut as wire. Jack shouted, but she was far too excited to understand, and the line began to run through her fingers to the shriek of the reel.

She never remembered afterwards exactly the procedure during the next few minutes; she only knew that by some miracle she had hooked a fish. She wanted Jack to take the rod, but he firmly declined, so she had to do her best to carry out his rapid fire of instructions.

Then followed moments of delirious excitement; instants of horror when the line went slack and the rod straight, and she thought she had lost her fish; gasps of relief when she again felt the strain, until at length her fears and her joys were merged in one intense feeling of satisfaction, when she had her first gleaming captive flapping safely at her feet on dry land and Jack's voice congratulated her on her success.

CHAPTER IV

SOME days after the landing of that never-to-be-forgotten fish, Jack and Janet were standing in the cove by the small boat.

Matters had progressed rapidly between them. They were no longer almost sworn foes; that little touch of common interest in the capture of the fish had put things on a new footing, and from that moment each had begun to discover a good deal to appreciate in the other. Janet had forgotten to be snappy, and Jack had gone out of his way to make the days for her as pleasant as he could. He had always arranged things for everyone else, but hitherto Janet would never let him do so for her. Now, however, she recognised that his little attentions made for her comfort; and soon he seemed to be devoting himself to her particularly.

Thira, who had so recently admonished Jack for his rudeness to the girl, did not seem satisfied with the change. It was all very well for Jack to leave off his ridiculous rudeness to Janet, but that was no reason why he need be always running about after her, waiting upon her as though he were her slave.

Jack was fully alive to Thira's views, though she had not said a word to him about it. He was in fact not displeased at the turn in affairs, for Colquhoun, his very good friend, had given him the run of his house and shown absolute confidence in him, and Jack had been perturbed by an occasional thought that he was not quite "playing the game." He liked Thira very much, but he had no intention of permitting that liking to develop into anything deeper; yet she had shown him plainly during the last month or two that she very much preferred his company to that of anyone else. Though flattering to his vanity, this was also embarrassing, and a little alarming; because, susceptible as he was to her charm, he was not quite sure how far he could trust himself. Therefore he had been rather pleased to have Janet to play off against her.

As for Janet, she had not realised the situation at all; she only thought that Jack was "awfully nice" when one got to know him, and regretted her previous behaviour to one who had proved himself, on closer acquaintance, one of the best of fellows.

At present she was not aware that Thira's attitude had changed, although she had noticed that her friend was not her usual bright self; she attributed this, however, to some passing whim, never for a moment to its true cause.

On the morning in question she and Jack had been standing on the terrace after breakfast, watching the sea. It was a lovely, warm, still day, and in a moment of thoughtlessness she said:

"How tempting the sea looks!"

"Well," answered Jack, "let's get the boat, and I'll take you out."

She hesitated, not being quite sure whether she ought to go alone with him, but he was so persistent (and, after all, conventions did not seem to count for much so far west) that at last she consented. A few minutes later they were gliding smoothly over the water, with only just sufficient wind to fill the sails. Jack had never talked to her so interestingly as he did that morning, and she, in return, told him many details about herself and her life. He was immensely interested, and showed it unmistakably; his sympathy, combined with his sensible suggestions as to the best way of getting on, encouraged her to still further confidences.

At lunch Thira made a few dry remarks to Jack concerning the folly of taking a girl out alone in a boat, among rocks and currents and tides entirely strange to him; but he only laughed, making light of the supposed dangers. He could see well enough, however, that she was anything but pleased.

She took him for an afternoon drive in an Irish car, leaving Janet feeling rather lost, and not quite knowing why; but somehow there seemed to be nothing worth doing after they had gone.

The drive did not prove a success. Thira was sweetness itself at first, though Jack did not appreciate her sweetness quite as she had anticipated; for soon after they had started, he inquired when she expected Colquhoun to join them. She had not thought anything about her husband, and was not at all anxious to have him, and she delicately intimated as much.

Jack, however, did not accept the opportunity offered by her mood, and expressed his opinion that is was rather queer for a host to absent himself, as Colquhoun was doing, without any apparent reason, since obviously there could not be much to keep him in town at this time of the year. Thira, quite huffy at this, said some rather nasty things, and he almost became angry, though he managed to check himself before he said anything which he would afterwards have regretted; but the slight clash of tempers produced a feeling of restraint between them which had never existed before. Thira felt that something was wrong, though she could not have precisely defined it; Jack felt it too. He knew the cause, and determined to find the remedy. On their return he wrote a note to Colquhoun, in which he said that they were all wondering if he meant to put in an appearance at all; that if he did not come soon there would be nothing left to shoot, and the best of the season would be over and gone. He did not mention to Thira that he had written, but now that he thought Colquhoun would probably soon come, he allowed himself more latitude with her, and took her about a good deal, reinstating himself in her good graces.

It was a dangerous situation for her. She had always liked Jack more than any other man she had ever met, and lately her affection for him had grown to such an extent that she was discontented; there was something missing if he was not with her. She had never analysed her feelings about him, or given any serious thought to the subject, until she noticed his growing intimacy with Janet; then she began to see things as they really were, and to feel that she would hate any woman who took him away from her. She knew that her attitude was a ridiculous one, her position quite untenable, but it persisted in spite of this knowledge, and she was light-hearted indeed when they resumed their old relations and he accompanied her as before. Her awakening to the strength of her growing love for him was not without its terrors; but as the days went by the secret gave up to her some of its sweetness, and she became more at ease.

Janet, meanwhile, had not been at all happy, though she would not acknowledge, even to herself, the cause of her vague trouble; she persuaded herself that she was simply wearied with the place and its surroundings. To outward appearance she and Jack were as good friends as ever. Occasionally he would take her fishing, or for a day's sail, but usually they joined a party, and the sense of friendship and intimacy which she had found so delightful seemed, somehow, to have vanished.

Then one morning came a letter from Colquhoun, saying that they might expect him immediately.

Thira did not appear unduly elated at this news, but Jack was delighted, for matters had been going too fast for him; also he felt highly pleased at the prospect of handing over his duties, which tended to become irksome; again, when Colquhoun arrived the position would be so much simpler with Thira. She had begun to turn to him for help in everything, which often entailed long *tête-à-tête* talks in her boudoir. He found the situation trying; he did not want her to care for him too much, and he was not conceited, but he could not help seeing that Thira was growing much too fond of him for her own safety and their mutual peace of mind.

* * * * * *

Jack met Colquhoun at the station. Thira refused to come, much to his relief, for he felt rather a traitor when his friend warmly gripped his hand, asking a string of questions as to how things had been going with them all and how Thira was. He looked round for her, obviously feeling disappointed at her absence; surely, after all these weeks, she might have faced the long drive in order to welcome him. The true state of the case never struck him; that Thira might not be glad to see him would have seemed absolutely impossible.

It was quite late that night when they reached Kilmona, and the meeting between husband and wife gave no signs of their relations to the uninitiated, though in response to Colquhoun's eagerness and delight Thira showed a matronly sense of propriety as to the extent of the embraces which she would allow in public. Some of those who saw the arrival, however, were not quite blind to the state of affairs, and to more than one the scene had its pathetic side.

Very soon the ladies retired, and Colquhoun was carried off to the smoking-room, where he was quickly placed in touch with the general customs and habits of his own house. He was grateful to Jack for taking charge, and said so, much to Jack's vexation, for he was aware that Seymour and a few others knew more of the position than they chose to show; therefore this public expression of Colquhoun's thanks for looking after his wife and household embarrassed him. He made haste to disclaim any right to thanks, saying how glad he should be to turn over all the responsibility to its rightful owner.

He spoke the truth; he was genuinely glad to have Colquhoun there. It was all very well to make up his mind to run straight, but when a really beautiful woman almost threw herself at his feet, danger was not far away. Jack was very human, and though he did not love Thira he could not help admiring her physical beauty. The constant presence of temptation might wear down his best endeavours to act honourably.

Early next morning Colquhoun was out with Jack, being shown round the place, of which he had a very hazy recollection, having been there only two or three times before. Jack made no secret of the fact that he had devoted much of his time to Thira, and Colquhoun seemed to think it quite natural that he should have done so; but Jack, with the wisdom of the serpent, was clever enough to bring Janet into his account of things in such a way that Colquhoun could easily imagine that there was more between these two than had ever existed. Knowing and liking both of them, he made up his mind that they should have as much of each other's company as he, at any rate, could manage, and from that time forward he invariably schemed to carry Thira off, or else arranged that someone other than Jack should be her escort when he could not go with her.

Thira fretted and fumed at this, but could do nothing but acquiesce. Under other conditions she would probably have rebelled, but a guilty conscience made a coward of her and she dare not make an overt move. Once or twice, when she happened to be alone with Jack, she did attempt to open the subject, but he never seemed to see what she was driving at; he was extraordinarily obtuse. His attitude maddened her, but she could do nothing; she simply had to leave matters to run their own course.

As for Janet, she so often seemed to be left with Jack as her partner that after a time it became an understanding that the two should go off together. Jack taught her to sail a boat herself, and they went for long excursions, seaward and along the coast. On several occasions they had gone after dinner when the moon was up, for there was a special charm on the water in the high-light, with the mysterious whispering of the waves and sigh of the wind.

At such times they would talk of many matters which in broad daylight would have seemed too "soulful" for open discussion, and as they learnt to know each other a mutual understanding, a sense that each had met a comprehending, sympathetic comrade, grew between them. Without actual love-making, this charming friendship and fellowship soon ripened, on Janet's part, into love. Jack found it as difficult as ever to define his feelings. He certainly liked the girl immensely, and was never so happy as when he was with her. He could not imagine himself quarrelling with her, nor could he fail to see that she liked him more than a little: but how far that liking went, or whether it verged on the deeper glow of love, he did not know. And he was not sure, yet, that he wanted to know; for full knowledge might disturb the even flow of life at Kilmona—so pleasant, so restful, so recreating.

CHAPTER V

A LOVELY warm summer's night, with the faintest breeze from the south-west; the moon, high in an almost cloudless heaven, a silver shield; the sea unruffled, tinged with a pale gleam that seemed not of this common world;—thus was the night which brought Jack to his fuller knowledge.

He and Janet were standing on the terrace, looking out across the waters, silently; speech seemed almost a desecration of such beauty. It was one of those long pauses, an interlude of quiet dreaming, only possible or bearable between two people who, as perfect friends, thoroughly understand one another.

Jack broke the silence first.

"Why not go out in the boat? I think there is just enough breeze to fill the sails."

"It's rather late, isn't it? It must be nearly ten o'clock."

Jack pulled out his watch. "Only just half past nine; besides, what does the time matter? No one ever bothers about time here."

"But what will Thira say if I go sailing at this time of night?"

"Why trouble what Thira says? She was out herself the other night till nearly midnight with Macintosh, and it's not the first time we've been out either. Do come."

"Very well. But you must promise to bring me in when I ask you, and not make excuses for staying out longer!"

"Right! Come along then, we'll get the boat."

A few moments later they were afloat, alone with the moonlit waves. Jack sat at the stern with the tiller in his hand, and the sheet hitched round a pin. Janet sat at his feet, as he said the boat trimmed better that way. They chatted about all sorts of themes, and presently touched upon the approaching end of this delightful holiday.

"I wonder whether Thira will go on with her music lessons when she gets back to town," Janet remarked.

"Why shouldn't she? She has always been keen on them."

"Yes, but I'm not so sure about it now. I don't think that she is as fond of me as she used to be before I came here. I don't know why, but I *feel* it."

Jack could have told her well enough why, but he had no intention of doing so. "Probably it is only your imagination," he said. "And a friendship between women is always a fluctuating affair. Everybody knows that."

"Well, I should be sorry to lose Thira as a pupil. I used to enjoy going to her, for it was a pleasant home and one met nice people."

"Was I one of the nice people? You met me there, among others!"

"I'm not quite certain. I didn't think so then. You were rather horrid to me in those days; but we needn't think about it now. We have discovered how silly we were."

"I have, at any rate," agreed Jack. "I know better now, but I, too, hope that Thira won't give up her lessons."

"Why? What can it matter to you?"

"Well, chiefly that if she does, you won't come there, and I shall not see you. That would be horrid. I can't afford to lose a friend, for I haven't many."

"It's nice of you to call me a friend; but even then you needn't necessarily lose sight of me. There are other ways!"

"For instance?"

"Well, perhaps the simplest would be for you to come and see me."

"Would you like me to come?" asked Jack, with earnest meaning in his voice.

Janet said nothing, but sat quite still for a moment, then, turning her head, looked straight up at him . . . .

The moonlight shone full on her face, and though he could not see the colour of her eyes, he could see the expression in them. There was no mistaking such a look. He knew then, though he had only dreamed of the possibility of it before, that she cared, more than cared, for him, and the thought thrilled him. It was new, and yet not new; he had asked himself the question more than once lately whether he loved this girl or not, but had not found a reply. Now, answering her long, deep gaze, he knew that he did love her; but *how*? It was not fair to fool with her, to make her believe that he really loved her if it were only a fleeting fancy doomed to fade when they had left this land of romance behind them; and yet . . .

Thoughts fly fast; after a few seconds, Janet lowered her eyes.

"You knew the answer before you asked me," she said. "Surely we are friends enough for that? I should hate to think that we were not to meet again after we leave this place."

"Yes, I did know, only I wanted to hear you say so. It was rather mean of me, but I couldn't help it."

"Then you will come and see me sometimes, when we are at home again?"

"Of course I shall; I simply couldn't bear to lose you now."

Silences fell between them, pregnant with possibilities, for they were both tensely strung. Jack was conscious only of the girl sitting at his feet, almost touching him. The desire came to him to stroke her hair; the inclination grew stronger and stronger until at last it was irresistible and he put out his hand and touched it. She did not move, and he let his hand stray among the loose curls at the nape of her neck; still she neither moved nor spoke, but a thrill seemed to run through her body.

Jack's hand slipped under her chin and turned her face towards him. Their eyes met; for a moment neither of them broke the hush.

"Janet?" he whispered.

It was the first time he had used her Christian name, and there was no mistaking his tone. Her eyelids drooped, and the long lashes caressed the ivory whiteness of her moonlit face; but still she did not speak.

"Janet—do you mind me calling you that?"

"Not if you like to. Why should I?"

"I don't know, dear, why you should, but you might. I want to tell you something, dear. I love you, Janet! Dear Janet, can't you love me too?"

Her answer was not in words; she simply kissed his hand. And in another moment she was in his arms, held close against his heart. She had never known the strength of a man before, but with all its surprise, its hint of terror, it was beautiful, almost divine; she offered no resistance, but was content to lose herself in the beauty of the moment.

She had loved him for a long time, even longer than she acknowledged to herself, but never allowed herself to dream that he might love her, or dared to hope for a moment like this. His lips were pressed to hers in burning kisses; all her soul in her lips, she responded. What she gave in those passionate moments could never be taken back; for when Janet gave, she gave with both hands, and now it was her all.

"Janet! How blind I must have been, darling! I knew that you liked me, but I never dared dream that you cared for me like this."

"I've known for quite a long time, dear, and I was horribly afraid you would find out, and think lightly of me for giving my heart unasked. I should have died of shame if you had thought that I cared while you didn't."

"I don't think you need have been afraid, darling. I, too, have known for some time that I cared, but I never knew how much. I have wondered a good deal lately what was wrong. I couldn't make out what it was I wanted; but I know now."

"Yes, that's it. It has been like that with me too. I soon found that I was only happy when I was with you, and I was rather upset, because I thought that you would never care for me like that, but only wanted me for a friend; and to be friends went such a little way along the road."

"What a lot of time we have wasted finding out, sweetheart!"

"No, not wasted; we have got to know each other so well these last few weeks, and after all we had hardly seen one another until a short time ago."

"I suppose it is a short time, really, yet it seems as if we had known one another somewhere, somehow, always. It seems so natural to love you, dear, to be with you, and to be loved by you. So divine, Janet; I wonder if you feel like that too?"

"Yes, Jack, dear, I think I do."

It was the first time she had called him "Jack"; hitherto it had always been the formal "Mr. Winthrop," and it was a moment he remembered.

They drifted idly, dreaming on, and neither of them could have said how the time had passed, until the boat gave an unexpected lurch over the slope of a long Atlantic roller.

"By Jove! Janet, look where we are!"

Janet looked, and to her amazement perceived that they were

far past the islands and fairly out at sea, in their frail shell of a boat. What time could it be? What would the others think? She uttered her thoughts aloud.

"What does it matter about the others? Let them think what they like, dear. But I had no idea we had drifted so far. We must be at least a couple of miles beyond the Black Isle, and we have come right through the race without knowing it. But the ebbtide was almost gone, and it's a still night, or we should have known it pretty quickly. Would you have been frightened, dear?"

"No, not with you."

"You darling girl! I feel as if I never wanted to go back to all those troublesome people. Why can't we stay out here, I wonder, or 'sail across the foam' as they do in all the best poems?"

"That *would* be nice, of course; but unfortunately one needs to eat and drink, and I don't suppose there is any food in the boat—you see I'm a practical person!"

"Well, we must turn homeward. But we go together and shall remain together."

"Yes, always together now, Jack; even though we have to separate for a little time."

Jack trimmed the sails and headed the boat towards the land, a good five miles away. The moon was already low on the horizon.

"I wonder what the time is," remarked Janet.

Jack looked at his watch, but remained silent.

"Are you wearing your watch, by any chance? Mine must have gone wrong."

"Yes, I have mine; but why do you think yours is wrong?"

"Well, just look at yours and see if it agrees."

"Oh, Jack! It really can't be that time!"

"That's just what I thought. Mine says one-twenty."

She nodded.

"Oh, Jack! What will Thira think?"

"Thira would think a good deal if she knew everything, but she doesn't yet, and we can choose our own time to tell her."

"But we shall have to tell her when we get in."

"I don't think we shall find many people out of bed to tell. They are all fast asleep by now."

"Well, I hope so!"

But neither of them was very anxious, for if it came to the worst they had that to tell which would close all mouths to scandal. The breeze freshened a little as dawn approached, and the boat sped lightly over the baby seas. They had left the ocean swell behind and were running under the shadow of the Black Isle's looming cliffs.

"Janet, dear, when you came out to-night did you dream how things would be when you went back?"

"No, oh no! If I had, I think I should have been afraid to come."

"Are you sorry, then?" His look anticipated her reply.

"Sorry? No, a thousand times no! But I should never have believed it could be so beautiful, or feel so natural in so short a time."

Her head was nestling against his shoulder and his free hand was round her waist; he moved it to stroke her hair.

Dawn paled the eastern sky as they stepped ashore, quietly made the boat fast, and stole up to the house. No glimmer of light appeared in any window, but the lounge door was never locked; it yielded to their touch, and they slipped in from the outer freshness to the heavy atmosphere of the room and the eerie hush of a sleeping house.

The clock on the mantelpiece warned them that it was half-past three. But as it was already so late—or early—another half hour or so couldn't matter, and four o'clock had struck before Janet raised her head from her lover's shoulder.

"Jack, dear, I really must go, or I shall sleep where I am!"

"Then good-night, my darling. You don't regret what has happened to-night, do you?"

"Regret it! No, no! You are not sorry you told me?"

"Darling! How can you say such a thing! It is the best thing I have ever done in my life. But what about to-morrow? Are we to tell the others about it?"

"Need we? Can't we keep it for our own secret for a little bit? I should hate to think the others were gossiping about us and making jokes over it. It would spoil things so. Let's just keep it secret for the present. It will be so lovely to have it all to ourselves."

"But are you quite sure it is wise, dear?"

"Why not? What difference can it make?"

Jack was not quite sure that it might make no difference, but thought it sweet of her to wish it, and such a secret, shared with her, seemed delightful. He agreed that they would say nothing just yet, and with a long, clinging embrace they parted.

Tired though she was, Janet lingered before her mirror, brushing her hair, for so much had happened since she had been in that room last. She could scarcely believe that she was the same girl who had stood there such a few hours ago. The whole world, life itself, seemed to wear a different aspect, and to have another, wider meaning than it had before; there was a new light on everything; she saw, where she had been blind. How blind, not to understand sooner! And to-morrow? What would it be like? Should she wake to find it a dream, and life just the same old, rather uninteresting routine which it had been for so long? No! That was where the beauty lay; she knew that the love that had come, had come to stay for ever; and life would never be quite the same again. It was so beautiful to know that when she went down she would find Jack, *her* Jack (that little pronoun made it so much more beautiful) waiting for her. It would be rather amusing, too, having this secret to hide from the others; she did not see what a false position she might place herself in by such a decision.

CHAPTER VI

LATER in the morning, Janet, looking from her window, could hear voices and laughter which proved that some of the earlier birds were already astir. She dressed and went down, feeling that the others must know all about last night; that even if they didn't know, they would as soon as they saw her. But when she arrived in the breakfast room no one read her secret joy, and it was almost a shock to find that they not only knew nothing, but apparently did not even suspect anything.

Jack had not appeared yet, and she wondered whether he would stick to their bargain, or would show by his manner that there was a new understanding between them.

At that moment he entered with Colquhoun, who, courtly and kind as ever, greeted his guests in turn, and had something pleasant to say to each. He held Janet's hand a moment longer than usual. "My dear child," he said, "you look quite brilliant this morning. What fairy has touched you with her wand?"

Janet felt that here at least was someone who could penetrate beneath the surface, but her blush and momentary embarrassment passed as quite natural in the circumstances, and Colquhoun had no suspicion of the truth; so she was easily able to turn his compliment aside with a jest about Erin, the elfin land. Jack's greeting to her, so far as the world could see, was what it had always been—frank, open, friendly—but his hand-clasp gave his thoughts clearly to her. Her pulses were throbbing as their hands parted, though his touch only lasted a couple of seconds, and, for all that the company could see, they might have been the most ordinary of friends.

Breakfast was in full swing before Thira appeared. Her greeting to the company was general; she made no invidious distinctions; yet it was fairly easy to see that she was not in the best of tempers. Her nearest neighbours happened to be Seymour and Jack. To Jack her manner seemed distinctly cool—she barely acknowledged his "good morning"; and even the genial Captain received scarcely any more recognition. As a result she was soon left to her own resources and her breakfast. Presently she joined in the conversation; but an observant onlooker might have noticed that she left Janet and Jack severely out in the cold. The two sufferers prepared for trouble.

"What time did you come in last night?" Thira enquired casually, as they rose from the table.

Janet expected some such question.

"I don't know exactly, but I think it was rather late."

"Yes, I'm afraid it must have been, dear; because after I was undressed and ready for bed I went to your room to say good-night, and you weren't in even then, though it was already getting on for twelve o'clock. I should have waited up for you, but I didn't want to alarm Richard, who might have thought you were in danger. I knew you were in good hands as you were out with Mr. Winthrop, so I went to bed."

The "Mr. Winthrop" sounded novel, and slightly formal, on Thira's lips. It was a long time since she had called him anything but "Jack." Janet made haste to express regret that Thira should have been anxious about her, and to explain that the wind had been very light and it had consequently taken them an unexpectedly long time to return.

"Oh, you went sailing, then," said Thira. "I didn't know where you had gone, though I did happen to know who you were with, because I saw you go, and as neither of you were in the lounge when I went up I concluded that you were still together. You know, Janet, it was rather incautious of you to stay out so long."

"Why? I don't see that it matters much; we all come and go as we please here, don't we?"

"Ye—es, perhaps we do; but you know, dear, people will talk if a young girl stays out with a man alone for a long time. Of course I know it was quite all right with you, but Mr. Winthrop has got himself talked about with other girls in the past, and it is as well to be careful; so I shouldn't stay out quite so late again if I were you."

It was a cruel shaft, deliberately aimed, and it hurt for a moment—but only for a moment. Janet was so certain that Jack had not been playing with her. The ring of truth in all he had said was unmistakable, and she realised that Thira's remark had some definite purpose, though exactly what it was she could not understand. Her woman's instinct warned her of danger.

It had been done so cleverly, and with such an air of kindness and goodwill, that she had to accept it in the same spirit; none the less she felt sure there was more behind it. However, there was nothing to do but to promise to be more careful in the future. She smiled inwardly at the idea of being careful about her absences with Jack, and instantly went in search of him.

On this she reckoned without her hostess, for Thira had no intention of letting her speak to Jack before she herself had done so, and had already sent a message to him to the effect that she wished for his advice on certain matters, and asking him to wait in her boudoir. She had also arranged that Colquhoun should be safely out of the way; and now, having finished with Janet, she hastened to tackle the much more serious business of bringing Jack back to his senses, and to his allegiance to herself. She foresaw difficulties, though she had no idea that matters had progressed as fast or as far as they had between these two. It was to prevent their doing so that she was so anxious.

She found Jack waiting for her, obviously chafing against the restraint. Serenely ignoring his impatience, she began by discussing various trivialities. Only after these had been satisfactorily settled did she open her attack, apparently in the most innocent manner.

"Oh, by the bye, didn't you say the other day that the boat wanted a new sail?"

"Yes, I did; if you mean to use her much longer you will have to get a new jib for her. The one she has now would split in anything more than a capful of wind."

"It was all right last night, wasn't it?"

"Last night? There wasn't any wind to speak of last night."

"No, I know there wasn't. Janet told me so."

"Oh! Then she told you we went out?"

"Yes. She told me all about it, Jack. You see, I asked her what time she came in."

Jack was rather nonplussed. Could Janet have told Thira everything—Thira of all people? He was wondering what he should reply when for once Thira overreached herself.

"You know, Jack," she went on, "it isn't fair to take a girl out and keep her out late like that. Of course I know there was nothing in it, and that it was only thoughtlessness on your part, but people will talk, and no one could help noticing that you two were out alone together all that time. You will get the girl talked about, and I know that is the last thing you would wish, because of course you don't want to get entangled with a silly little thing like Janet."

"So she hasn't told, after all," thought Jack. "Not wish to get entangled with a silly little thing like Janet!" He could have laughed in her face. He was almost inclined to tell her the whole truth himself. It would be uncomfortable news for her, but it would serve her right for her duplicity. As he had promised Janet that the others should not know, he refrained.

"Oh, hang it all, Thira! Surely we are not so straitlaced here as all that? You and I have done a good many unconventional things since we came."

"That's quite another thing! We are very old friends."

"Ye—es; but I wonder whether Richard would think the same if he knew?"

"Don't talk nonsense, Jack. He will never know, because no one can tell him except ourselves, and we are not likely to be such fools."

"Why not tell him, if there is no harm in them? And if there is, why must I be more careful in one direction than another? Surely your reputation is worth as much as any other woman's, Thira? And if I am safe company for you, I am for Miss Baxter."

Unable to meet this argument squarely, she caught at a straw.

"That's just it. She is 'Miss Baxter' to you, and you are 'Mr. Winthrop' to her, while you and I are Jack and Thira. Everyone knows it and knows that Richard approves of it. If you two had known each other long enough to be Janet and Jack, it might be different."

"Well, suppose we were Janet and Jack to each other, would you be satisfied then?"

"*No*, I shouldn't! You know that without asking, and I won't have you going out all night with the girl like that."

"My dear Thira, don't let your imagination run away with you! We weren't out 'all night'; but if we had been and chose to go out again, I don't see how you are to stop it, unless you asked us to leave your house. Naturally it is your house and you can order your affairs as you choose; but I must say I don't quite see how you would explain having one set of rules for Janet—shall I call her?—and myself, and another for yourself and the rest of your guests!"

Thira felt sick and unhappy at this spirit of rebellion which she had raised in Jack. She made no pretence to herself that she did not love him, though she had long been half afraid that the feeling had been almost entirely on her side. She did not think that he cared for Janet, either, but she felt that in taking this line she had made a mistake, and had probably driven him in the very direction she wished to avoid. It would be just like Jack to make a fuss about the girl and spend most of his days with her, by way of showing his independence; and at the same time he would be sure to do it in such a charming manner that she could neither take offence nor do anything to stop it.

What a fool she had been! If she had only been content to work from the other side—it would have been so easy to upset Janet and make her show Jack the cold shoulder! But now she had made a hash of the whole thing. She knew quite well that she was really powerless to prevent Jack doing just as he chose; of course, it would be out of the question to request either of them to go away. Even if she could have asked him to do so she would never have found strength of purpose enough to do it, because she felt she could not do without him. In fact, now that she had assumed this attitude, her chief terror at the moment was that he might go, without any definitely expressed wish on her part.

She was madly in love, ready to forget everything for him; pride, modesty, her honour, even her marriage vows might go for his sake; yet she knew quite well that although he liked her very much—might even be fond of her—love itself was lacking. It was a cruel situation, and she was not altogether to blame for it. She could not help loving him, and argued that if Richard had never brought him into her life, this trying position would never have arisen, and she might have gone on to her dying day more or less contented. But now . . .

"Oh, Jack, don't be horrid to me! You know I didn't mean anything of the sort: but you also can't help seeing that the conventions must be respected to a certain extent, even here, unless the others are to think all kinds of things; so do be reasonable."

"I'm ready enough to be 'reasonable,' but as no one saw us either go out or come in last night I don't see that they are likely to be shocked, or to have their sense of propriety jarred. Except ourselves and Janet no one knows that we did go out, and why should they?"

"Very well, then; leave it at that, and I will tell Janet that she had better not mention that you were out last night; but you won't do it again, will you?"

"I don't think that will do: Janet may feel hurt at having things put to her in such a crude way. Leave it to me; I will tell her."

"I don't see why I should leave it to you: I think she would take it much better from me."

"Perhaps so, but if I am to play the game to your rules I must do it in my own way or not at all, so please say which it is to be: whether I am to have my own way in this little business and afterwards play your game, or let you have yours, and then please myself."

"You put things most disagreeably, Jack, but if I let you settle with Janet, will you, on your side, promise not to take her out alone at night like that again?"

"Yes, I will go as far as that if it pleases you, Thira."

"Of course it pleases me; I don't want you to get yourself into a mess, or Janet either."

"Very well, then; and now may I consider this little lecture closed? You have never given me one before, and I don't much care about it."

"Neither do I, Jack. I hate having the slightest row with you. Please forgive me if I have been interfering, but, believe me, I did it with only the best intentions, very much against the grain."

"Very well, let's forget all about it, and go out for a ride. I want you to try that new mare Richard and I bought for you yesterday. She's really a ripper, and I feel sure you will like her."

Thira's heart leaped for joy at the thought of a ride alone with Jack. She had not had one for some time, and it meant that she would have him to herself. Better still, it would mean that Janet would be left out in the cold.

"Oh, I should love it. When shall we go?"

"As soon as ever you can get ready. How long will that take you?"

"Let's see, it's just half-past ten—how about eleven o'clock?"

"Right; I'll have the horses ready by then. Will you come round to the stables, or shall I have them brought to the door?"

Thira hesitated a moment. If she had the horses brought round, everyone would come to see them start, but if she went to the stables they could slip away without being seen; so she elected to go to the stables.

"All right, I'll be there in time," said Jack, and hurried off to find Janet. He had promised Thira to warn her not to mention last night's sail, but that was not the reason for his search; he knew well enough she would say nothing about it. His heart had been aching for hours to be with her, and he felt he must see her before he went out, even if it were only to explain why he were going.

She was not in the lounge or on the terrace, and after he had learnt that she was not in her room he began to search the grounds.

Fifteen minutes of precious time were gone before he found her sitting disconsolately alone in the little boat-house arbour, looking out across the sea.

She sprang up with a little cry as he came in, and ran to him.

"Oh, Jack! I thought you were never coming. Where *have* you been?"

"Darling!" was all Jack could say for a moment; he folded her in his arms and held her there.

He explained as fas as he thought necessary, and she was rather sore at being deserted, but she could not gainsay the wisdom of his decision, and saw that if they were to keep their secret they must play to the gallery; though, as he pointed out, if she chose to make it public it would be easy enough for them to be left alone all the time.

However, she had no hesitation as to which it should be, for she wished to keep her happiness to herself and could not bear the idea of being a mark for the critical curiosity of the others; so, reluctantly, she let him go, first obtaining a promise that they should have the afternoon together.

CHAPTER VII

THE new mare which Thira rode, a beautiful creature, gave every indication of an excitable nature, but as his companion was a good horsewoman and Jack had often taken her out before, he had no anxiety. She soon put the mare through her paces, expressed delight with the acquisition, and was her bright and happy self again.

"Is she really fast?" asked Thira.

"Fast! By Jove, I should think she was! It was a treat to see her yesterday; we tried her thoroughly."

"Come on, then, I'll race you to the corner of that hill!" said Thira, pointing to a bluff about half a mile away.

"Race me! Why, I should never see your heels on this horse!"

"Oh, nonsense! He's not all that slow. You are afraid of being beaten!"

"I don't mind being beaten a bit, but it wouldn't be a race, it would be a foregone conclusion."

"That doesn't matter. Come on, see if you can catch us!" She started off at a gallop, and Jack had to follow.

"Be careful, Thira!" he cried; but she gave the mare her head, urging her to the top of her pace, even giving her a cut or two with the whip. The mare resented this insult, snorted, and shot off like an arrow.

Jack knew before they started that there was no question of his catching her, but he sent his horse along as fast as he could, and managed at first to keep him within hail, though he lost ground every minute.

Nearing the bluff, he fully expected to see her steady a bit, but instead the mare swung round the corner at breakneck speed.

"Stop! Stop!!" he yelled, but Thira, flying on over the soft turf, did not seem to hear him. She could not stop; she had hustled the mare, and the high-spirited animal had now made up its mind that if there was to be any hustling two could take part in it. Thira's little hands were doing all they could, but for any impression they made she might have saved herself the exertion; the mare was mad now and quite out of hand. Thira hoped she would get blown soon and stop of her own accord. For the next mile or so the going was sound; but then came a nasty bit of loose, stony road on the spur of the hill. As they neared this, Thira realised her danger, and redoubled her efforts.

Jack, labouring a quarter of a mile behind, saw the danger too, and knew that the mare had taken charge; he could do nothing but hope for luck. They disappeared round the corner, but came into sight again in a moment or so, where the track skirted a low hill. He could see that Thira was trying hard to stop the mare, but her efforts did more harm than good, for they only distracted her attention from the road. For a hundred yards all went well; then, whether the mare put her foot on a stone, or in a hole, or crossed her legs, Jack could not see, but she stumbled, pecked, and went down heavily, falling over and over down the slope, horse and rider in a confused heap. The mare scrambled to her feet, hesitated, then galloped away, leaving a motionless grey figure on the ground.

Jack suffered in the next few moments an agony of fear.

Thira lay huddled up with one arm twisted beneath her, her ashen face showing no sign of life. His heart sank, If she were dead? What should he say to Colquhoun?

He knelt by her and placed her in a more natural position, but she did not move. He felt for her pulse, but could make nothing of it. He put his hand on her heart, but it seemed still. In desperation he tried to pull off her habit, but the fastenings were strange and his fingers were awkward; at last he loosened it, but she did not apparently breathe. He looked wildly round for water, and quickly filled his hat from a burn a hundred yards away; splashing it in her face, he was in despair, for her eyes remained obstinately closed. Again he tried to feel her heart, but her clothes impeded him; he loosened them still more, and a moment later, her breast, free from restraint, rose and fell softly, and she sighed.

He continued bathing her temples and chafing her hands, and at last was rewarded. The blue eyes opened lazily, dreamily; at first she did not seem to recognise him, or to realise in the least where she was; then slowly consciousness came back.

"Do you feel better, Thira?" asked Jack. "Are you badly hurt?"

"Why? What has happened? Where am I, and what are you doing with me, Jack dear?"

"You have had a nasty fall, and I thought you were very badly hurt, but you will be all right soon."

"Oh yes. I begin to remember a little now." She shut her eyes and lay quite still again, much to Jack's alarm. He continued to bathe her forehead with water until she opened them once more.

"Oh, Jack! You are good to take care of me like this. I must have been unconscious, too. What happened? I have a kind of recollection of the mare falling, but I can remember nothing more."

He told her what had occurred, then tried to discover if she was seriously injured, persuading her to move her limbs gently to see if they were sound. She tried to stretch herself, then gave a little cry.

"Oh, my arm!"

Jack, examining, found at once that it was broken above the elbow. She bore his touch very bravely, and, when he told her, seemed more concerned over a spoiled holiday than over the actual injury.

Then she saw that her dress was disarranged, her bosom exposed, and flushed crimson.

"Oh, Jack! How did my things get like this?" She tried with her uninjured hand to adjust her costume.

"I'm awfully sorry, Thira, but I had to do it, to try and make you breathe. You simply wouldn't come round. Forgive me, won't you?"

"Oh, it isn't a case of forgiveness; I don't much mind, as it was only you; but you must never tell anyone that you have seen me like this, please, Jack."

"Tell anyone? Of course not! Let me fasten you up again—you can't possibly do it yourself with one hand." Quietly he began to refasten her garments, but stopped suddenly. "What a fool I am! I ought to make that arm comfortable first." For splints he broke his ash stick in two; then carefully bound up the injured limb with his handkerchief. His touch was light, and hurt her very little, though now and then she gave an exclamation at some sharp twinge. Turning again to the task of restoring her clothes to order, he managed this after a good deal of difficulty and some whimsical comments from Thira, with a laugh or two in spite of her pain. When she had been made presentable he found for her as comfortable a position as possible, and went in search of horses. There was no sign of the mare, but his own horse was quietly nibbling the turf not far off. He caught it easily enough and went back. Thira was looking very white, but wonderfully cheerful. The immediate problem was to reach home. Jack suggested that she should wait there while he rode to the house to fetch a carriage, but she would not hear of it.

"Oh no, please, Jack! Don't leave me—I should be dreadfully frightened. You must either put me on your horse, or we must both just wait until some of them come to look for us. They are sure to, if we don't turn up at lunch."

"We might wait a deuce of a time before they did, though," remonstrated Jack, "and you would catch your death of cold sitting out here in the damp after a shock like that—to say nothing of your arm, which must be properly set as soon as ever a doctor is available."

"Very well, then, you must manage to get me on your horse."

There was no alternative, so he assented. Fortunately the horse he had been riding was a very well-mannered one. He picked Thira up and placed her in the saddle. For a moment she rested in his arms like a child, with her cheek against his hair. She seemed quite contented to be there; it was a joy to feel herself in his strong arms. Never, till that moment, had he held her so.

Slowly they set off homeward, Jack leading the horse, and picking the way carefully to avoid any jar to her arm, which now gave her a good deal of pain. He had rigged up a sling to make it easier, and she was very plucky about it, though now and again a little spasm flitted across her face. Jack was thoughtful and gentle with her, and in spite of everything she was happy; his care of her was sweet. She tried to make him tell her his feelings when he saw her fall, and afterwards when he found her unconscious, and was thrilled when he told her, in his bluff way, that it had frightened him out of his senses when he saw her lying so still and white, and could not bring her round. How, for a moment, he had fancied she was killed, and his despair, and his joy when she breathed again and spoke. He happened to look up at this moment; their eyes met, and she blushed.

"Jack, if I had been killed, would you have been sorry?"

"How can you ask such a silly question, Thira?"

"Well, would you have minded very much, I mean? Of course you would have been sorry; anyone would."

"Of course I should have minded frightfully, because you are one of the best friends I have, and I couldn't spare you. And it would have been all my fault for tempting you to ride that mare and not taking proper care of you."

"It wasn't your fault, it was my own. It was I who started that race; you hadn't any chance of stopping me, because I was gone before you knew that I meant to start; afterwards you could do nothing, because you couldn't possibly catch me up; and as for taking proper care of me, if you hadn't been so clever I might never have come round at all. You were just a dear—you thought about everything and were ever so sweet over it."

"I didn't feel a bit clever; I never felt so helpless in my life. If you had been a man, I should have known what to do; but I never had to do with a woman in such a case before. You women wear your things fastened up queerly, and all your buttons are on the wrong side, which makes it awkward; and when it came to corsets"—Jack grinned—"I was awfully afraid of hurting you if I was rough: yet I had to use a certain amount of force to get them undone at all."

Thira blushed again as she remembered her "divine disarray" when she had first recovered consciousness, but Jack was looking the other way and did not notice it.

"Jack, dear!"

"Yes, Thira?"

"I would rather you didn't tell the others about that part of the performance. I should prefer you not to—let's keep it to ourselves, please."

"Right—I won't tell. I expect they already know there has been an accident, for the mare is certain to have galloped home and created a fearful scare."

"Poor dears! What a state they will be in. We shall have Richard out directly, driving furiously to see what has happened to me. It will be very nice of him, but it will also be very trying!"

They were nearly half-way home by now, clear of the hills and on the road, where the shade made it pleasanter going for Thira. The strain was beginning to tell on her; and she felt almost ready to fall from the horse's back, but with an effort she kept her seat.

Suddenly, far away, they heard the sound of galloping hoofs.

"There they come! I knew they would!" she cried. "They will be here in a minute."

"Well, I shall be glad to see you safe in a carriage, no matter what kind. You ought to be in the doctor's hands already."

"Jack, I think I should like to get off before they come. They might make this horse frisky, and I don't want another tumble just yet."

Jack stopped the horse and lifted her gently down, carefully avoiding the poor wounded arm. How soft and round she was, he thought, as he held her for a moment before setting her on her feet. Thira stood perfectly quiet for a while when she reached the ground, clinging to him with her uninjured arm.

"Thanks, Jack. You are wonderfully gentle, and yet so strong. I can't think how you manage to be both at once."

She did not want to move; the support of his arms thrilled her, and in a moment or two others would come, and things would slip back to their usual groove once more. For a wild moment she thought he was going to kiss her; but he gently disengaged himself, and almost as he did so a pair-horse car, smartly driven, came into view and pulled up with a clatter beside them.[10] The horses were white with lather, and Colquhoun, sitting by the driver, looked grey with anxiety.

"Thira! What has happened? Thank Heaven you are not killed!"

Thira tried to explain, but now that the first strain was over, faintness suddenly overcame her. She would have fallen if Jack, whom Colquhoun had not even noticed, had not caught her.

"She isn't fit to walk yet," he explained. "Get her home as fast as you can—I'll tell you all about the accident later. I will go for a doctor—her arm is broken and she has had a bad shaking."

In the car she soon recovered, and was full of regrets for having been so silly as to faint. Colquhoun got up beside her, while Jack swung himself on his horse, and vanished in a hard gallop up the road.

Thira did not speak more than a few words to her husband. She did not feel inclined to explain matters to him just yet, and after his last attempt and its results he feared to cross-examine her again. Anxious to get her home as quickly as possible, he dared not urge the horses for fear of jolting her too much; at last, however, the house came into sight, and a few moments later they arrived, to find the whole party waiting to receive them.

"Good heavens! What's happened?"

"I don't quite know, but Thira has had a bad fall, and broken her arm."

A volley of questions followed this announcement, but Colquhoun set them all aside.

"You shall know all about it by and by," he said abruptly. "Get this poor child to bed first."

---

10 Pair-horse car: type of carriage that is pulled by a pair of horses.

"Yes, that's the best place for her," said the practical Mary, taking charge of Thira and bearing her off.

Janet was looking on, white and frightened, one question on her lips which she was compelled to repress. Where is Jack? If anything awful had happened to him what should she do? Luckily for her, someone else had the same thought, though not the same fears.

"Where's Winthrop?" inquired Bertie Wilson.

"Oh, he has ridden over as fast as he can to fetch the doctor."

"Sensible chap! but hasn't she seen a doctor yet?" asked Seymour.

"No. How could she?"

"Then who tied her arm up?"

"I really don't know. Winthrop, I suppose; no one else was there."

About twenty minutes later the doctor arrived; and Jack was left to tell the story of the accident, for the first knowledge of which the mare was responsible. She had come in riderless, with one pommel smashed, and only one conclusion could be drawn from that.[11] Colquhoun had rushed out at once for a carriage, and only after the horses were in and he was ready to start did it occur to him that the direction the two had taken was uncertain; none of those present could help him. It was rumoured, however, that they had gone up the valley, so he set off.

Anxious as the rest of the party were, nothing could be done; they could only wait and hope for the best. Janet was almost beside herself; if Jack had been unhurt, she thought, he would never have let the mare get away; it never struck her that he might not have been able to catch the animal, and until Colquhoun told them that Jack had gone off for the doctor and she knew that he was at least not seriously hurt, she had been in an agony of fear.

---

[11] Pommel: rounded knob at the front of a horse's saddle.

She felt so relieved that she was almost unsympathetic about Thira. She went away to her own room to recover herself, and once there in solitude, away from observation, she broke down, and much to her own surprise, gave way to tears of relief. Even while she lay on her bed with her face buried in her pillow, sobbing, she felt happier.

The doctor's report proved fairly satisfactory; he had found no damage beyond the broken arm, and a slight concussion accompanied by a general shaking. Thira was to be kept absolutely quiet for the present, and to remain in bed.

"Where's Janet?" asked Mary. "I want her to help me nurse Thira. Someone will have to stay with her to-night in case she is feverish, and as she knows Janet better than anybody else, I think she will be the best one for the job; she and I can divide the work between us."

She went upstairs and knocked softly at Janet's door; knocked again more loudly; and after an interval a voice from within said, "Who is it?"

"It's me—Mary! May I come in? I want to speak to you."

"Just a moment, please."

The moment was a long one, but at last the key turned and the door opened. Mary went in and immediately began to explain her scheme for nursing Thura.

"You will do it, won't you?" she said. "I'm sure she would rather have you than anyone else; you know each other so well, for you have been with her more than the rest of them, even more than I have. She must have someone with her, and we can't trust a maid in an emergency like this."

"If you really think she would like it, of course I will do it with pleasure," said Janet; "but I'm not so sure that she will."

Mary had not noticed Janet particularly until then, in the

eagerness of her request; but now she looked more closely, and could not help seeing that the girl had been crying.

"Why, child, what on earth have you been crying about? Things weren't so bad as all that!"

"Oh, I don't know. It was all so horrid, I got frightened and upset."

"Well, cheer up, dear—there isn't anything seriously wrong except the broken arm, and that will soon get well. The doctor said that the way Jack tied it up makes all the difference, because it was practically set at once. He had very little to do except to cut her sleeve off and replace the amateur splints with the professional ones. She's asleep now, and all we have to do is to keep her quiet; but someone must be with her. Would you like to go there now, or take me off duty later?"

"I don't mind which," said Janet.

"I think I should prefer being day nurse, because I sleep so heavily—I mightn't wake if she wanted anything. It's just about four now. Suppose I stay until eleven, and then you come for the night? I would relieve you again about seven in the morning."

"Very well, that will suit me all right; if you are sure there's no one else who could manage it better than I can."

"Quite sure, dear. Don't cry any more—there is really nothing to cry about."

It was evident that she ascribed the tears to Janet's concern about Thira, and never dreamed of attributing them to their true cause. Janet, not displeased at the error, took care to remove all traces of grief before going downstairs.

CHAPTER VIII

LATER in the day Jack and Janet managed to escape together, and he told her the whole story, omitting only the details which Thira had made him promise not to reveal.

"Oh, Jack dear, I'm thankful it wasn't you who were hurt. I was in an agony until Thira was brought in and Mr. Colquhoun told us you had gone for the doctor; after that I didn't care any more about anything, because I knew you were safe."

"My darling! I am so sorry you were frightened. I believe if I had thought of it I should have been heartless enough to ride home and send a man for the doctor, but somehow it never struck me that you would think anything had happened to me."

"I thought of you first; in fact, I never thought of Thira at all. She will be laid up for some time, I am afraid. You know, of course, that I'm going to help nurse her."

"I hadn't even thought hat she needed nursing. Somehow a broken arm didn't associate itself with nursing in my mind, but I suppose she was a good deal shaken and knocked about, poor girl."

"Dense person! Of course she was; didn't you tell me yourself that she was quite dazed? If people are hurt as much as that they have to be taken care of. Mary is looking after her now, and I am to relieve her later on for the night."

"But you are not going to sit up with her all night?" protested Jack.

"Yes, I am. Why not?"

"You will knock yourself up, getting no sleep."

"Oh, I shall get plenty of sleep. I can go to bed in the morning when Mary comes back."

"Then you'll be in bed all day to-morrow and I shan't see anything of you. It will be simply unbearable. What am I going to do without you?"

"Selfish boy, to think only of yourself! If it's a little trying to you don't you think it will also be for me? Sitting there all night with nothing to do but think, possibly of somebody who doesn't deserve it, and having to go to bed meekly in the morning instead of being out and about?"

"I am a selfish pig, Janet; but it's only because I hate the thought of being kept away from you."

"Well, if you really care, you will like me all the better afterwards; and if you don't, you will have time to find out."

"Really care? You know I care! I shall be miserable all the time."

"Silly boy, it won't be so very long, after all, before you have me back again."

"How long do you expect it will last? I mean how long will it be before I can have you alone again?"

"How long does it take a broken arm to set?"

"Oh, I don't know; when women take to sick-nursing one never knows what to expect!"

"You really are provoking, Jack; you deserve to be punished; so I just won't come with you again until . . . " She stopped and looked up mischievously at him.

"Until when, you little sinner? Be merciful, and put me out of my suspense."

"Well, shall we say until about three o'clock to-morrow afternoon?"

The road was secluded, and she was irresistible.

Jack, however, was not quite happy. He felt uncomfortable about the whole situation, for much as he liked Thira (and with her he included her husband) it was evident that she desired something deeper than mere liking, and this he never would, or could, give her. He had known for some time that there was danger, but after her fall there had been no mistaking her manner, nor had it been possible to overlook the repeated "dear" which had slipped into her sentences when she was speaking to him. He was horribly vexed that things should have come to this pass, more than ever now that he and Janet had arrived at an understanding.

He sat down and gently drew her on to his knee.

"Are you happy, darling?" he asked.

"Blissfully happy. Are you sure you won't get tired of me, and be sorry by and by that you have given yourself to me? You may find somebody else you would like better."

The assurance came, and their tongues ran on as lovers' will until the night closed in around them. It was nearly half-past ten when Janet awoke to her self-imposed responsibility.

"I must go in—I promised Mary to relieve her at eleven."

"Well, if you must, you must, I suppose," sighed Jack, and a few minutes later they said good-night in the shadow of the house.

Janet slipped in and upstairs, while Jack lighted a cigar and strolled off to the smoking-room, where he found some of the others immersed in a discussion on horses and bridles, which arose from a question as to how Thira's mare had been bitted that morning. It ended by one of his guests asking Colquhoun for permission to take the mare out in the morning if she was fit and sound, to try her. Colquhoun was only too glad to consent, admitting that he would be a little anxious about the animal, after what had happened that day, until she had been thoroughly tried again by an experienced rider.

The party gradually broke up, and the house was wrapped in sleep, except for one weary little watcher.

* * * * * *

Janet sat very still and quiet by Thira's bed; she had a book on her knees, but she could not read, for somehow her thoughts would not follow her eyes.

Every now and then Thira moaned a little and moved restlessly. The shock and the pain of her broken arm had made her feverish, and though she was asleep it seemed to be more a series of nightmares than wholesome slumber. A constant stream of half-defined horrors seemed to haunt her; partially memories of what had really occurred, and the rest distorted dreams of what might have been. Now and again Janet would bend over her to see how she was, occasionally moistening her lips, or arranging her pillows. As the night went on Thira's restlessness increased; her moans gave place to vague words, and then to sentences. Janet was rather alarmed, but took no notice till Jack's name, spoken in an unmistakable tone, attracted her sudden attention. She could not help listening then.

* * * * * *

It was broad daylight before Thira's wanderings ceased and she sank to sleep, but in the intervening time Janet felt she had grown a thousand years older . . . . What did it all mean? Surely it wasn't true? And yet, if not, why should Thira's sick brain have conjured up those pictures? Was the man to whom she had given her love, given her whole soul, as black as that? She would not, she could not believe it! And yet . . .

She remembered how he and Thira had always been together when first she came there. Also, in this new and appalling light, she remembered how often she had found him and Thira alone in the old days in London. Yet how could she reconcile the two situations? How associate the Jack she had learnt to know and love with the story those lips had revealed that night? It seemed utterly impossible.

It was a very weary, careworn little woman whom Mary found when she came on duty a few hours later, with dark rings round her eyes, something strange about her which Mary could not understand. Surely one night's nursing could not have had such an effect? She was distinctly puzzled.

Janet made her report, then slipped away to her own room, but not to sleep. Miserable beyond words, she lay prone trying hard to sleep and forget, but she heard all the movements of the house, as its occupants rose for the day, and all the time she wondered how she would meet Jack at three o'clock. She could not.

About one o'clock she dressed. What did it matter how she looked now? And yet she would look her best if possible, so that at least she need not feel that it was a question of appearance, and that she was not so good to look at as that other woman whom he loved, and with whom he had sinned. If love must go, pride at least should stay.

A very beautiful Janet made her way downstairs. The house appeared to be empty, but from the garden she heard voices, and following the sound came upon the whole house-party standing by a low fence, watching Jack—on the new horse which had caused the accident yesterday, and which to-day seemed quite mad. They told her that the mare had only just missed dashing the brains out of one rider as she bolted through the stable gates; Jack, who had seen the whole thing, had vowed that he would teach the devil manners, and, in spite of all protests, had fetched her out again.

He had changed her bridle so that he could hold her more easily; that did not stop her from trying to get rid of him, yet, in spite of every trick she knew, her tormentor was still firmly seated. There was a grim look on Jack's face that showed he was not likely to be vanquished. He had had some hurdles put up and was trying, much to her annoyance, to school the mare over these. She could jump, but she would not be made to go where she did not wish. He had already got her over twice, by coaxing and driving, but each time she became more restive, and when Janet arrived she was turning round and round, rearing and plunging, doing all she could to get her own way.

Jack's whip came down smartly on her shoulder; she promptly wheeled and bolted, but only for a few yards; she could not fight those hands and that bit; then in a fit of desperation she reared madly. Jack dropped his hands, but it was too late—she lost her balance and came right over backwards.

Man and horse fell apparently together, and Janet's heart stood still. There was a cry from the onlookers, but almost before they had time to recover their breath, Jack was on his feet again. He had the reins in his hands before the mare, thoroughly shaken and frightened, could get up.

The others thought this was the end of the performance, but a second later it was clear that he meant to remount.

"For God's sake, man, don't get up again—the brute will break your neck!" cried Seymour.

Jack either did not hear, or would not heed, but raised his foot towards the stirrup. In a moment the mare swung round and tried to get away from him, but although the reins slipped over her head, he held her. Very quietly he tried again, with the same result. Again he put the reins back, patted her neck, and placed his hand on the peak of the saddle, while the mare stood trembling, waiting for the foot to go up again; but she waited in vain, for with a clean spring her adversary was in the saddle.

With a snort of surprise and rage she dashed away, and while Jack gathered himself together she went as she pleased; but then matters changed. He had his feet in the stirrups, and his reins well in hand, and before the mare knew what was happening she was swung round and going the opposite way. Until then she had been going for her own amusement; now she had to go for his.

They raced round the field, and for a moment the mare looked like taking the bank and making for the open, but about fifty yards from it her head was wrenched round, and back she had to go. Then she tried to slow down, but there was a nasty surprise in store for her. The whip cut her ribs stingingly; she sprang forward, tried to stop and kick, but the whip fell again, harder. Round she went, and round again as the gag tore her mouth; and round yet again. She tried bucking, but with no effect, except that every time she bucked the whip came down on her ribs or her shoulders. There was blood mixed with the foam in her mouth now, and her satin skin was wet with lather and lined with weals.

Desperate at last, up she went again on her heels; but Jack was ready for her this time. The whip came crashing between her ears and drove her down to her feet, and before she fairly knew that she was on them it lashed her ribs. She had had her fling, and she was to pay for it; her rider had tried persuasion, but now he meant punishment, and no half-measures. Round and round the field she had to go until her flanks were heaving, and her eyes dilated with terror. Gradually she was allowed to drop into a canter, and then into a trot, but there was no peace for her yet. She was taken to the hurdles and ignominiously made to jump them backwards and forwards; but she had had enough of resistance and meekly did what was required. Finally she was pulled up. Her conqueror dismounted, patted her, and spoke kindly to her, then made her stand still while he remounted. She bore it all, for she knew that she had found her master.

The battle was over. Jack rode across to where the stablemen were standing open-mouthed, swung himself off, and handed the reins to the head groom.

"There you are, Pat; I don't think she'll give much more trouble. It all came from letting her think she was boss. Give her a good rub down; she needs it. I'll take her out again to-morrow to see if she's cured."

"Cured she is intoirely, I'm thinking!" said Pat, as he led the mare away.

Jack was met at the garden gate by the whole of the party.

"Man alive! You ought to be ashamed of yourself," said Mary. "You might have broken your neck! I never saw such a performance in all my life!"

"Oh, there really wasn't any danger, but it was hard exercise. I'll go in and have a hot bath, or I shall be stiff to-morrow."

"Well, you may say there was no danger," said Seymour, "but it was a bit startling to see the horse turn turtle like that! I can't think, even now, why you weren't crushed to death."

"Oh, that's an old trick; easy enough when you know how. It's only circus-riding!"

"Well, I'm glad that you are safely on the ground again. I wouldn't get on that devil for a thousand pounds!"

Jack wondered why Janet did not speak. She would not meet his eye. He fancied she must be vexed with him for having taken what she might consider unnecessary risks; but all the same it was rather unkind of her to hold aloof. He felt hurt, but consoled himself with the thought that one can never quite tell what a girl will do, and went off with some of the men to change and get something to drink. He would settle with Janet later; the present was neither the time nor the opportunity.

If he had only guessed the state of Janet's feelings just them, he might not have been so certain that he was going to settle it so easily by and by.

Until the immediate danger was over she had forgotten everything except that the man she loved was risking his life; nothing else was of any consequence. Then, after he had succeeded, she was full of pride in him. How beautifully he sat the horse; how masterly his control seemed to be! But when it was all over and he dismounted, remembrance came to her, and she felt that her love must be torn out of her heart, at no matter what cost; yet realising that, come what might, she could never help loving him. At least he should not know it. At the very first opportunity she would tell him that things were at an end between them. He would want to know why, but she would not betray that. There would be a scene, but she did not mean to tell him what she knew, or how she came to know it. Yet in spite of all his voice was still music to her, though his apparent openness and honesty made her feel almost faint when she thought of the hypocrisy. She made up her mind to face the crisis as soon as possible.

She went to the appointed spot to wait for him, but her courage failed her, and she fled back to her room; locking herself in, she threw herself on her bed an gave way to tears.

Jack sought her in vain. Naturally he waited at the arbour, but as she did not come he went to look for her elsewhere. He could neither see her nor hear of her, though he ventured several inquiries as to where she was. It was Mary who at last told him that she had gone to her room, no doubt tired after being up all night; she added that she had seen Janet coming from the arbour about half an hour before.

Jack cursed himself for a laggard in love, and for having kept the girl waiting until, no doubt, she had given him up. What an idiot he had been to change; there really had been no necessity for it, except that he hated feeling dirty and untidy, especially when he hoped to spend the rest of the afternoon with his little love. However, as there was no help for it, he must just wait until tea-time.

But she did not appear at tea, or even at dinner: a message came that she had a headache and was going to bed.

To Jack the evening seemed endless. When he went to bed, he could not sleep, but lay there thinking, until the dawn glimmered through his curtains. He felt sure that there was more the matter with Janet than the conventional headache, but what was it? There he was at a loss. He felt that his heart could not have ached as it did if all was well with her. About six he could stand it no longer; he got up and dressed, and visited the stables. There he found his previous day's adversary quite well, although still bearing the marks of the gruelling he had given her with the whip.

"Poor old girl! Never mind; let's make it up and be friends," he said, as he patted her neck.

The animal seemed to understand, and turned her head, looking at him with big, soft eyes. He stroked her muzzle; she rubbed her head against his sleeve in an inarticulate answer. Jack felt quite touched, and presently he had her saddled and took her out.

All the stable lads came to see him mount, rather hoping for another "show"; but they were disappointed, for the mare proved to be absolutely quiet and docile. She had met her match and knew it.

CHAPTER IX

AT breakfast, when asked where he had been, Jack told them he had been out on the mare, who was now as quiet as a lamb.

"Ah yes, it's the old story. 'A woman, a spaniel, and a walnut tree, the more you beat them the better they be!' " laughed Colquhoun.

"That's a silly proverb. It all depends on who does the beating," said Mary. "Doesn't it, Janet?"

Janet flushed, but did not look up, then said:

"I don't think it would work with all women, no matter who did the beating."

"You'll learn better than that some day, Miss Baxter. Won't she, Miss Macintyre?"

"Why appeal to me? Do you think I have learnt from experience? I have never found the man who had pluck enough to try the recipe with me! And it isn't all of you who could, you know. Perhaps Jack might, but I don't think he would want to, would you, Jack?"

"What, beat you? I would cut off my head before I'd lay a finger on anything so charming!"

"Oh, you hypocrite! You would beat me fast enough if I were the right girl. Probably there's some other girl you would like to try your hand on; but you are too deep to show it!"

"You girls are always making romances for other people; but I can't imagine Jack keeping a secret like that. He would be certain to give the show away," said Colquhoun.

Jack was glad to be saved answering Mary's banter, and quickly took advantage of a remark from the other end of the table to change the subject.

Janet felt as if the secret in her heart would burn its way through when Colquhoun made that remark. He, of all men, to suggest that Jack could not keep a woman's secret. The thought of what she half knew, half guessed, made her shudder; and to think of what might have been, what she had hoped would be! Her heart seemed turning to stone.

For two nights she had been in revolt against her fate, against this unsought knowledge which had come to her. At first, she felt utterly incredulous. It could not be possible! And yet, the more she thought over it, the worse it seemed, and the more points she found to hang suspicions on, until at last it became a conviction, a certainty, which she could not ignore.

Now the first agony of it had passed, to leave a dull ache: a void in her heart which could never be filled again. But she had quite made up her mind about one thing at least; there must be an end to her romance. She had meant to have it all over and settled yesterday, but her courage had failed; she had lain awake through interminable hours, tossing and thinking, until her brain reeled and she was sick with the fear of the scene which she knew must come. This morning she had resolved that there should be no running away. She must face the music; and afterwards? Well, there would be time enough to think of that . . . afterwards.

Jack was just as anxious as she was to come to an understanding. He was quite at a loss to know what she had meant by evading him the day before, so evidently on purpose.

As soon as he could escape from the house he wended his way to the arbour by the sea where they had so often met before, expecting to find Janet. She was there; but at sight of her hard, set face, his greeting froze on his lips.

"Janet! What is it, dear? What is the matter? Why did you avoid me yesterday, and why are you so quiet and strange?"

Her hand was lying on the table; he tried to take it, but she drew it away.

"Janet! For Heaven's sake tell me what I have done to hurt you? Surely it was not because I kept you waiting a few minutes yesterday evening?"

"No; as if that could have mattered!"

"Then what is it? What have I done, darling?"

"You mustn't call me that any more, please."

"What do you mean? Surely you don't intend to throw me over!"

"You may call it 'throwing over' if you like, but what I mean is that there must be an end to everything between us."

"An end to everything? But why, why? What have I done?" persisted Jack, utterly at a loss. "You must at least tell me that!"

"There is no 'must' about it. I can only tell you I have found out that I have made a mistake."

"Found out . . . And so you just throw me over without any further explanation. I suppose it's nothing to you to wreck a man's life? That counts for nothing because you have 'made a mistake'! Do you think I am going to believe that? Do you think that I will believe that you, of all girls, could do a thing like this without some reason, and a strong one too? You *shall* tell me! I won't be just thrown aside without a fair reason!"

"You may believe it or not as you choose, but I can't give you any other reason."

"I have a right to some sort of explanation," said Jack, more calmly. "Is it fair to give me no chance to defend myself, or explain whatever it is that has upset you?"

"I acknowledge no right on your part. What rights have you? And as for asking you to defend yourself, I shall never ask for any defence from you; if you made it, I couldn't believe it, because I know the truth beyond all doubt."

"Well, at least tell me what this wonderful truth is, which has so changed you in a day and a night? Surely I have a right to ask what it is?"

"No, you haven't any right, and I shan't tell you any more."

"But you haven't told me anything at all yet, and though you refuse, I have a right. Any man would have a right to expect some sort of explanation in such circumstances; you gave me that right when you made me love you, and pretended that you loved me in return. Good God! To think that I should let myself be fooled like that!"

"It wasn't pretence!" exclaimed Janet, in her own defence.

"Wasn't pretence? What else can it have been? If there was love, where has it gone, and why?"

"There was love, but it was for the man I thought I knew, not for the man I now know you to be!"

"What on earth do you mean? Am I not the same man whose arms you lay in, whose lips you kissed, whom you pretended to love?"

"I didn't pretend; I did love you!"

The strain was too much for Janet; she gave way, and began to cry. Till that moment Jack had respected her evident desire that he should not touch her, but he could not see her cry and not try to stop her tears.

"Janet, dear, for Heaven's sake try to tell me what is this all about!" he cried. He slid his arm round her waist and tried to draw her to him, but she simply wrenched herself away.

"Don't touch me! How dare you touch me!"

Jack was utterly bewildered.

"Good heavens! One might think I was some loathsome creature whose touch would contaminate you, to hear you speak!"

"So it does! I can't bear it! I can't bear to remember that I let myself lie in your arms, let your lips touch mine, listened to your words of love and believed them true!"

"Believed them true? They *were* true! Love you! I loved you then, I love you now—love you with all my heart and soul, even though you are trampling them in the dust. You must know it is true. You believed it then, why don't you believe it now?"

"Oh yes, I believed it then. I was just a foolish trusting girl. You took advantage of that to make a fool of me and ruin my life!"

"Good God! Is it I who am smashing our lives up now? Is it I who say 'Go away, I find I have made a mistake'? If anyone is ruining lives, it is you, yourself, all for some idiotic, mysterious reason, which is nothing but imagination. For Heaven's sake tell me what it is, so that I may wipe it away; I could in a moment if I only knew what it was; there is nothing to cause you to treat me like this. I know I have done nothing deserving it."

"Perhaps our ideas on that subject may not be the same, but at any rate I am not going to discuss the point with you." Janet's sobs ceased, and her voice came more steadily.

"Janet, don't do a thing like this without giving me a chance to clear matters up." Jack's tone had become very grave. "I assure you there is no real foundation for your mistrust, nothing in my whole life which would warrant such punishment. And, Janet, if you still love me, think of yourself as well as me," he pleaded.

He again tried to touch her, but she started away from him.

"You shan't touch me! I don't love you; the man I thought I loved never existed. Love you! I simply loathe you. Go, go! Never come near me again!"

"You mean that?" Jack's tone was stern now, and not pleading.

"Because if you are not quite, quite certain about it, take back your words; if I go now, it will be for always. Think a moment before you answer. I don't know what idea has got into your brain, but you may be sorry later for what you are doing, when it is too late. Janet, don't speak in haste!"

For a tense moment there was silence, then in a very low but quite clear voice, she said:

"I mean it—go!"

If she had looked up and seen the pain in his face she might have relented; but she did not raise her eyes, and with a long look at her bowed head, Jack went away.

Could it be true? Was he the same man who had walked down that same path such a short time before, full of hope and joy at the prospect of seeing his girl again, and lightly brushing away the misunderstanding? What could be the explanation of it all? Well, she had chosen, and it was evident that she had no intention of retracting what she had said; but what was it all about? In vain he turned things over in his mind to find some reason, but none came. At any rate one thing was certain: he could not stay in that house any longer; he would go, and go at once. It would be fairly easy to make an excuse to Colquhoun. Thira would have been more difficult to hoodwink, but she was safely out of the way.

He did not hesitate, but went quietly up to his rooms and packed, then sought Colquhoun, whom he found in his writing-room.

"I have come to bid you good-bye. It's an awful nuisance, but I have had some news this morning which leaves me no choice in the matter."

"My dear fellow! You really can't mean it; it would be too bad! How shall I get along without you? I shall have to go back myself soon, and I was looking to you to clear things up for me after I had left. Must you really go?"

"Yes, I must, this morning, if I am to catch the night train. I'm awfully sorry to put you to any inconvenience, but I really have no choice in the matter."

"Well, if you must, you must, but we shall be very sorry to lose you. I shall miss you awfully, and I think the others will too."

"Some of them, perhaps, but you'll get along very well without me."

"My dear boy, you talk as if we might never meet again, whereas, at the worst, we shall see you in town soon; we can't extend the holiday much longer."

"Well, I hope so! Anyhow, good-bye, and good luck, I have taken the liberty of ordering the cart, and have told Tom to come with me to bring it back." Five minutes later, Jack was off. Colquhoun, still mystified, went out to see him start, but as no further explanation was offered, he could not very well say more.

"Say good-bye to the others for me, Colquhoun. I hope Thira will soon be down and about again. But I shouldn't let her ride that mare again if I were you."

"I shan't, you may be certain. But she won't be too well pleased when she hears that you have run away without even saying good-bye to her."

"Well, it was best not to go up and disturb her. Perfect quiet is what she needs for the next few days. Cheerio!"

"Good-bye, and good luck, old chap. I'm awfully sorry you have to go." With a hearty grip of the hand it was over, and the cart spun away.

It was a nine days' wonder to the others when they discovered that Jack had gone. With him the whole spirit of the party seemed to depart; things fell flat, had not half the "go" in them.

"There's no devil in things now that old Jack is gone!" grumbled Bertie Wilson.

"What do you want with devils?" asked Mary.

"I like them, that's all; so do you, if you speak the truth!"

"Well, if Jack Winthrop's a devil, perhaps I do!"

Thira was simply astounded when she heard the news. That Jack should have gone away in such a hurry, without even a word of farewell to her, needed explanation. No one seemed to have heard anything of his sudden departure until after he had vanished. She could not make head or tail of it. She tried to ascertain what he had been doing that morning, but beyond the fact that he had come down unusually early, even for him, and had exercised her mare, all was a mystery. What he had done, or where he had been, between breakfast and the moment when he announced his impending departure to Colquhoun, no one could say.

Janet, who of course could have told her, remained silent, and even went so far towards misusing the truth as to say that she knew nothing about it. She had no intention of letting the real facts be known to the others. She was pretty certain that whatever he might or might not do, Jack would keep silence on the subject; so she wore a brave face and showed no sign that she was specially affected by his departure, and no one knew the torments that raged in her heart. She had never for a moment dreamed that he would take her literally at her word and go, without even letting her see him again. And now that he had gone, and her anger and wounded pride were left victors, she began to realise what she had done. The love that she had tried to crush and strangle rose up and took revenge—took it in full. Her thoughts tortured her. What a fool she had been—what a brute! Suppose it were all true—all she had heard that night from Thira's lips? All men were like that sometimes, and she had gathered that he had not been the most to blame. Suppose he had fallen; if he loved her, Janet, best, if all those beautiful things he said were true, and she had turned him away with love overflowing in his heart for her. She knew, no matter what he was, what he had done, that she loved him still, always must love him, even though through her own folly she might never hear from him again. At any rate she would manage to meet him when she got back to town, would show him, as fas as she could, how ashamed she was of herself.

Would he ever forgive her? she wondered. That was her greatest fear: that he would be too proud to forgive her. Perhaps he would not even speak to her if they met. And so she fretted her soul with tears, paying over and over again for those moments of pride and folly.

CHAPTER X

LATE autumn—and those happy days at Kilmona, with their final disastrous ending, a memory. Janet, back in town, had resumed the weary drudgery of life, had faced work as though love and pain were shadows, unreal and meaningless.

She had neither seen Jack nor heard from him since her return, nor did any fortunate chance give her news of his movements.

The Colquhouns had gone away, and not a line had come from Thira. Unkind, she thought, not to have written! Did those long night hours of nursing, those willing efforts to amuse the invalid during the last few weeks at Kilmona, count for nothing? Janet felt that there was something on Thira's mind which she would not speak about; and she was right.

Thira had more than a suspicion that Janet could have explained the mystery of Jack's sudden departure, though, try as she might, she remained baffled. She had tried to "draw" her friend on the subject of Jack, but Janet never betrayed anything deeper than the most conventional feeling for him. Her woman's instinct, however, whispered restlessly of secrets unpublished. Had Jack run away to avoid temptation? She felt that he must know her love for him, yet he could not have fathomed its depth. If he had stayed she would have shown him even there, for she was past caring for any sense of modesty or shame where he was concerned. She thought she could have made him love her, if she had only more time in which to do it; but his flight had upset everything. She had written to him, addressing her letter to his club, a week after, asking him for an explanation of his sudden departure without even a "good-bye"; avoiding any phrase or expression which could have been misconstrued if read by anyone else, or which was not quite correct; knowing, however, that he would read certain meanings into certain words. Impatiently she waited for the answer which never came.

A few days after her return home, to find him out of town, she and Colquhoun had themselves gone off again. That was nearly two months ago; now again she was back in town, but had already found that Jack's rooms were in charge of a care-taker, and that he had not been seen at his club for months. Her husband, in response to her subtle hints and apparently chance remarks, brought news, after a week or so, which she had not anticipated. Jack Winthrop had gone abroad almost immediately after his return from Ireland, having secured a responsible post as supervising engineer on a large construction contract, almost at the other side of the world. The duration of this absence was uncertain; the job itself would not be finished for years, but of course he might not choose to stay and see it through. His position was sufficiently independent to allow him to come home if he chose.

To Thira, life suddenly seemed futile. She could not deceive herself by imagining that this was only a passing disappointment; she knew that for her, only one hope, one joy remained—a hope and joy now immeasurably distant.

With heavy heart and smiling face she took up once more her daily round—the ordinary treadmill of social life—went about as usual, perhaps a little more cynical, a little harder.

Walking down Bond Street, one day, a few weeks later, she almost ran into Janet.

"Thira! Where have you dropped from? I didn't even know you were in town! Have you been back long?"

"Oh no, a week or two, perhaps."

"You never let me know! I had given up calling to ask when you were coming back."

"I have meant to write to you for some time to ask you to come and see me, but something always made me put it off."

"Well, I'm glad that we met now. I have been frightfully dull lately, and wanted somebody nice to talk to."

The sight of Thira had seemed to bring Kilmona and all that it meant nearer again, back from dreams to reality; Janet felt a pleasant thrill of memory at the sight of her old friend. Thira, also, was pleased, sharing, it seemed, the same feeling. Janet was at least a link with the past, and they would be able to talk naturally of Jack and the happy holiday.

"Come home and lunch with me and chat over old times, Janet, unless you are too busy just now. If you are, come in some other time soon. It will be nice to have you again after so long."

"I have nothing particular to do," said Janet. "I shall be delighted to come."

They hailed a taxi, and drove off. As usual, Colquhoun was in the City, and they were quite alone.

During lunch, with the servants present, they spoke of ordinary matters, though the same subject hovered in their minds. Janet was impatient for news of Jack; Thira wanted to talk about him. When they adjourned to the boudoir, she steered at once to the pressing theme.

"Have you seen anything of our Kilmona friends since you have been in town?"

"Yes. I saw Miss Macintyre one night. She was sitting in the stalls at the place where I was singing, and later came round behind to have a little chat; but she didn't seem to know much what had happened to the rest of the party." Janet was trying to give Thira an opening without actually mentioning Jack's name.

"One or two of them have been to see me lately. Captain Seymour called two or three days ago; he was very much interested in Jack's new venture."

"What is that?" asked Janet casually.

"Oh, didn't you know? He has gone to the other side of the world, to look after the building of a big harbour, or something of the kind."

Janet felt for a moment as if the earth was falling away from her. She heard Thira speaking, but her voice sounded very small. Then she heard herself make a reply which seemed to come independently of her own volition.

"No, I hadn't heard. Will he be away long?" She recovered her balance, concentrating her attention upon Thira's answer. Had Thira been looking at Janet she would have known her secret then and there.

"No one seems to know; for months, at least, and perhaps much longer, for it will take some years to compete the work, they say."

Years! And she had hoped, day after day, that she might meet him by chance in the street.

She knew why he had cut himself adrift. The agony of it was almost intolerable; yet she must make no sign, must wear a smiling face. At any rate Thira, of all people, should not know. She wondered vaguely what Thira's own thoughts on the subject were; after the unforgettable things she had heard that night, she could hazard a guess. Some little consolation lay in the thought that he had gone because he was trying to forget her, Janet, and therefore must have loved her most. It showed her what she had done: she had thrown away that which she valued most of all things in the world. And so the two sat chatting about the past, about the months spent at Kilmona: often speaking of the man they both loved, yet betraying no emotion.

It would be hard to say which one of them loved him the more. Their love differed, each demanding a different standard. The one was all self, the other self-less, save for regret and sorrow and self-reproach. She knew how much she must have hurt him, to drive him to exile; but he loved her, she was certain; and while she could hug that secret to her heart, there was hope. Even if there had been another love, she had triumphed.

The conversation marked the beginning of a new era for Thira and Janet. Each for her own reason, which was really the same, liked the other's company, because opportunity came of speaking of Jack. The one knew, the other suspected, was almost certain, that her friend loved him too; yet each assured her heart that she was the beloved, that it was to avoid her that the man had put half a world between them. So a queer bond, partly of affection, partly of jealousy, arose between them.

Janet grudged Thira Jack's photograph. There were several in the house, the best being in Thira's boudoir; Janet had not even one. She was better off than Thira in another way, however, for her work kept her busy, and helped to distract her thoughts. Thira had nothing to do but amuse herself—the most trying of all occupations when carried to excess. Possessing apparently everything that a woman could want, she was never happy, never contented, ever brooding over her unattainable desire. She had written to Jack directly she knew where he was, and after a weary interval received a letter, full of news, of his work out in Purnam, drawing joking comparisons between his present life and the old one at home; but there was nothing in it which spoke of love, past or present. Other letters were exchanged, but it was always the same. She wrote, striving to suggest meanings for him between the lines;

he only answered what was actually written, and not always all of that. Yet, few and infrequent as these letters were, they kept her in touch with him, and she spoke of them to no one.

As the winter wore away the constant fretting told on her; she lost her energy, her colour, her cheerfulness. She caught a bad cold, which developed into a persistent hacking cough. Doctors spoke gravely of complications and the advisability of sunnier climes, and her husband, seriously concerned about her health, threw up all business and took her to the south of France. Even there she made very slow progress, and finally he bought a yacht, in order that they might follow the sunshine and leave the cold north, with its winds, mistrals, and other inconveniences behind.

It would be dull for Thira, he thought, with him alone for company, and the idea of arranging a party occurred to him. The selection of its members, as they would probably be thrown together for some months, was a matter for very tactful consideration. Oddly enough, Thira wanted to have Janet; but it appeared that her musical engagements would not allow her to leave London for so long a period. Colquhoun himself wrote to Janet, and offered to make good any loss which she might sustain; "if you will only come," he said, in his odd business-like manner, "I shall be pleased to settle this beforehand." Janet, inclined to be annoyed at the suggestion, realised after a moment's thought the kindness which inspired it, and instead of refusing indignantly, wrote a letter of regret, explaining that it was not entirely a question of finance, but that she felt she ought not to leave her mother for so long.

Finally a party of six was decided upon, all of whom had been at Kilmona except a Miss Boston, whom Thira invited as she fancied the girl was a rather particular friend of Bertie Wilson. Mary Macintyre and Captain Seymour were also included on her list.

CHAPTER XI

THE graceful s.s. *Siren*, answering excellently to the description "well-appointed" which is so favourite a term with agents desirous of disposing of yachts or houses, drew slowly in to the harbour at Port Said, and came to anchor. It was a magnificent evening, full of that indescribable sense of mystery which sunset and twilight always lend to strange scenes, and every member of her party thrilled to the lure of the gateway of the East, felt the nearness of the desert sands, the appeal of Egypt, the subtle influence of ancient, immemorial things.

With practically no time-limit to interfere with their arrangements, they would be able to wander at will; but as yet their plans were indefinite. It seemed, in fact, that there was no "programme"—that they drifted on from day to day with no set purpose; yet each stage carried them onward, eastward. No one bothered to wonder how this came about; but it might have been noticed by an observant onlooker that Thira invariably had the casting vote, that it was she who always decided the trend of their journey.

For Thira, the voyage had but one end, and that was Purnam. It was she who had really originated the project of this cruise, though her husband imagined it his own idea; and she meant to carry it through.

She had not written to Jack that she was on the way to him, nor had she told anyone of her purpose. It was to appear a matter of chance that they found him at a certain point in the course of their travels. Day by day she counted the miles that remained, and planned the quickest possible time in which those miles could be covered without undue haste; therefore it was not likely that their stay in the land of Isis would be prolonged.

* * * * * *

There was a cool freshness in the morning when Bertie Wilson, some days later on, began the leisurely process of awakening. No one else seemed to be astir but the crew of the dahabieh, who were busy at the usual preliminaries, making things shipshape for the day.[12] Bertie sat up, stretched himself, yawned, and went off to wash and dress, though the heat made him long to remain in his pyjamas.

Living on the dahabieh, the party had been up the Nile, through the cataracts, and were now lying off Philæ. They had gathered many new experiences, had explored pyramids, tombs and temples, visited Arab villages, and seen all that could safely be seen of the country.

Colquhoun was perhaps the happiest member of the whole company, for it had been one of the dreams of his life to spend a long holiday investigating the ruins of Egypt. The rest of the party seemed to take an almost equal interest in these wonders, with the one exception of Thira. She had done her part to make life pleasant for the others, and had been very sweet to Colquhoun, trying to share his enthusiasm; nevertheless, it was clear that her pleasure had no deep feeling behind it. This was ascribed to the state of her health, for she had seemed to flag a little during the last week or so; only the day before Doctor Smith had taken Colquhoun aside and suggested that the heat was too much for her, that it would be better to turn northward for the recuperating sea and its cooler air.

Thira, however, had been playing a deep game, and only bided her time. She was longing to get on, but felt that it would be unwise

[12] Dahabieh: traditional Egyptian houseboat used on the Nile.

to show urgency just now, when perhaps she might want to linger when the others did not. She thought, however, that it was time to move, and with consummate skill arranged for the suggestion to be made to her.

There was an air of renewed cheerfulness about the party now that they were starting down the river again; they had had enough of Philæ and the dam for the present. The women were looking forward to Cairo and a little social gaiety, before rejoining the *Siren*, and the men were keenly discussing the probable results of certain polo events which, if back in time, they would see.

After several uneventful days they tied up one night alongside a little native village, which they had already called at on their way up. A French exploration party, said to have its headquarters there, had been missed before, having proceeded inland to "burrow for mummies," as Bertie put it. It was an expedition working under the French Government sanction, and Colquhoun learnt that Professor Tremaine and his party had returned to the village after a very successful venture, and were now in residence there for a time. He at once decided to call and invite the party on board for dinner.

He was warmly received by his fellow-Europeans, who were glad to have a brief interlude of social talk; they had seen no one but each other and their native helpers for weeks, and were tired of the monotony, though their enthusiasm for Egyptology was undimmed.

The Professor was full of a wonderful find he had recently made in the hills some distance back from the river, which he asserted would revolutionise much that had been previously accepted as true on a certain period of history; he promised to tell them all of his discovery later.

A merry party gathered round the dinner-table that evening. The Frenchmen were all pleasant, interesting men, even outside their special archæological interests, and kept up a vivacious chatter, especially with the ladies; they included the whole party, however, with that facility characteristic of the Latin races, who never seem to tolerate dullness or restricted conversation at table.

When the stage of coffee and cigarettes arrived, the Professor, in response to a request from Thira, began his story. It seemed that from traces they had found on a previous visit, he had felt sure that at a certain spot there was more to be unearthed. Literally unearthed, for treasures and even cities of old are buried so deeply that only long, patient excavation and research can discover their exact sites. Six weeks ago he and his friends had begun their search, and though for days no result encouraged them, they persevered. At last they disclosed the entrance to a series of tombs, hitherto untouched by any previous party, even having apparently escaped the marauding Arab through the long centuries. Here they had lighted on several examples of early Egyptian sepulchre, with contents which the Professor described as "specimens" in a state of perfect preservation. They had already removed several mummies, and were hoping for further "finds," when one night, during their absence, the natives raided the tombs, knocking their watchmen on the head and doing what the Professor described, almost in tears, as incalculable damage in a very few hours, breaking open sarcophagi, rifling their contents, and scattering all they thought of little value on the floor. Fortunately in their haste they had not had time to ruin the place entirely, and the explorers at once decided to camp at the entrance to the tombs. Since then the site had been guarded night and day, and no native had managed to elude the vigilance of their sentries.

The Professor went deeply into detail of dynasties and periods beyond the comprehension of most of his hearers; but interspersed with the dryness of the archæologist was much of ordinary human interest. Among the mummies discovered, he said, was one that they considered to be some priestess of Isis, who had been put to death by suffocation with the wax cloth which appeared to have been a regular punishment for priestesses in those past ages. Unluckily this lady's coffin was one of those which had been despoiled, and the Professor regretted beyond words this gap in their knowledge. He had managed to collect enough, however, pieced together from mural paintings and writings and oddments recovered, to give him a general idea of the lines of deduction which might be reasonably followed.

The mummy itself had not been disturbed, but much was missing, and he felt that if only he himself had opened the sarcophagus and mummy-case he would have found jewels and other evidence to complete, as far as might be, the tale; for it was known that almost every mummy was accompanied by articles which fixed its rank and designation, thus enabling the skilled decipherer to read its history almost as in a book. Alas!—only enough remained to tell that the mummy was that of a priestess, and that she had been put to death probably as a penalty for some breach of priestly law. That at present was all he knew; he could not yet supply the details of her story.

The whole party were immensely interested, and his invitation that they should all join him on the following day in an expedition to the scene was unanimously accepted, even Thira showing some enthusiasm.

It was fairly late when the gathering broke up, and the Frenchmen departed to their temporary home, but the company on board the *Siren* still sat on discussing the gruesome history of the unfortunate priestess, and the strange way in which, thousands of years later, it had been brought to light.

Thira, to whom mysticism and the idea of reincarnation appealed strongly, had much to say, Mary scoffed at most of her theories; Seymour and Colquhoun supported them, while Bertie, and, to everyone's surprise the retiring Doctor Smith, pooh-poohed all such ideas. Presently, tiring of their arguments, they separated for the night, and the stillness of the East was unbroken save by the murmur of the water, and the queer, haunting sounds from unseen things of the river and its low, long shore.

CHAPTER XII

TO avoid the heat, an early start was made. The Frenchmen had undertaken the necessary arrangements and provided the inevitable donkeys for all, and before the sun was high the whole party was on its way into the desert. A motley crew of natives accompanied them, urging on the beasts and acting as escort.

For some time they followed the bank of the river; then, leaving it, they passed over ground which became gradually more rugged and broken until they suddenly emerged from hummocks of agglomerate into a sort of rocky arena, entering it through a narrow passage between huge boulders. At once they seemed shut off from the world, for the entrance vanished, merged in the barrier behind them.

At their feet lay a floor of level, yellow sand, roughly circular, and about two hundred yards in diameter. A wall of terraced rock faced them; on either side wings of a similar nature extended to meet the barrier they had just penetrated. The face of the cliff, scored vertically with deep grooves and fissures, resembled a rough corduroy. No sign of vegetation appeared, and the only suggestions of life within the field of vision were a couple of small bell tents, and two statuesque sentries at the base of one of the fissures. It was such a spot as might be chosen for a burial place, where the departed, safe from the strife and turmoil of this world, should rest in peace until time had passed away and ceased to be; where no desecrating force should stray, and silence reign for ever.

Professor Tremaine stopped, and the others formed a group round him. They felt that they were trespassers already, even though as yet they had seen nothing of those to whom the place belonged by right of possession—the silent shades from a long-dead past.

For a moment or two a complete hush reigned; then the Professor spoke.

"It was here we first began to feel that we were nearing our goal. From this spot we made the final start that was to bring to us those who had rested undisturbed for thousands of years, those who had lain here from before the days when Romulus laid the first stones of Rome; before Hector slew his thousands, or was in turn slain and dishonoured by Achilles; before Moses wrought miracles; even before Abraham journeyed from the land of Chaldea into Egypt. Here they slept through the slowly passing centuries, undisturbed and forgotten; it was left for us, men of the present day, to unveil their tombs and record their history for a people who will find it difficult and strange to understand the meaning of it all. I will show you something of what they were, how they lived, how they died, what is left of them to-day."

He dismounted and moved forward on foot, followed by the others. Before them opened a gap in the cliff, perhaps twenty feet across, running back some thirty or forty yards until it narrowed to three or four feet. The sandy floor of this inlet was flat, but it had evidently been deeply silted up, for on either hand, outside, were heaps of sand which had been removed by the men, leaving a passage between about twenty feet high.

"By Jove! You must have had a job to get all this stuff cleared away!" said Seymour. "But what made you think of trying here rather than in any of those other clefts?"

"We had a great deal of work before we could be certain that we had found the right spot, and of course we searched in many places without success. It needed a strong hope to keep us going, but just here we perceived indications that everything was not as nature had made it, though whether by the lapse of time or on purpose to prevent sacrilegious hands from breaking in, it is impossible to say, for little remained to indicate that man had been at work. However, there was something. If you glance at the rocks you will see that here and there they show markings that are not visible higher up; these led us to believe that the rock had at some time or other been cut away. Examining the face of the rock at the back, that opinion became confirmed, for the farther we got below the surface of the sand, the clearer became the markings; finally we hit on a spot that had undoubtedly been worked, though the replacement had been so cleverly done that it was difficult to see that the rock had actually been cut away and afterwards rebuilt. Come and look."

At the end of the gully, on the right-hand side, he pointed to a narrow opening in the face of the cliff; it was perhaps six feet high by half that width; within the gully everything was pitch dark, though outside the landscape shimmered in the heat.

"Those who happen to be afraid of getting dusty or soiled had better not join us," said Tremaine, smiling, "for the way is not easy, and some climbing and stooping is necessary. I think it was purposely made difficult; but one can get in with a little trouble."

No one seemed discouraged by this friendly warning, and a moment later they were all scrambling along the narrow ways, by the doubtful light of candles, led by the Professor. The change from the burning sunshine at first made the place seem delightfully cool and shady, but after a few minutes the atmosphere became decidedly close and stifling—there being no apparent outlet and no ventilation other than that offered by the narrow entrance. The stillness was so uncanny that they spoke little; in itself it was enough to remind them that they stood in a death-chamber.

Whether by design, or whether in the course of ages nature, by earthquakes and subsidences, had changed the various levels, it would be impossible to say, but the path rose and fell surprisingly, widening here, narrowing there; out of sight above their heads at one moment, and then again so low that they had to stoop, almost crawl. After. time they emerged into a large chamber, where the air was still close and heavy, but the increased space brought some relief. Here the Professor stopped and began looking about him.

"Wait a moment, please," he said; "there is more here than you can see by candlelight, and we have provided the necessary illumination."

Suddenly a brilliant blaze of electric light flooded the chamber.

"That's better!" he said. "We put this little installation in because we found it impossible to work properly by candlelight. Now I will try to interpret some of the things which you will see."

The place seemed to be an anteroom to a larger tomb beyond, also lit up from the same source. It was about twenty feet high by as many broad, and about twice that length. The walls were covered with figures and writings, the former plain enough to read and, to some extent, conveying their meaning to the uninitiated, the writings undecipherable save to experts.

The visitors listened to his explanations with breathless interest as he unfolded the history of people who had for thousands of years been dust. Wonderful indeed, that now, in the twentieth century, for the first time, these stories should be told from the actual work of those who painted and wrote! Still following him, they passed through a lofty, narrow doorway into a far larger chamber, which, like the anteroom, was coloured and decorated. He pointed out one scene depicting a marriage feast, the principal actors being a reigning prince and a priestess—highly honoured, he concluded, from the special care apparently being taken of her by the guard of many soldiers and attendants. The prince, he said, named Amenhotep, was evidently a person of great power and authority. He would show them, farther on, another fresco which he thought bore on the same matter, though it would be a long time yet before the whole story could be unravelled; it might take him months of study to arrive at a satisfactory interpretation.

The pictures were wonderfully lifelike. They suffered from the lack of individuality common to almost all Egyptian paintings, yet a distinction of feature was traceable. The adjoining fresco showed Amenhotep in council, issuing a sort of manifesto, the gist of which was that the priestess, Ohora, having mysteriously disappeared, he offered a great reward for her recovery, or any information which would lead to knowledge of her. It appeared that the last occasion on which she had been seen was when she went to worship at the temple, fully guarded as usual. In spite of the guards, and without any visible reason, she had vanished, and no search had hitherto been successful. The proclamation went on to relate how sore was the grief of Amenhotep at the loss of his beloved, whom he valued above all else, and to state the reward.

Two other pictures on the same subject Tremaine exhibited. One commemorated the throwing down of a temple, and the massacre of its priests by the royal guards because they were suspected of conniving at the disappearance of Ohora; the other showed a funeral, evidently of Price Amenhotep. That was the last picture he would explain; "but," he added, "if you would like to see all that the earth now holds of that same priestess, come with me."

He led them from the great chamber into another passage: this, unlike the first, was smooth and unobstructed. Here, too, the walls were frescoed and inscribed heavily. It brought them to a smaller chamber from which others seemed to radiate; into one of these the Professor passed without a moment's hesitation. In the centre lay a huge stone sarcophagus, of which the lid had been removed and lay on the floor. It was only the case; the mummy itself, he said, was already in the Museum, having been sent down some time since. This was the tomb of the Prince. The painted face on the case showed a man of middle age, and, in spite of its quaintness, one could discern an attempt at portraiture; it bore a baffling expression which must have been on the living features. It seemed to tell of a struggle lived through, of bitter experience and a hard fight; whether the fight had ended in victory or defeat, who should say?

"How strange it is," said Seymour in a low voice, "to stand here and look down on this effigy of a man who actually lived, and whose remains were brought here ages before our history began. It makes one feel very small and insignificant, doesn't it?"

Colquhoun answered him.

"Yes, in a way it does; but on the other hand it makes one feel that this short earthly life, which is all we know, cannot be the end. There must be something beyond; when the spirit leaves the body it does not die, but is still living somewhere else."

"Do you really believe, then, that the spirits of these people are still hovering somewhere about?" asked Kathleen. "Perhaps even here, near the scene of their last resting-place?"

Thira, who was standing by, shivered at the suggestion.

"What an uncanny idea, Kathleen! It makes me feel creepy all over. We may see the ghost of one of them directly!"

Most of the party did not take Thira's remark seriously. Kathleen remained thoughtful, however, and curiously enough Bertie Wilson, the last person to whom superstitious fancies would be attributed, seemed uneasy.

Professor Tremaine smiled. "There are stranger things to see yet," he said. "Stranger—and perhaps more disturbing."

He led them back to the chamber they had left and turned along another narrow passage.

"I take you to the burial chamber of the servants of Isis, priests and priestesses. Many are buried here, but only one will I show you. Time does not suffice for more."

The apartment to which he now conducted them was oblong in shape, about thirty feet by twenty-five, and hewn out of the solid rock. Pierre, one of the French party, produced an electric torch, which shone upon walls of absolutely bare stone, without any attempts at decoration; in some places even the markings of the workers' tools could still be distinguished. From this the deduction was made that this chamber was of later date than those previously inspected, and that for some reason time had been wanting for its completion. The roof rose in pent-house fashion. Round three sides ran a stone bench, three feet wide and raised about two feet from the floor, broken at intervals by arched niches or recesses, as far as Tremaine could tell leading nowhere, though he admitted that he had not had time to sound the walls thoroughly. The floor was smooth stone or cement, it was impossible to say which.

In the middle stood an oblong raised coping about a foot high, from the corners of which square stone pillars ascended almost to the roof; a heavy stone lintel united them at the top, with a heavy transverse stone across the centre.

"Now come and look," said the Professor, "but with care, not rashly."

Gazing over the edge, at first nothing was visible but a black, yawning hole, its first few feet lighted by Pierre's torch. The sides, as far as they could see, were smooth, evenly worked stone, with no projections or means of ascent or descent.

"What on earth is it?" asked Thira. "It looks horribly eerie and mysterious; and how deep it is!"

"Not so deep as it looks; one can easily go down on a rope. I am not yet sure of its original use. Perhaps it was intended to be another chamber such as that which we have just passed through; if so, it was never finished. It may have been used as an embalming chamber, though it seems strange that it should have been placed almost at the farthest point of these catacombs, and not near the entrance, where one would more naturally have expected to find it; at any rate it has ended as simply a tomb, for there is another sarcophagus with its contents down there."

"Only one?"

"Yes, only one. There are sundry jars and vessels, stone slabs, and other things, but only the one occupant, so far as we have yet discovered."

"That seems curious," said Seymour, "for in the other chambers there were many tombs."

"Yes, but we shall be a long time before we complete our investigations, and even in this chamber where we now stand there are other mummies. It was, as I told you, the place of burial of the priests and priestesses, and in most of those niches there are slabs either occupied or ready for occupation. Those which are occupied have stone sarcophagi such as that which we have already seen, inscribed with the name and title of the occupant, and some dates of which we are not yet quite sure of the meaning. But the one below bears no name, which has so far puzzled us. The marauders who broke in must have removed the means of identification, but they did not remove the designation from the coffin, for it has never had one! Who will go down?"

"How the deuce do we get down?" asked Bertie, gazing into the gloomy chasm. But the Professor had not given the invitation without being prepared beforehand.

"Look there!" he said, pointing to the stone beam above. They looked, and saw a running pulley with a rope passed over it, which ran through another attached to the farther lintel, and ended in a coil lying at the foot of one of the pillars.

"But who's to do the hauling?" questioned Seymour. "Not everybody knows how to handle a tackle like this. Probably Bertie and I could haul you others up and down; but we don't want to be left behind."

The Professor smiled, and clapped his hands; from the archway through which they had entered appeared four native helpers who had followed through the first stage of their journey, but had since dropped unobtrusively into the background.

"Here are your haulers, Captain Seymour; there will be no need for anyone to stay behind."

"I'm going to stay behind, anyway," exclaimed Thira. "I haven't any intention of being dangled in space at the end of a rope."

"Oh, but, Madame! It would be a pity, having come so far, to miss seeing that which of all is most worth it!" protested Tremaine, visibly vexed at the idea that he should not be able to show his chief object of interest to the lady whom he evidently accepted as the most important person of the party. But Thira refused to alter her decision, and after a brief argument Mary agreed to remain with her; Pierre was to conduct the operation of lowering and relifting those who descended.

Gustave, the Professor's other assistant, went first; soon his voice came uncannily from the depths assuring them that he was safely aground, and the rope was quickly hauled up. Bertie was second, and then the Professor said Kathleen had better go. She was the only lady of the party to descend, and extra care was taken; a sling was looped in the rope for her to sit in, and a folded coat made the seat more comfortable. The Professor took the further precaution of having her tied in.

As her feet swung clear of the floor, and she felt herself dangling over the black space, beginning to drop into the unseen, Kathleen wished she had not come; but the lowering was done quietly and skilfully, and the novelty of the experience overcame her momentary fear. Nevertheless, she was relieved to find herself at the bottom, with the cheerful Bertie at her side; she had unbounded confidence in him as a protector in any difficulty or danger. He and Gustave quickly freed her from the rope, which vanished above them.

"Weird!" said Kathleen, as they awaited the next arrival. "It is rather uncanny to think what our fate would be if that rope never came down again. We couldn't possibly get back to daylight; we should be trapped. Finis—for us!"

Bertie nodded. "It would be a trifle on the grim side; the walls of the shaft seem absolutely smooth. My word—the idea gets on one's nerves! Is there much farther to go, Monsieur Gustave?" he asked, turning to the Frenchman.

"Only a few steps, Monsieur," replied Gustave.

A moment later Seymour appeared from the enveloping gloom, and shortly after the Professor and Colquhoun joined them. The torches were switched on, and the chamber became visible. Long and very low, its roof, or rather "ceiling," could easily be reached by the hand; the floor widened, fan-shaped, from the foot of the shaft. Along the sides ran shelves or benches similar to those above, upon which stood jars and pots and slabs of stone small and large. At the far end they could vaguely discern a grey coffin, towards which Tremaine led them.

The lid was closed, and upon it lay a number of little round cylinders of pottery or ivory, each about two inches in diameter by a foot long, and each bearing a similar device. Tremaine picked one up, and stated that he had not yet discovered their significance. The inscription seemed to be a seal or emblem; by it they knew that the remains within the coffin were those of a priestess of Isis, but beyond that he had been able to make nothing of it, though there was undoubtedly more to be revealed.

"Now I will show you what, to me, is the most wonderful of all—that which seems to bring one more nearly and really in touch with the remote past than anything else. Far more so than even the mummies, writings, buildings, and all their wonders and grandeur; for here is something which makes us realise that the poor atom of humanity which rests here has lived, suffered, and died. Makes us sympathise with the soul which once inhabited the body in a way in which none of the paintings and writings has ever affected me before. It is a touch of humanity, not merely dry archæology, or mere recounting of events without a human element in them. Gustave, let us remove the stone.

Very reverently the two raised the stone slab. The Professor motioned to the others to come and look. There was a general gasp of horrified surprise as they gazed upon the contents of the coffin.

Lying yellow-white against the greyness of the stone was the outline of what had once been a human being, so shrunken and withered it seemed that it might crumble to pieces at any moment, even as they gazed. From the feet to the shoulders the form was swathed in yellowish wrappings, which looked as though they had been intended to prevent all possible movement, not as a light, enveloping shroud for the dead. Over the face was an opaque veil of a different texture, wound round the throat and passing above the forehead, so as to cover in part the head-dress. Through its tightly drawn folds the shape of the human skull and features beneath could be perceived. There had been an outer wrapping of a canvas like material covering both head and body, but this had been removed, and now lay torn and thrown back along the side of the coffin, the ruthless work of the despoiling Arabs.

"Good heavens!" exclaimed Colquhoun. "It looks almost human, even now. How long do you suppose she has lain here like this, Professor?"

"It is a hard question. Perhaps three thousand, perhaps six thousand years. Many times the period since William of Normandy invaded and conquered your England; a stupendous time, is it not? But we archæologists do not measure time as you others. Isn't it wonderful that these people could so preserve the human body that it should endure for ages, even in a dried, desiccated form? Even now there is more below the shroud than the mere bones; under usual conditions, even the bones would have long ago been dust; notice how the outlines of the poor hands and arms show through the bandages as though they had madly tried to burst their bonds. To me it seems the poor creature was cruelly done to death. See the cloth upon the face—it is no shroud; touch it—the texture is hard, unlike any usual material. It was the waxed cloth used for suffocation by those priests."

He laid his fingers lightly, reverently, upon the covering of the face. The men, one by one, followed his example. Kathleen seemed unwilling to touch this poor shell of humanity even thus, but finally did so. She drew back her hand in an instant with a slight shiver.

"How dreadful a death! Poor thing! I wonder whether it was done in the coffin or before they put her there. I feel as if I could cry, just as if it had happened to someone I knew. What fiends men can be!"

"Yes, Mademoiselle; men can be devils at times. I doubt not that these ancient priests did this because she knew more than they thought was safe with her. Their law did not allow them to shed her blood; doubtless they had reasons for secrecy, and brought her here to finish her. She must have been a person of some importance or they would have left the corpse in the sand to decay; they may have been afraid it would be discovered. They little thought that thousands of years later their sins would be found out, that the secret of this woman's history and death would be published to the world, though too late by many ages to affect them. Still, if my reading is right, I think those who did this deed, or at any rate those who were responsible for it, paid for their misdoings even then, thousands of years ago, in their lifetime."

"Why do you think that, Professor?" asked Seymour.

"I will not attempt to tell you just now; but there are reasons . . . We must not linger too long. The air of these tombs is trying, and our friends are waiting for us above. I may tell you more when we have returned to the vessel."

He motioned to Gustave, and they gently replaced the cover of the coffin. As he turned to go, Kathleen laid a gentle hand on his arm.

"Please, Professor Tremaine, may I take one of those little cylinders away with me? I should like to have something to remind me of this visit, and to assure me that it has not been all in a dream. There seems to be a lot of them, and they are all alike."

The Professor looked thoughtful. To give up even one of his treasures required some self-sacrifice on his part; he weighed the matter well before he replied.

"If you really wish it, Mademoiselle, you shall have one, but do not take it unless you will value it. I should not like to think that it was to be treated as a mere curio, a souvenir of travel."

"I do really want one, and I shall value it and take great care of it. If you ever want it back, I will give it up at any time."

So the little memento was chosen and given, and they turned away from the scene of sadness.

The rest of the party were glad enough to see them again. Both Thira and Mary had begun to feel anxious, and the flickering candlelight, emphasising the darkness around them, had made them long for the open air once more.

When the last visitor swung up from the black hole, Kathleen confided to Bertie that she would not have been left down there alone for all the world could offer her, and Bertie agreed that he was glad Gustave had been the last to come up. Kathleen had been sent up first of all, so had escaped anxiety on the score of loneliness, but she seemed uneasy and uncomfortable, and Bertie, noticing it, kept near her, talking cheerfully.

As they entered the passage, Kathleen turned her head for a last glance at the temple-like structure over the well. She had to look past both Bertie and Gustave, who were each carrying candles. Her face went deathly pale, and if Bertie had not caught her she would have fallen.

"What's the matter?" he cried.

"Oh, look! Look!" she gasped, pointing backwards towards the well. Both turned hurriedly, but could see nothing but the pale glimmer of their candles' light on the grey stone of the pillars.

"Oh! Come away—I am sure I saw it!"

"Saw what, my dear girl?"

"I can't tell you. At any rate, not here! Let's get out as fast as we can!" Kathleen, unnerved, hurried forward and joined those in front, managing to place as many of them as possible between herself and what she had left behind her.

When they came to the tunnel, the order of their going was fixed by Tremaine, two of his natives being sent on to help the visitors at awkward places. Kathleen had Bertie, Dr. Smith, Pierre, Gustave, and Tremaine himself behind her; she had recovered from her fright, but Bertie's protecting presence was welcome. Captain Seymour, being just in front, joined with Wilson in assisting her over the troublesome spots. She began to feel more cheerful, and blamed herself for being a coward and letting her imagination play tricks with her. Presently Bertie ventured to ask what it was that had alarmed her.

"I really am rather ashamed of myself," she answered; "of course it must have been only my imagination, but when I looked back I suddenly saw, or thought I saw, the figure of a draped woman standing by that well, gazing at me with the most awful expression of fear, horror, and hatred. I seemed to see her absolutely clearly for a moment, then I went dizzy. When I looked again there was nothing; but it had been so frightfully vivid that I couldn't shake it off for a time, I just had to run away from it. I feel better now, and rather silly."

Bertie was very sympathetic, agreeing that their recent experience was enough to make anyone nervy.

They made good speed on their return, for now that their visit was over the electric torches were allowed to burn as long as they could, and sufficed to light them through the passage. It chanced that as they emerged from the final tunnel, Bertie and Kathleen were separated from the others by a few yards.

"Have you got your little cylinder safe?" asked Bertie

Kathleen had forgotten it for the moment, but produced it triumphantly.

"Isn't it quaint? I wonder what it was meant for, and if the Professor will ever find out."

Bertie's answer changed to an inarticulate shout of warning; he tried to drag the girl aside, but was too late. A mass of sun-dried sand detached itself from the wall of the fissure above them and slid down, just missing Kathleen's head, but hurling her to the ground and tearing her hand from his grasp; oddly enough, leaving him with the little cylinder, which she had held in the hand he caught at, in his own hand. Kathleen lay half buried beneath the mass, which nearly blocked the opening to the tunnel. It was evident that it would need more than their unassisted labour to extricate the poor girl.

The Professor sent his men at full speed to the tents for shovels, and in a few strenuous minutes they managed to set her free.

She had lost consciousness, but recovered sufficiently as they worked to tell them that she was not much hurt, and to their great relief they found that she could stand up and move her limbs. She could not walk, however, for one of her ankles had twisted, and she felt bruised and sore.

A donkey was fetched, and, riding gently, she was taken to one of the tents, where the Doctor examined her and made her as comfortable as he could.

The men of the party returned to inspect the scene of the mishap, for the Professor said that nothing of the kind had ever occurred before; that to all appearances the sand and mud had been so hardened by time and weather that they were practically homogenous, and it had often been necessary to cut through its stone-like substance before they could move it. The remaining face of the fissure appeared to be as he described it, hard and solid as rock, with no sign of a cleavage.

In the cool of the evening the party reached the river again, by no means sorry to rest. Even without accidents, it had been a heavy day. The ladies, tired out, disappeared to their cabins until it was time for supper.

CHAPTER XIII

PROFESSOR Tremaine, who had been urgently pressed to spend the evening on board, arrived in due course with his friends Pierre and Gustave.

The adventures of the day had been discussed, and now he was fulfilling his promise, giving reasons for his belief that the authors of that age-old tragedy had paid the price of their sins in their own lifetime. He drew his deductions from some of the painted frescoes which they had examined that day, telling his interested audience that he felt fairly sure that the priests who had done the deed were the same who were depicted as being massacred, and having their temple pulled down on their heads. He thought it more than likely that the unfortunate woman was the lost priestess Ohora, whom Amenhotep was seeking high and low, far and near. It was evident that he never discovered her fate, or he would have fetched the corpse from its dishonoured situation and placed it in one more suitable to her rank. The priests kept their secrets well.

"Why were they so anxious to get rid of the poor woman?" asked Colquhoun.

"Most probably she knew too much of them and their secrets, so they took the only way to keep her quiet. As a priestess in the royal palace, and the king's favourite, she would be able to use her knowledge as she chose, and her power would be immense. Women in those days wielded great influence in the life of the East."

"I wonder what it was she knew that they were afraid she might reveal, and how they managed to get hold of her without their dirty work being found out," said Wilson.

"The reasoning of priests, in all ages, has been different from other men's, and their secrets have often been such that they would do almost anything to prevent them from becoming known. Priests, from the beginning until now, have no reason to love the light. They are workers of darkness."

"Aren't you an orthodox Roman Catholic, Professor Tremaine? I thought, as a Frenchman, that you were almost sure to be," said Seymour, so intent upon the subject that he hardly realised the exceptional directness of his question.

"*I* a Roman Catholic! A follower of priestly mischief-makers? No! Had I my wish, I would do away with them all to-morrow."

"You speak strongly, Professor," said Thira. "Are you an atheist, then?"

"Madame, I do speak strongly. I am not an atheist. I believe in a good God, try always to do those things which I conceive He would wish me to do, to leave undone those things which would displease Him. But to believe there is a God does not necessarily mean that one need believe the nonsense that men teach who choose to set themselves up as His interpreters. What man of sanity could believe all the fairy tales they try to make us swallow? They are for children, for savages, not for men; at any rate not for men who have brains and who use them. The more one knows, the more impossible it is not to believe in a God who rules everything and is just. How can one study the world, its history, the marvels of science, and be an atheist?"

"Then, Professor, if you believe in God, to what creed do you belong?" asked Mary, tempted by his frankness.

"I am of no creed, Mademoiselle. I am not of creeds or dogmas; little petty rules which men have made; thou shalt, or shalt not. The commandments of Moses are for my guidance, and those he did not make; they existed thousands of years before; he only codified them and gave them to the Israelites. If one uses those rules, and tries to do to others as he wishes them to do to him, I think there is not much need of more."

"Then do you believe in a hereafter with a heaven and a hell?" asked Thira.

"Yes, Madame; in a hereafter. To one who pursues such studies as mine, that almost must be. I do not attempt to define it. I am not a priest, to make rules. As for heaven or hell, are they not here with us, to-day? What greater happiness than to feel one had done rightly, or that one had made another happier by self-sacrifice? For hell, we have remorse, shame, fear, regret for evil done which can never be undone. Seeing our evil actions reflected on others, perhaps those whom we love; loving vainly someone who may despise us; oh—and many other hells on earth. Why not believe in hell if these things are to be through eternity?"

"What about the reward and punishment, then?" asked Seymour. "We sailors have ideas on those subjects; we often think that the punishment falls here, in this life, without having to wait for the next."

"Most surely it does, Captain. Do not we see it in our lives? For instance, take what we have seen to-day: the woman who broke her vows to become a queen, her cruel end. Then the king who stole her from the temple to please his whim; he was punished by losing her. Those priests were perhaps only half found out, but they were wiped away, most likely their religion with them. Every day one sees it. Yes, the price is always paid, somehow!"

"What a terrible creed, Professor! I thought you said that you had no creed," said Thira, smiling.

"I have not, Madame; I have facts only—facts I have seen

hundreds of times proved. One gets nothing without a price. If we take without leave, we pay later."

Thira shivered a little, and soon after said good-night. Mary went with her, and the men were left alone.

"Why have you such a grudge against the priests, Professor?" asked Bertie.

Tremaine hesitated before replying, then seemed to take a decision.

"That is a subject I do not usually speak of," he said; "but of you I make an exception; you will please not repeat what I have to tell, nor ask me for any continuation of the story. You know I am a Frenchman, of some family. I was brought up a rigid Roman Catholic, as all my people for centuries have been. It had been the custom of our family, when there have been many daughters, for one to enter a convent; it had never occurred to one to ask the reason for young girls being put away thus, within walls which kept secrets. It was accepted; a sacrifice to God, or rather to the Church, which usurped authority and had made its own laws and customs. They went into those convents, generation after generation, and usually no more was heard of them, though occasionally one became an abbess and a person of some importance. To humanity and their family, however, they were lost.

"In my generation there were several daughters, and my favourite sister was chosen for the convent. She was willing, but she hated the thought of losing me; on the other hand, the priests had taught her that it was a sacrifice—one that would bring fortune to all her dear ones; so she felt she should make the great renunciation, and went. Nevertheless, she and I agreed that we would not quite lose each other. We arranged a means of communication—no matter what. At first, while she was a novitiate, there was no difficulty about my mother or sisters going to see her. They told us she seemed happy and contented, had a pleasant life, and that everyone was kind. Then she took the veil, after which it was only occasionally that anyone might see her, and never alone.

"Gradually there seemed a change; she was not bright, not happy as she had been, but frightened, anxious, as if she wanted to speak of something, but dare not. Finally came a day when she whispered to my mother, 'For the love of Christ, get me from this place!' That was all she was able to say, for, foolishly, my mother lost her head, and not thinking of the nun who was near by, said:

" 'Why do you want to leave? Are you not happy here?'

"My poor sister paled to the lips. She knew the other would hear that she had spoken forbidden words. The nun had heard, and came forward, saying that the interview must end. So, my mother left, not dreaming that matters were really serious.

"Next visiting day she called, to be told that Sister Agatha—my sister—was ill and could not be seen; several times afterwards my mother failed to see her. Then we grew anxious. I had been away, but when I returned I determined to communicate with her by the means which we had arranged. After many attempts I succeeded. It was not much that I could learn, only that she was in great trouble, and prayed to get out at all costs. Well, to shorten my story, we did get her out, but only after we applied to the civil tribunal to help us. Even then it was a slow process.

"She came to us, nearly dying. There was scandal. The priests who came within the convent could not be found. My sister died heart-broken in a few weeks; but she had told her terrible story. The poor nuns were altogether under the domination of their priests, believing the things the hypocrites told them. Can you wonder I feel bitterly against priests, and hate their self-righteousness, when it hides only hideous sin, made safe by laws of their own making? Things are different in France now. The State has closed the religious houses, set the inmates free, if they would be free; but many are so steeped in what they have learnt that they prefer their slavery, and seek it elsewhere.

"That is all I have to tell; perhaps it will be enough to supply you with reasons for my hatred of priests."

There was a brief silence among his listeners when he ceased. Seymour spoke first.

"And yet, in the face of evidence like that, we are giving home and sanctuary to such people in our old England! Surely that is setting the door of hospitality a little too wide!"

The others joined in, and for some time a general discussion took place, other experiences of a similar nature, of which they had heard, being related by one or two members of the party.

It was late when they separated, to forget in sleep the wonders and horrors which they had seen and heard during the past few hours. While undressing, Wilson discovered Kathleen's little cylinder in his pocket, and put it away in a safe place where it was not likely to be disturbed.

The next day saw the dahabieh and its occupants on their way down the river, after good-byes to the Professor and his friends, mutual hopes of meeting again, and promises on Tremaine's part to let them know the results of his investigations when he had arranged them in methodical form.

Kathleen could hobble about with the aid of a stick, the stiffness and soreness being troublesome. Her two most attentive cavaliers did their best for her. Bertie Wilson expressed his candid annoyance with "that damned Doctor Smith" for "everlastingly poking his nose in where he wasn't wanted"; while the Doctor showed a strong objection to having his patient "so constantly disturbed by that aggressive young Wilson." Meanwhile the patient herself seemed quite content to be entertained and cared for so assiduously.

There was a general feeling among the party that enough had been seen of Egypt's tombs and temples. The journey down river provided several minor mishaps, and on one occasion they only just missed shipwreck. At the end of a long, tedious day they reached Cairo, heated, tired, and inclined to be cross. Their train had behaved badly, breaking down and delaying them for several hours; some of the luggage which they specially wanted was left behind with their indispensable servitor, Tom, who had gone back to look for it and would not return for some hours. Colquhoun had telegraphed for rooms, but when they arrived the hotel could not provide so many at such short notice; therefore the party had to divide.

Thira was restless, for she felt that she must be getting forward. All this time in Egypt meant time wasted for her, for she was longing to be with Jack, or at least to hear something of him. She worried her husband until he set aside the wishes of the rest of the party to please her, though she took good care that his excuses should not include her name. It was arranged that they should leave in two days to rejoin the yacht, and when the necessary telegrams had been dispatched Thira felt better. She declined, however, to take part in any amusements, but spent her time idling in the hotel, chatting with such acquaintances as she met, and writing home. She took it into her head to write to Janet, among others, telling her some of their adventures, and expressing the hope that they might meet again some day; though, she added, as they contemplated returning *via* the Antipodes, they could not be back until, at the earliest, the following year. She was cruel enough to scribble a postscript to the effect that they might call at Purnam, where, probably, they would see Jack Winthrop. That, she knew, would make poor Janet wince, and the knowledge added a little piquancy to the pleasure of writing it.

The postscript caused Janet many unhappy hours. She was hard at work as usual, and had to a large extent managed, not to forget, but to put aside useless regrets for her folly; Thira's words brought them all back again and added fresh ghosts to haunt her. She had not yet paid in full for her impetuous dismissal of the man she loved.

CHAPTER XIV

THE sun was setting, a ball of fire, over the African coast, shedding its deepened radiance upon a fagged and fretful world. The first hint of a breeze for the day ruffled the water, but it brought little relief; it might have come from a furnace. As Mary said, it was the sort of temperature that might have suited Shadrach, Meshach, and Abednego, but was not agreeable to twentieth-century Christians.[13] Ever since they left Port Said they had endured this terrible heat till they felt faded and sun-dried to a degree. Thira, limp as a rag, was so irritable that she was not fit company for anyone, but the other two women had managed to keep wonderfully cheerful. Seymour said that it was really nothing, that he had known it much hotter; regarding him suspiciously, the others compelled him to confess that he should not be sorry to be clear of that sun-trap, the Red Sea. Colquhoun seemed depressed, though whether from the heat or because Thira did not seem to improve in health or spirits, it was impossible to say; he rarely took anyone into his confidence. Kind and courteous as ever, he left nothing undone which would add to the comfort of his guests, but it was evident that he did it all with some effort.

Kathleen, quite recovered from the effects of her accident, was as lively as the thermometer permitted anyone to be. Naturally, her distressing experience specially interested Dr. Smith; he often spoke of its cause, of Tremaine's discovery, and of the poor murdered

[13] In the Bible, Shadrach, Meshach, and Abednegothe were thrown into a fiery furnace by Nebuchadnezzar and came out unharmed.

priestess, evolving various theories upon her history and its tragic close. He and Bertie were discussing it, as a relief from the ever-present theme of the heat, when Wilson suddenly remembered Kathleen's cylinder, which still remained in his charge. She had not asked for it, and he did not know whether she thought it had been lost in the sand, or whether she preferred not to be reminded of it; therefore he had refrained from mentioning it. He had noticed that she avoided speaking of that expedition unless the course of conversation compelled her to do so.

He went below, and brought it up for Smith to examine. They were alone; the others had their own favourite retreats during the heat of the day. Deep in their scrutiny, they were speculating upon the origin and use of the curiosity, when they heard Mary's voice not far from them.

"Thank Heaven," she said, "another day of this has gone; to-morrow we may hope to be where there is at least a little air. I am not surprised that Moses and the Israelites were able to cross the Red Sea on dry land; the wonder to me is that it isn't always dry land; this sun ought to evaporate every drop of water."

"It might if the Sea wasn't always filling up from the South. The water is always running into the Red Sea and never out; the saltness and specific gravity of the water in it is greater than that of the ocean that feeds it." It was Seymour who spoke.

"Oh, don't let's have any learned discussions yet, Captain; I haven't sufficiently recovered from to-day's broiling. I want something lighter than gravitation, specific or otherwise—not that I understand in the least what that means. Hello, you boys! What are you putting your heads together over?"

She leaned forward and looked at the cylinder in Bertie's hand. It was the first time that she had seen it, for it had been in Kathleen's pocket until the moment of the accident.

"What is that queer thing?" she asked.

They explained, and Mary, interested, took it for a closer inspection; at that moment, Kathleen appeared. Mary called to her to come and claim her property.

"What is it?" she inquired.

"The little cylinder Tremaine gave you."

"How on earth did it get here?" exclaimed the girl. "I thought it was buried deep in the sand where I fell."

"If you recollect," said Bertie, "it was in your hand at the moment, and when I caught your hand it was left in mine. If you hadn't been holding it I might have pulled you quite clear, but the thing prevented me from getting a good grip. I slipped it in my pocket before I began burrowing for you, and afterwards put it away, intending to give it you when you asked for it, but you never have yet. Will you take it now?"

"No, thanks, you may keep it! I don't want it; it brings back unpleasant recollections."

"Don't you want it, really?" asked Mary.

"Not a bit!"

"Then may I have it? I am frightfully interested in anything that had to do with that poor girl, and it has no unpleasant memories for me."

"Certainly—take it and keep it if you like; though I suppose it really belongs just as much to Mr. Wilson as to me, for he saved it and has kept it all this time."

"Don't forget," put in Bertie, "that Tremaine gave it to you, and you promised to return it to him at any time. He may ask you for it."

"Oh—I had forgotten. If you take it, Mary, you must take the contract with it."

"Right. I am quite willing to give it back if it is asked for; but meantime I should like it."

They sat for some little time longer, discussing the event. Kathleen drifted away without saying much more, and presently Mary went below, taking her treasure with her.

At supper-time, the whole party assembled except Mary. They waited awhile for her, and then, as she still did not come, began without her; but as the meal progressed and she was still absent Thira expressed surprise.

"What can have happened to delay her?" she wondered, aloud.

"Well, it can't be anything serious," replied Colquhoun. "Tom, go and ask the stewardess to find out if Miss Macintyre wants anything."

In a short time Tom returned with a message.

"If you please, sir, Miss Macintyre has met with a slight accident and hopes you won't wait for her; she will be with you before long."

No one thought much of it, the men guessing at some slight trouble with her toilet—no rare occurrence with ladies; Thira, however, was not quite happy about it, and her troubled glance sent Kathleen quietly from her place to find Mary.

When she reached the cabin, she found Mary bathing her forehead, with a towel wrapped round her head and the place reeking of eau-de-Cologne.

"Mary! What *is* the matter?"

"Nothing much, dear," replied the girl, her face still lowered over the basin. "Only a knock on the head and a little cut and a bruise or two."

"But how did it all happen? And are you much hurt, poor dear?"

"No—I shall be all right directly, but it was odd. I came down to get dressed for supper and went to my locker to put away that little cylinder you gave me. I had opened one of the drawers and was putting it in, when suddenly I received the most terrific blow on the back of my head. For a little while I must have been knocked silly, for when I came round I was lying on the floor. My small trunk was also on the floor, and gradually I remembered. Of course the trunk must have fallen from the rack. It has been there for days, and the sea is as calm as a pond, yet the beastly thing falls and stuns me! It is really rather sickening to be laid out like that."

Kathleen was sympathetic, but looked grave. For a moment or two she said nothing; then she seemed to make up her mind.

"Where is that cylinder?"

"In the drawer, I believe. At least I think so."

She looked in the drawer. "Yes! There is is." She put out her hand to pick it up, but Kathleen restrained her.

"Don't touch the wretched thing! I am sure there is some curse attached to it. I wish I had never asked the Professor for it!"

"Why on earth should you think that?"

"Well I do, anyway, and I have some reason. I was carrying it when that sand so unaccountably slid down and nearly smothered me."

"That is only a coincidence. I don't see why, on such a small basis, you go and build up a theory of a curse."

"It isn't only on that I build." And she then told Mary of the apparition she had seen, or thought she had seen, in the tombs.

May listened attentively, but was not convinced or ready to accept Kathleen's suggestion, though her friend had fully made up her own mind on the subject and went on to elaborate her theory, pointing out that since the cylinder had been with them bad luck had seemed to haunt the party. First, her accident; then the several small *contretemps* which had befallen them on their journey down to Cairo, and sundry other things: not the least being the terrific heat they had experienced in the Red Sea, unusual at that time of the year; and now this accident to Mary herself. She begged Mary to let her throw the thing out of the porthole, but Mary refused. To begin with, she said, she would never think of letting herself be frightened into doing a silly thing like that; further, they had no right to do it, considering the promise to Professor Tremaine. If they threw it away, how could it be restored to him—supposing that some day he wished to have it? At last they agreed to leave it where it was for the time, and Mary retired, as she felt considerably shaken.

Kathleen went back to report progress, but left unmentioned her ideas as to the part the cylinder might have played in the accident.

* * * * * *

Mary, next morning, looked far from her usual bright, cheery self. She said the most horrible nightmare had quite spoiled her sleep, and for long afterwards kept her awake, though when she did drop off she slept like a top, and really did not feel as bad as she looked.

"You, of all people, suffering from nightmares!" said Seymour. "That's about the limit. I thought you were proof against such things."

"Well, it isn't a weakness to which I am often subject, but on this occasion I certainly have had more than enough of it. It was distinctly unpleasant."

"Why? What did you dream, Mary? Will it bear relating?" asked Kathleen.

"Oh yes, it's strictly proper, if that's what you mean. In the middle of the night I woke, and began thinking of your cylinder and of its unfortunate original owner.

"After a time I got up and fetched it out, and studied it. Of course I could make nothing of it, and must have fallen asleep with it in my hand, and having my head full of all those gruesome tales,

I suppose gave my dreams a queer turn; anyway, I thought a veiled figure was bending over me. I could see it quite closely, and I felt sure, though I never saw the poor mummy, that it was the Princess Ohora. At first I only felt a sort of languid surprise, as one does in dreams, then I felt uncomfy, and at last I was seized with an awful terror. I could not move hand or foot, and though I knew I was in my berth, it never occurred to me that it was impossible for anyone to have come on board, much less a mummy dead for thousands of year.

"I tried to cry out, but I couldn't. Then the figure leaned closer and closer over me. I could see its eyes simply burning, for it seemed as though the veil melted away and I was looking on a real face.

"Then I was seized and crushed down on the bed, and something was pressed over my face. I was half suffocated, and in my desperation began fighting for what seemed an eternity, but without avail. Then suddenly I woke up, I was trembling all over, wet with perspiration, and the sensations of my dream were still horribly vivid; but I was awake and the pressure had gone off my body. Something was certainly over my face though, but it was only my pillow! I must have managed in my restlessness to push my head under it, though how on earth I did so is a mystery. I can tell you I was jolly glad to be awake again.

"I lay awake for quite a long time, for fear that if I went to sleep again it might return; but when I did no more dreams came to worry me."

"Good Lord! How rotten!" exclaimed Bertie.

"We shall have to be careful how we discuss unpleasant things in your hearing, Miss Macintyre," said Captain Seymour. "It won't do to have you getting nerves."

"What happened to the cylinder?" asked Kathleen.

"I don't know. I forgot it. I expect it is in my bed still."

"In that case the servants will find it and put it aside for you, so you needn't worry about it," said Thira, and at that moment Tom arrived with something on a salver, which he took to Mary.

"If you please, Miss, this thing got damaged while the servants were making your bed. One of them trod on something, and looking to see what it was, found this. Unfortunately it seems to have got cracked, but it was really not the man's fault, for it was on the floor under the berth and he only found it by treading on it."

Mary picked up the cylinder.

"It really doesn't matter. No one is to blame," she said, then gave a little cry of surprise.

"Why, look! It is broken, and it is hollow!"

Everyone crowded round her to see. There was a distinct spiral crack running round the cylinder and terminating at one end, where also a small piece of the ivory had been broken right out, showing a hollow space beneath. The end, which appeared to be all in one piece with the rest, was really a cleverly fitted plug fastened in with some sort of cement. It passed from hand to hand for examination. Kathleen would not touch it, but suggested that now it was broken it might as well be thrown away. Dr. Smith remarked that it could very easily be mended if only the missing bit could be found.

The ever-practical Bertie solved the last difficulty by shaking the cylinder; a rattling sound seemed to indicate that the lost piece was inside.

Teed, the captain of the yacht, who had now joined the party, gave it as his opinion that before repair was possible it would have to be further broken. "You can't apply cement to the edges unless you can get at them, which at present is impossible," he said.

A moment later he added: "There is something else inside besides that bit of broken ivory; I can see it through the crack. Looks like leather, but I doubt if any leather could have lasted so long. May I try to open it, Miss Macintyre? I will be as careful as possible not to do further damage."

"Oh yes! Do let's have it opened," came in a chorus from the onlookers.

"I haven't any objection; but, after all, it is really Kathleen's. What do you say, Kathleen?"

The girl seemed to hesitate a moment.

"I really don't know what to say; it might bring us bad luck to open it. We don't in the least know what we shall find."

"But why should it be unlucky to open it?" asked Thira.

Kathleen looked confused, and hesitated again, so Mary explained.

"She has an idea that there is a spell about that cylinder, and that it brings bad luck to anyone who interferes with it. I chaffed her for it yesterday, but I am not quite so cocksure about it now. At any rate, I haven't had a very pleasant time since it came into my possession."

There was a murmur of surprise, for it was unlike Mary to be superstitious; if it had been Kathleen the others could have understood it, but from Mary such a speech was quite unexpected. Bertie intervened:

"Well, I have had the thing for days past, and don't remember any special bad luck. Nothing fell on my head, nor was I troubled with nightmares."

"There's your answer, Mary," said Thira. "I think it would be rather silly not to open it and see what is inside. It isn't likely that anyone would take the trouble to secrete anything so carefully unless it was of exceptional interest. Anyway, the thing is open already in a sense, with that bit out of it."

After a little more persuasion Kathleen gave way, and Captain Teed was permitted to try what he could do. Taking an end of the cylinder in each hand, he applied a gentle pressure to it. The result was unexpected, for the partial crack widened, and then with a dull sound it broke in two and the captain was left with half in each hand. The contents were revealed: a long spill of yellow papyrus, dry as dust and light as a feather.

"It won't do to unfold it in this state—it will crumble to bits in our hands; but I think I can soon remedy that. Just wait a minute or two." The captain went below; Bertie and Smith followed to help.

It seemed long before they returned, and when at last they appeared, Teed was carrying what seemed a square board; on closer inspection it proved to be the back of a glazed frame. Being a sailor he was neat, and had prepared his specimen most carefully.

"Well, Teed! Have you found anything worth looking at?" called Seymour.

"That depends. To my mind it is a marvel, though what it is we have found it will take someone cleverer than any of us to tell." He laid the frame on the table.

Inside, carefully flattened under the glass, and mounted on a sheet of white paper, lay the quaintest-looking document that any of them had ever seen.

The material was evidently papyrus, which they had all often heard of, but of which hitherto they had only seen fragments. This bit seemed perfect, except that one tiny corner was torn.

All over the papyrus were drawn hieroglyphics and little pictures. There were figures of men and women, buildings, boats, fishes, unfamiliar beasts and mythical creatures, easily recognisable, for the drawings were perfectly clear, though the ink had faded. At the bottom appeared the same sign or seal which had been on the outside of the cylinder.

"Why, it's a letter!" cried Mary.

"It looks more like a legal document to me," said Teed.

"Possibly her burial certificate," suggested the Doctor.

"I wonder whether those other cylinders contain papers similar to this," said Seymour, "or whether they were all different. We must let the Professor know of this find. It may mean a lot to him."

"We will write from Aden," agreed Colquhoun, "then he will be able to follow it up at once. I will ask him to send us an interpretation, for anything dating from such an immense antiquity couldn't fail to be intensely interesting."

"Yes, that would be the right thing to do," said Thira. "What do you think, Kathleen? You must express an opinion; it was confided to your care."

Kathleen did not hesitate. "By all means send it back at once. I am sure we ought to; the Professor would never have parted with it had he dreamed what it was."

"But what do you think it may be, Kathleen?" asked Mary. "You haven't made any suggestion yet."

"Oh, how should I know, or anyone else? It might be anything."

"Perhaps a passport into Paradise!" suggested the ribald Bertie.

"More possibly her death-warrant," replied Kathleen.

"What a gruesome idea!"

"Well, the whole business is gruesome. If you had seen all that was left of the poor woman, with that awful wax cloth tied tightly round her face, and had stood by her coffin imagining what she had suffered before death came to relieve her, you wouldn't be surprised at any ideas as to the evil fortune hanging about the thing."

"Well, Captain, have a good sound box made to pack it in," said Colquhoun. "I suppose it won't be long before we reach Aden, will it?"

"No, only a few hours, with any luck."

He turned to go, then suddenly stopped.

"By the bye, I had forgotten—there was something else inside."

He put his hand in his pocket and produced the two fragments, and then unfolded a little packet of tissue paper and disclosed a small object which he offered to Kathleen. She would not touch it, but put her hands behind her back, and said she did not want to have anything more to do with the "find"; Mary also, to everyone's amusement, refused to accept it. He passed it to Thira, who took it at once.

"It's a seal, or something like one. A scarab—the sort of thing they sell to tourists in the bazaars, only a different colour. Mounted in gold, too. How interesting! And the engraving is the same as that on the cylinder."

The scarab was passed round, but the other two women still declined to handle it.

"I had better send that with the document, I suppose?" remarked Teed.

"I don't know—the Professor won't need it, for the same markings are on the papyrus. I should like to keep it as a memento."

"Oh, please don't, Thira!" broke in Kathleen. "It will bring us bad luck; do send it away."

"Oh, don't be silly, Kathleen! One would think you were a schoolgirl."

"Well, it hasn't been much good to Mary or myself."

"But it didn't hurt Bertie."

"Perhaps the charm, or curse, or whatever it is, only works with ladies!" said Bertie, laughing.

"Then to make Miss Boston happy, why not let Colquhoun keep it for you?" suggested Seymour.

Thira gave a little contemptuous laugh.

"Very well, if it pleases Kathleen, I will give it to Richard; though it seems a little unwifely to saddle him with the curse, doesn't it?"

Colquhoun smiled quietly and picked the scarab up.

"I am quite willing to risk it, my dear, especially if it will relieve you from a possible danger," he said, slipping it into his pocket. "Now let us see about packing the papyrus before we get to Aden."

CHAPTER XV

A FEW hours later they were lying off Aden, and the launch was ready to go ashore for fresh provisions and the mail. It was nearing sundown, so none of the party accompanied it. The package directed to Professor Tremaine, care of the Museum at Cairo, was sent, with a superscription asking that it might be forwarded to him whatever his present address might be.

Kathleen gave a sigh of relief when the cylinder and its contents had left the yacht, though she was sorry that Thira had insisted on keeping the scarab.

Everyone seemed cheerful on the next morning and eager to land; even Thira was full of suggestions as to the programme. Among the garrison at Aden they had several acquaintances, and their anticipations of a warm welcome proved correct. Bertie found an old friend, the companion of many sporting excursions, and promptly became lost for all practical purposes, absorbed in discussion of sport, chatting over old times, and the planning of other trips later, when opportunity should arise.

Polo and tennis passed the hours for the others, who were treated to a very creditable show in the cool of the evening. Not until long after the sun had set—and, incidentally, long after a convivial supper—did they return to the launch by the light of a brilliant moon.

Kathleen, sitting apart from the others in the bows of the boat, looked up with a little smile as Bertie joined her, but made no attempt to speak.

"Anything on your mind this evening, Miss Boston?" asked Bertie, smiling in return.

"Nothing special. I can't help thinking how extraordinary it is that all this was practically the same—the rocks and sea and moonlight—thousands of years ago, even at the time that poor woman was put to death in that tomb. It seems to come back more vividly to me every time I think of it. After all, she was a girl like me—the only difference being in her ideas and habits, corresponding with the time and place she lived in. I suppose I feel for her more than you men can."

"But we do feel it, though not in quite the same way. At any rate I do, and I think the others do, from what they say. We have had several long discussions on the subject; it began the last night Tremaine was with us. He told us some horrible stories. I can't repeat them, but they were enough to make anyone, even the most sceptical, realise what awful things may and do happen in this world of ours."

"But those things don't happen now. They wouldn't be allowed."

"Many things are done which wouldn't be allowed if they were known. Clever people often hide their evil deeds; more often than most people think."

"But it is seldom that anyone is murdered without the police tracing the criminal. One sees such things in the papers day after day."

"Yes—if they discover a murder has been committed; but what about the crimes that are never heard of? Even in London, dozens of people disappear without a sign."

"But surely most of them are cases where people want to disappear for some reason of their own—debts, or unhappiness, perhaps."

"Not always; quite a lot of poor people are picked out of the river every year, for instance, whom nobody owns or recognises. They are generally buried in nameless graves, and no more is heard of them beyond the Coroner's verdict of 'found drowned.' "

"How dreadful to think that there can be so much wickedness and misery! It's such a grand world, really, if people would only take what is best in it and leave it as God intended it to be. Just look at the sea to-night! Could anything be more lovely?"

"Perfect! Yet even here, in this beautiful sea, everything isn't so peaceful and happy as it looks; there are evil brutes underneath the surface. It wouldn't be safe to fall in; apart from any danger of drowning, one would stand an excellent chance of being made a meal of by a shark."

"What a grisly notion! I shall feel creepy until we are safely on board the *Siren*."

Bertie smiled at her.

"It doesn't matter much where one is, there are always chances of unpleasant occurrences. Best not to worry about such things, but just to take responsible care and let Providence do the rest."

"Are you a fatalist, then? One of those people who believe that it isn't any good worrying, because whatever one may do, things will happen just the same, whether or no?"

"No, I don't quite believe that, but I do believe that some power greater than ourselves takes a hand in the game and usually sees fair play, and looks after its own people. I have seen a good many queer things happen in my short life—things which, from a human standpoint, seemed so utterly unlikely, so almost impossible; yet they *have* happened, so I can't help feeling that we are watched over and kept in order for our own benefit most of the time. I agree with Seymour that if we are punished it is for our own faults."

Kathleen showed her surprise.

"I should never have thought you held such ideas, Mr. Wilson; you are so practical, as a rule, and always seem so well able to look after yourself—and other people too. You have shown me a new side to-night: and I am rather pleased, for I like to know my friends' inner thoughts."

"Thanks for calling me your friend. I have very few friends; I think the best of them is Jack Winthrop. He and I understand one another as few men do."

"There is a good deal more in him than he shows to the world, I imagine. It always stuck me that if one could pierce his shell of self-possession, one would find much that was very attractive; but he wouldn't be an easy man to get to know."

"Oh yes, he would, if he liked you and thought that you were genuine; but he has no use for anyone who is superficial."

"Do you think we shall see him on this trip? We are going somewhere near him, aren't we? What on earth made him run away to the end of the world? He didn't need money, I suppose?"

"I can't say why he went. He went off without a word to anyone; certainly he never even hinted to me that he had the slightest thought of leaving, and we were together a short time before."

"Everyone seemed surprised," said Kathleen musingly. "I wonder what it was."

"Well, we won't try to decide. Jack would have told me, I think, if he had told anyone, but as he didn't choose to, I shan't trouble about his reasons."

The conversation ended, for the *Siren* loomed above them in the velvety darkness, and the bustle of climbing aboard separated them.

CHAPTER XVI

KATHLEEN was awakened by the unrestful angle at which she was lying, and for a few moments drowsily wondered where she was; then she realised the familiar surroundings of her berth, and the memory of the previous evening and her conversation with Bertie came back. The quiet talk had seemed to bring them nearer to each other than had all the previous weeks and months during which she had known him. Hitherto she had recognised in him a straightforward, strong character, to be depended upon in any time of trouble or difficulty of a practical nature; but it would never have occurred to her to ask him for help or advice in any moral or mental problem. Now, however, he appeared in a new aspect, and she looked forward to their next meeting.

Lost in day-dreams, it was some time before she noticed that while the yacht was rolling rhythmically the familiar vibration from the engines was absent. A strange stillness pervaded the ship, and she got up to look through the porthole.

Spreading to the distant horizon an unbroken expanse of sea, a sea of brilliant blue, was flecked with little feathery patches of white foam. No land was in sight. The *Siren* was slipping along at a good pace, under sail for the first time since they had entered the Red Sea. It was just 6.30, and Kathleen, wide awake and alert, dressed quickly and went on deck.

Aloft, snowy canvas rose to the dizzy height of the top-mast—an exquisite picture. There was a considerable list to leeward, for though the breeze was light, with such a spread the vessel responded sensitively. The deck was clear, except for a few sailors at odd duties.

She stepped to the side; the splendour of the sea, the hint of land far astern, the water whirling alongside in little eddies and flounces of foam, thrilled her.

"Cheerio, Miss Boston! you are up early," said a deep, cheery voice behind her.

Captain Seymour had appeared, looking very much at home and with a contented smile on his weather-beaten countenance.

"Good morning, Captain Seymour. Yes, the movement of the ship woke me, I think. Where are we off, and why did we make such a mysterious departure? It reminds me of stories of blockade runners I read years ago."

The old seaman laughed.

"Ah well, I shan't be surprised if there is trouble about it. But it was on our programme to get away from Aden some time to-day, so when I turned out and found a splendid chance of a little real yachting—sailing instead of steaming—I persuaded Teed to steal a march on the sluggards and get under way as soon as possible. I hope Richard and Thira won't be annoyed with me."

"I don't see why they should be. How did you manage it without disturbing anyone?"

"Teed arranged all that. Special orders were given for silence and dispatch. Sailors can be very quiet at their work if necessary."

"They can, undoubtedly—I never heard a sound. Where are we going?"

"I don't know. Even Teed hasn't any definite orders, except that we are to run clear out to sea and keep off the African coast. You see, the boat is very well provisioned and carries a lot of coal; with spells of sailing we could make quite a long trip without absolute necessity to put in anywhere. I asked Colquhoun yesterday where we were bound next, and he said he wasn't quite sure. He pays the piper, but I rather fancy it's his wife who calls the tune. Perhaps we shall find out when she comes on deck."

There was no more to be learnt for the present, and Thira, who took life lazily, might not appear until luncheon, so the two strolled about, content with the delight of the swift motion through tropic seas. To Kathleen there seemed to be something lacking to make it perfection; she did not realise what it was, or, at any rate, would not acknowledge to herself that she did.

"Hello, Bertie!" called Captain Seymour, catching sight of Wilson. "What have you been doing idling below when you ought to have been lending a hand? It isn't often you lose a chance of handling a rope."

Wilson laughed, and denied the accusation of idling. "The Doctor and I have been overhauling tackle," he explained. "He is a bit of a deep-sea fisherman, and last night we thought we were going to have some sport among those rocks. We hadn't reckoned on stealing away like this. And when we found that we were sold, we thought we might as well have things ready for the next chance, and not be caught unawares."

"Rotten luck—Teed and I have spoilt your sport. You might have come off sooner last night and have had a quiet fish."

"I wouldn't have given up last nights experiences just for a bit of fishing," replied Wilson, with a glance at Kathleen.

Kathleen blushed and looked away, and before Seymour could reply Mary and Dr. Smith appeared; then Colquhoun joined them, looking quite cheerful. He received the captain's apologies and explanations with amusement, saying that for his part he was only too glad to be at sea again with a fair breeze; and as for Thira, he had not seen her so gay for weeks as she was that morning when she woke to find that the *Siren* was under way.

"I expect she is about as sick of the heat and airlessness of the Red Sea as we all are, and the Nile wasn't much better either. We shall all be as fresh as paint after a good blow," said Seymour. "Here comes Tom—breakfast is served, ladies and gentlemen! Let us prove our appetites!"

CHAPTER XVII

THE days that followed passed pleasantly enough, with glorious weather and steady breezes; and the *Siren*, under sail, stood away along the African coast. This was no journey where speed was all-important, and the travellers were able to choose their own time and touch at whatever points they chose.

Captain Teed was consulted as to their next port of call, and gave them the necessary information. He was a man of many years' seafaring experience; there were few spots near the usual track of ships that he had not visited, and those he had seen he knew all about. It was agreed, after discussion, that they should touch at the Somali coast, and from there work along to Socotra, from which point they would sail across the Line and into the Southern Hemisphere.

These were days of idleness, and the travellers, thrown much together, grew to know each other better. A pretty little romance seemed developing between Bertie Wilson and Kathleen, noted by the others with interest. Captain Seymour, as an elderly man, took pleasure in watching the love affairs of young folk; and Mary, being a born matchmaker, could never resist the temptation of giving a helping push to anything suggestive of matrimony which might be proceeding in her neighbourhood. It was plain enough, however, that not much extraneous help was needed. The young couple were almost always together, but so far neither Bertie nor Kathleen had acknowledged in their own hearts that they were in love, though each felt the world was empty when the other was absent.

Seymour was never so happy as when criticising the sailing of the ship, but in spite of arguments he and Captain Teed were excellent friends. Bertie, content among ropes and sails, and always willing to take a hand, to take his turn at hauling with the crew, and even to go aloft with the best of them, was naturally very popular with the men.

It was one of Kathleen's nightmares that Bertie would some day fall from aloft and either break his neck or go overboard; at the same time she could not help admiring his cleverness and agility in the rigging and feeling a pride in it. She once suggested that he should not risk life and limb unnecessarily, but he seemed so surprised that she should think there was any danger about it that she hid her fears.

A good deal of rivalry existed among the men as to who was the smartest aloft. By way of amusement, Captain Seymour suggested a competition, and offered a small prize. Conditions were made and the test was arranged, when Bertie, who had been listening, announced that he did not see why he shouldn't be included; true, he was only a volunteer and not a professional, but in his opinion enterprise and merit should be encouraged.

Seymour and Teed asserted that he would not stand a chance, but, after argument, he was permitted to compete *hors concours*; further, he himself offered a prize for any man who could beat him at any work aloft which the crew among themselves should select.[14]

The contest was fixed for the same afternoon, and during lunch Bertie bore heroically a considerable amount of chaff from the rest of the party. Kathleen did not join in it; she was anxious, and heartily wished that he would rest content to be a spectator. She realised that even if she could persuade him to refrain, he would feel miserable at the thought of backing out at the last moment; but she felt that she must say something to him.

[14] *Hors concours*: without competing for the prize.

Her chance came after lunch when everyone turned in for a siesta.

"Mr. Wilson," she said, as he was strolling past, "I want you to promise me not to be rash this afternoon. You know, as a friend, I have a right to ask that—at least, I think I have."

Bertie looked rather at a loss and also somewhat overcome.

"But, Miss Boston, why should you worry about it? It isn't likely that I shall come to any harm; but, of course, if you would rather I gave it up, I will."

"That's decent of you, but I shouldn't like you to do that now, after the teasing you had; it would look like backing out. But do be careful."

"It never occurred to me that anyone would worry about me. It's awfully jolly of you! I never dreamt that you would care one way of the other."

"But I do care a good deal one way or the other," she answered, looking away.

Bertie thrilled at the realisation that this girl cared for him, and that there was a very genuine anxiety behind her words. He gave her his promise, and they separated, each feeling that a definite step forward had been taken in their friendship, each aware, for the first time, that love was knocking at the door of their hearts.

* * * * * *

The sun was dipping towards the horizon; on deck, ready for the show to begin, the company grouped at various vantage-points. The general competition was to come first, and then Bertie's match. Captain Seymour was to be the judge and referee in one, and no appeal against his decision could be allowed.

The *Siren* carried a press of sail, for she was a three-masted schooner, and her spread of canvas was more like that of a racing yacht than a cruising one, though her powerful engines made her independent of wind and weather.

The men entered into the spirit of the entertainment, and showed great enthusiasm and skill. Bertie was quickly outclassed, for many of the tasks which were set had not previously come his way, whereas the crew were old hands at the work; still, he had a shot at them all and acquitted himself by no means badly. He felt, however, that he stood no chance in the competition that he himself had started. No one yet knew what form this was to take, for it was to be decided by lot, the seamen having selected a certain number of feats, any one of which was suitable.

At length Captain Seymour's competition was over and the prize awarded, and for two at least of the party the critical moment came. Captain Teed asked Thira to draw the lots. The task selected on the one drawn was to replace the mizzen-top, it being supposed to be split, and to be taken down.[15] The man who could do the work in the shortest time would be adjudged the winner. Each competitor was to be allowed to choose a crew to help him, selecting in turn from those not competing; Captain Seymour again to be judge.

Only two men offered themselves for competition, and they were the best men of the crew at such tricky tasks. Lots were again drawn as to the order of going aloft, and the second place fell to Bertie. The assisting crews were then chosen, and Seymour, watch in hand, gave the word to go. A moment later the first crew were racing up, watched with breathless interest by those below. Quickly and cleverly they did the work, and in a very short time were on deck again, with the other sail neatly folded at Seymour's feet.

---

[15] Mizzen-top: a platform on the mizzenmast (the mast aft or next aft of the mainmast of a sailing vessel).

It had been of great advantage to Bertie to see how the thing had been done, for although he had often been aloft on similar work before, he had not the experience of the others.

"Stand by!" shouted Seymour. Almost before he had time to realise that his turn had come, he and his crew were scrambling aloft. Bertie did not mean to be disgraced altogether, and buckled to with a will, his men playing up to him splendidly.

Kathleen watched, hardly breathing, as Bertie reached the top of the swaying mast. Would he lose his hold and fall? Would be he beaten? She knew the time the other team had taken, and, watch in hand, counted the seconds as they passed. It seemed they could never possibly finish in equal time, but they even beat the previous record, much to the surprise of the men, and not least to Bertie himself.

Seymour judged everything to be well and properly done, and then came the turn of Dick and his crew. He was probably the smartest man on board, and it was accepted as practically certain that he would bear off the prize.

The third crew got to work in a silence of breathless interest from those below. Even Thira excitedly borrowed Colquhoun's watch to follow the test. And, as they stood there, the sound of something snapping broke the hush of strained attention. The men were hanging out on the end of the gaff, fixing the sail; the man aloft was waiting for them.[16] The sail was seen to be falling, leaving the men clinging on to such hold as they could find. It all happened so suddenly that almost as the agonised shout of warning died away the whole thing was over. The sail, gathering speed in

---

[16] Gaff: a wooden spar at the top of the sail, extending diagonally from the mast.

its descent, rushed down on those below. Part of it caught Bertie and Kathleen, who were standing together, and knocked them into the scuppers; the tag end of the rope knocked Captain Seymour's watch out of his hand; but the chief weight of the sail fell on Thira and Colquhoun, dragging them heavily to the deck and enveloping them.[17]

In spite of the suddenness of the catastrophe, Teed and his men kept their heads. He shouted to those aloft to make good and come down, and even while he was shouting was helping to lift the sail from the prostrate forms beneath it. They found the victims lying stunned, but apparently not otherwise injured; in a few minutes they were able to sit up and speak, though both were badly shaken and Thira's right wrist was sprained. Dr. Smith made a rapid examination, and assisted Thira to her cabin. Colquhoun would not go below, but stayed to investigate the cause of the accident. No one could explain how it happened, for the rope that had parted seemed perfectly sound, and, as far as the fracture showed, had been so up to the end. It had snapped clean through without warning, and it was a miracle that none of the men had fallen; but no one seemed to be hurt except those on deck, and of those only Thira's injury was worth mentioning.

She had suffered from the shock, as well as the actual sprain, and did not appear again that evening. She told Mary, who went to look after her, that her head was aching and that she was bruised all over. But the description she gave of her sensations at the moment of the accident interested Mary particularly. As the sail struck her, she felt convinced that her end had come; and before she was knocked senseless by the smashing fall on deck she felt

[17] Scuppers: openings in the side walls of a vessel that allow water to drain.

as if she were being choked, as though the sail had twined itself deliberately round her face and throat—it felt as if it were being held there by unseen hands. It was the most ghastly sensation; then she supposed her head struck the deck, and everything vanished until she came round and found herself lying in a chair.

"Thira," said Mary, "you were holding that scarab, on Richard's watch-chain, at the moment. Everyone who touches it seems fated; Kathleen and myself have reason to think so. I thought when the cylinder and the parchment had gone, the bad luck would go with them, but the scarab carries it too."

Thira pooh-poohed the idea; but Mary persisted.

"You may scoff as much as you like, my dear, but you won't shake my conviction that the detestable thing is unlucky for some reason or other."

"Well, it isn't of much consequence now, for no one is wearing it. Richard's watch got smashed, or at any rate the glass did, and as there isn't a jeweller on the yacht he won't be able to use it for a bit!"

"Well, I only wish Richard would take it off his chain and throw it overboard, but of course he won't; he has such queer ideas about the rights of property, and he would say it must be send back to Professor Tremaine. But I shall speak seriously to him at the first opportunity."

Mary aired her theories pretty freely among the party, seeking their help to induce Colquhoun to get rid of the scarab; but she was quite unsuccessful. Colquhoun had a perverse temper at times, and the very suggestion that there was some reason to fear in keeping the scarab was enough to make him mulishly obstinate about parting with it. He promised, however, that he would not let Thira have it again, and that he would send it back to Tremaine when a suitable chance occurred.

CHAPTER XVIII

"AN oppressive sort of day, isn't it?" said Wilson, who was sitting with Mary under the awning, contemplating the oily, dead-calm sea. They were well out in the Indian Ocean, and for the last few hours the aspect of the weather had entirely changed; instead of a limitless expanse of blue water, a sort of coppery haze seemed to brood over the sea, bringing the horizon within a mile or two.

"Yes, it's uncanny, somehow," answered Mary. "I suppose we needn't worry about weather in the *Siren*, with two such good seamen aboard as Captain Teed and Seymour, but if we were on land I should expect an earthquake, or at least a terrific thunderstorm."

"How about a cyclone? We really ought not to go back without examining one specimen. It would be an awfully interesting experience."

"Do you think so? It is the sort of experience I could do without."

"I wonder what Seymour thinks of it. I'll try to draw him out, though the old chap isn't exactly communicative at times."

He strolled off, and Mary joined the other ladies. She found them sitting forward, limp and depressed, trying to catch the slight breeze created by the movement of the ship. Thira, recovered from her accident, had been sociable for days past, but at present seemed to have very little to say and was not even roused by Mary's suggestion that they might be in for a typhoon. Kathleen, however, rose to the bait, and she and Mary compared notes and consoled one another with tales of storm and stress, until they expected the worst. They were still at it when some of the crew came along in charge of the bo'sun and began to unlash and take down the awning.

"Why are you doing that, Jacob?" asked Thira.

"Captain's orders, ma'am," he grunted.

Meantime Bertie had found Seymour and Teed in serious conference.

"Hello! What's up?" he inquired.

"Well, the glass has almost fallen out at the bottom. There's a dose of very nasty weather ahead, so we are having a pow-wow; it's just as well to be prepared, especially in these latitudes. I wish we could get the ladies down below out of the way for a bit on the plea of dressing for dinner. I don't expect any trouble just yet, but it might come at any moment."

"I'll get Tom to hurry up. I needn't tell him what's wrong—merely that we want dinner sooner." Bertie went below. In a few minutes the first dinner-bell sounded, and Bertie was duly blessed by the two experienced sailors on the bridge.

* * * * * *

"Where is Captain Seymour?" asked Thira, noticing two vacant places in the saloon. "And Captain Teed?" No one seemed to know, but shortly afterwards Seymour came in full of apologies. Teed sent word that he was detained on deck.

Dinner was over except for the coffee stage when an unusual clamour of voices sounded above, and doors and hatches could be heard quickly shutting. Seymour rose quietly and moved towards the companion-way. "I think it would be well," he said, as he went, "if you all remained below. We are in for bad weather."

Darkness had already fallen, but there was a wicked streak of yellow light along the western horizon, which told his practised eye what was coming. The sea was barely visible as a sombre expanse, dead calm, and flecked with gleams of phosphorescent light. Teed, on the bridge, greeted Seymour's arrival with relief.

"She's as snug as possible, and there isn't a spar which we could get down," he said, glancing aloft. "Even now we have all the top-hamper we shall care for."[18]

As he spoke a subdued roar filled the air; the rigging began to hum softly, the note rising higher as the distant roar grew louder and stronger. Advancing towards the boat, they could see a white line stretching far across the sea. Teed gave an order to the man at the wheel and shouted some directions to the crew, and the bows crept round to meet the storm.

Stout vessel and good sea-boat that she was, the *Siren* staggered under that first onslaught. A wall of seething water towered above her, and though she rose gallantly to meet the assault, a huge sea broke over her forecastle and rushed along the deck.[19] Even on the bridge the impact was felt, and for a moment everything was obscured from view.

It was well that everything loose had been cleared and the remainder made fast; as it was, when she shook herself free, shuddering and drenched, from that smashing blow it was seen that one of the forward boats had been carried away, and another was simply broken wood and splinters, with the davits twisted like bent pins.[20] The force of the wind was terrific. There was no ordered onset of regular seas; the waves seemed to rise and threaten from

---

[18] Top-hamper: upper sails, spars, rigging, etc.

[19] Forecastle: forward part of the upper deck.

[20] Davits: crane-like devices used for supporting, raising, and lowering equipment, such as anchors and boats, from a ship.

every side; each one, to the inexperienced eye, seemed that it must swamp the vessel.

In the saloon the party had settled comfortably; but the breaking of the storm scattered all other thoughts. The whole ship seemed to quiver and come to a standstill as if she had struck.

"Good heavens! We have run into something!" cried Mary.

All around was chaos. Everything that was loose rushing about madly; all that remained of the table-service went crashing to the desk, adding to the confusion. The noise was appalling; but though the women turned pale none of them were cowards, and there was no screaming or foolish panic. Most of the party were soon glad enough to seek the refuge of their cabins and lie down.

The night wore on, but the violence of the storm continued. Sleep was impossible for anyone. On deck, the nerves of the watchers were taut as they endeavoured to defeat the fury of the seas. In the stokehold the firemen, on reeling floors, shot coal into the furnaces continuously to keep a good head of steam, while the harassed engineers clung to stays and rails as they crept round oiling crossheads and crank-bearings, tightening nuts and feeling the brasses. On their successful work depended the whole safety of the ship.[21]

At last the dawn broke, suddenly, as it always does in these latitudes; but the light brought little relief to the haggard men on the bridge. Their faces were white with rime; their eyes were red and weary with the bite of the spray, their clothes dripping, but they were not beaten.

The ship herself showed many traces of the strenuous hours.

---

[21] Brasses: the high-strength, corrosion-resistant alloy sheathing usually used to construct the parts of a ship that sit under water, such as that produced by Muntz's Metal Company.

Most of the boats were either carried away or smashed, and gaps showed in the bulwarks where the solid seas had broken the rails.[22] The usual trim rigging was in festoons; more than one spar hung broken and useless; but in the main she had battled through better than they had dared to hope.

Bertie struggled on deck to lend a hand, and was not encouraged by the sight that met his eyes. He was no coward and feared death as little as any man can, but he was young and in no hurry to leave this world; besides, he could not forget the women. He wondered how they had passed the terrible night. Kathleen had been very brave when the trouble began, and he could still see the expression of her face when she left him; but his heart ached for her during those long hours of sleeplessness.

Some time later, Teed sent him below again for a spell of rest. In the comparative warmth and safety of the saloon chaos reigned, and except for Dr. Smith the entire party had succumbed. He seemed decidedly glad to see Wilson, and wanted to know how long this sort of thing would last, and if there was any real danger. Bertie did his best to reassure him, and sent him off, as a privileged man, to comfort the ladies, envying his errand.

A moment later Mary appeared, looking grey and tired, but still full of energy, and, to his astonishment, she began to attack him vigorously.

"You know you weren't any earthly good up on deck; you weren't wanted there. Why couldn't you stay below, instead of risking being washed overboard?"

"But, my dear Mary, why shouldn't I go if I feel like it? I don't

[22] Bulwark: a protective structure along the sides of a ship, above the upper deck, that acts as a railing and prevents crew and passengers from falling overboard.

see that there is any more danger to me than anyone else—Seymour, for instance; he's there, so why shouldn't I be?"

Mary looked at him solemnly.

"Bertie, you are several sorts of an idiot. Who's worrying about Seymour? He's an old dear, but no one is specially interested in him."

"He's worth a dozen of me in any emergency," said Bertie.

"No doubt," retorted Mary. "Quite likely. But other people are soft enough to think that you have a special value. Can't you understand what you have made that poor girl suffer by risking your life? She's worried herself ill about you."

"Good Lord! You don't mean that Miss Boston was anxious about me?"

Mary signified by a gesture that he was hopeless. "I give you up," she exclaimed. "Go away and wash and get into some dry clothes; you make me tired."

Bertie, his brain in a whirl, went off to change, and then routed up the stewards and had some coffee made; with much care he managed to carry it to the ladies' cabin, and transferred it to Mary, to whom he suggested that it might help to make the others better. Mary smiled at his peace-offering and his careful inclusion of "the others," but took it, and presently came to give him Kathleen's thanks. She hinted that if he would turn in and rest, perhaps she would reward him later by telling him how "the others" were getting on.

Bertie meekly did as he was bidden, though it was a long time before he slept, for he rolled and pitched about on his berth like a cork; but eventually, accustomed to the motion, he fell into an uneasy slumber.

A tremendous crash over his head woke him suddenly. In a moment he was on his feet, clutching the berth to steady himself, and the next minute he was rushing for the deck, quite forgetful of Mary's sermons. If there were things to be done he must be there to help.

* * * * * *

On deck, disaster and confusion; the mizzen mast had gone by the board and was hanging in a tangle of spars and ropes. Already the boat-swain and a gang of men were cutting it away to prevent it from doing irreparable damage by battering on the ship's side, and Bertie plunged into the thick of the work, hauling and slicing at top speed. They had nearly hacked it free, so that it would fall clear, when a huge sea broke over them and Bertie felt a stunning blow across the face. In a moment they were fighting for their lives to avoid being swept overboard.

Captain Seymour hurried from the bridge, gave a few orders from Teed, and then noticed Bertie.

"What brought you here? I thought you were safely below. I sent you long ago."

"So I was, sir, but the smash brought me up to see what had happened, and of course I had to take a hand."

"No 'of course' about it! You ought not to have been here. Go below again at once, and stay there this time!"

Bertie, rather annoyed at being dressed down, turned to go without a word, for he realised that the Captain was not to be trifled with.

"And look here, you had better let Smith see to that cut on your face."

Bertie put his hand up and was surprised to find it wet. He had a nasty cut on his forehead; in his excitement he had scarcely noticed the blow. In the main saloon an unexpected chorus greeted him. The terrific crash had frightened everyone, and the apparition of a member of their party soaked through, with pale face and apparently a broken head, was not precisely reassuring.

Poor Kathleen had endured the strain and horror of the night pluckily, thinking less of herself than of the impulsive Bertie on deck in the thick of the storm. Mary had comforted her fears by persuading him to rest; but then came the crash, and, with the others, she had rushed out to find that Bertie had gone again, no one knowing what had happened. In those moments she had lived through a thousand imaginary terrors for his sake, and when he appeared she forgot everything save that the man she loved was hurt, perhaps badly.

"Bertie . . . oh, Bertie, what is it? What have you done?" she cried.

His look set the blushes flaming in her cheeks, but the sound of his voice, full and strong as usual, assuring her that it was nothing bit a bit of a cut and not at all serious, more than compensated her for betraying her feelings. In the babel of questions which followed she was able to recover herself, and no one seemed to have noticed her sudden, anxious exclamation.

The damaged hero explained that for the moment there was no need for alarm, though he did not conceal the fact that the situation demanded careful handling if they were to pull through safely.

"And that head of yours, old man, demands a little careful handling," interposed Dr. Smith. "Come into my dissecting-room and let me make you a presentable object instead of a scarecrow."

He carried Wilson off for bathing and bandaging, and left the others to regain their composure.

Thira's opinion was that they would all be drowned; Colquhoun, trying to console her, received snubs for his pains. Mary, choosing the better part, bore Kathleen off to her cabin to soothe her ruffled feelings.

CHAPTER XIX

THE battered *Siren* was steaming easily through a smooth sea, and the crew were engaged in making good, as far as possible, the damage. The storm had passed none too soon for the safety of the ship. After it was over, Teed confessed to Seymour that at one time he had been doubtful if she would weather it. Not a man had been lost, although several had been badly knocked about; one was in hospital with a broken leg, and others were in the Doctor's hands for minor injuries, including Bertie, whose head was decorated with a good imitation of a turban, and whose face bore sundry bruises and strips of sticking plaster. The blow had been more severe than he had realised, and though he asserted his dislike for being fussed over, it was noticeable that he made no objection when Kathleen offered to rearrange his bandages.

Their destination had been discussed, and, as usual, Thira settled the question. To the others it was not a matter of much moment, but to her it was the whole purpose of the journey; they must go to Purnam. So to Purnam the course was set.

Thira, hitherto often listless and fretful, seemed to revive and was full of gaiety, taking an active part in everything, and becoming again the charming hostess of old. Mary remarked upon the change to Kathleen, who had also noticed it. But Thira's moods concerned her less than someone else's, and that someone else seemed uncertain himself as to his mood. At one moment he would be jovial and the best of company, and then suddenly he would retire into his shell and become almost unapproachable. Poor Wilson, in short, was in a state demanding sympathy of all who have ever been in love.

Kathleen cared for him, he thought, but how much? He feared to upset his "prospects"—he smiled as the word crossed his mind—by being premature; if she did not love him, but had only a rather more than ordinary sense of friendliness towards him, it would make such an awful hash of things on board if he were to propose and get a refusal. He was sure enough now of his own feelings; unless he could win Kathleen, life would be empty. But his experience of women had been very limited—he was no man-about-town—and he read a wrong meaning into many trifles which sometimes had no significance at all, giving himself unnecessary torture, and keeping Kathleen in a similar state of puzzled suspense.

The day soon came when the captain laid a finger on the map and said, "We shall sight land to-morrow morning, if all goes well, and should make Purnam towards sundown, so you will soon be able to get ashore, Mrs. Colquhoun. I am afraid the trip has been rather monotonous, but it couldn't very well be helped.

Thira laughed.

"Naturally, Captain Teed, one doesn't expect a magic carpet. But though it has been very restful and pleasant since that awful storm, nothing but sea, day after day, does get on one's nerves a bit. I shan't be sorry to land again."

There was a suppressed excitement about the party at sunfall; for various reasons several of them were anxious to reach the end of this section of their journey. All of them, of course, knew that Jack Winthrop would probably be found at Purnam, though Colquhoun attached no special significance to that fact. He would be glad to see his young friend again; it did not occur to him that the encounter might affect the whole tenor of his life. Simple-minded, frank, and sincere, the idea that there could be any feeling between his wife and Jack, other than ordinary friendship, never entered his head.

To Mary and Captain Seymour matters had another aspect. Both looked at things from their respective points of view, but both remembered vividly the state of affairs at Kilmona before Janet had appeared to intervene, and Janet was not here. They were uneasy as to what might happen if the stay at Purnam were protracted. Both of them liked Thira and Jack, but with a fairly extensive experience of the world they knew that the meeting meant a delicate situation.

Wilson, however, had no suspicions; to his innocent eyes the friendship between Thira and Jack had been the most platonic of sentiments, the harmless *camaraderie* which might exist between any man and woman who were thrown together and were fond of sport. He was looking forward keenly to meeting Jack, as his best friend, and at the back of his mind lurked the thought that he might profit by a wrinkle or two from Jack upon how to bring his affair with Kathleen to a successful issue.

As for Thira, to-morrow meant heaven. Since her accident—how many long months ago!—she had not seen Jack. She could only guess at his real feelings, but she had convinced herself that it was on her account he had gone. It was a process of willing self-persuasion. She knew him so well, she thought. He would feel, honourably, that he simply could not take advantage of the situation in which he had been placed, and rather than risk it, he had sought to avoid temptation by absence and distance from the temptress. She did not for a moment pretend, even to herself, that he could be in any doubt as to her feelings for him—had she not made them plain enough?—and she flattered herself that she was not the sort of woman who would offer herself in vain. She was beautiful; how often had he reminded her of it in the old days! She felt almost certain that he loved her, even as she confessed to herself that she loved him, but . . . Jack's temperament must be reckoned with.

His was not a weak nature to be easily swayed, and if he had really made up his mind to give her up, it would take all her power to shake his decision. He was such a loyal friend that he was not likely to forget Richard, who had brought them together; nor that it was to Richard's faith in her that they owed their intimacy; and that in itself would be enough to armour him against her charms. Well . . . to-morrow might solve the problem.

As the day drew out its interminable hours, she became restless; her patience wore thin; and presently Dr. Smith, regarding her professionally as a mild case of "nerves," advised her to lie down, finding a couch for her in a quiet corner, and warning the others that she was overstrung by the heat and must not be disturbed. But no sleep came to soothe her. Her excited mind, over and over again, traced the past and imagined the future. She felt that it was rather mean to have taken advantage of Richard's care for her; to let him provide the yacht, and give up everything for the sake of this voyage, and to repay him by giving her whole heart and soul to another.

And when she had met him . . . what then? Time enough to think when they faced one another. After all, was it very wrong? She soothed her conscience with the thought that she only wanted to see Jack, to be near him again for a while, to know how life went with him.

She could not or would not see that by deliberately running into temptation she was making matters infinitely more difficult for herself; and that if Jack's object had really been to avoid her, as she imagined, she was acting unfairly and cruelly towards him in pursuing him. She had been so spoilt since her marriage that it seemed to her she need only wish for a thing to have it. And her conscience was lulled into convenient drowsiness by the lightest of anodynes.

CHAPTER XX

NIGHT had long fallen when the *Siren* felt her way into the harbour in charge of a local pilot, but even in the gloom her passengers could dimly discern the ghostly outlines of towering cranes and spidery derricks on the wharves of the new harbour works—Jack's works. Threading her way through the shipping, she came to rest, her neighbours an ocean-going tramp and a huge liner. The noise of the anchor chain running out through the hawse-hole sounded pleasantly in the ears of that little party after so many days at sea.[23] Soon silence fell, and everyone sought their berths.

It came as a shock to Thira that this important enterprise should be under the control of the man she was seeking. It seemed strange that Jack, whom she had treated and looked upon as her tame cat, should be so tremendously competent in something really big—something that demanded a high degree of engineering skill and the ability to handle rough men. Her thoughts, and the nearness of . . . her success?—kept her awake most of the night. Tossing and turning in her berth; longing for daylight so that her suspense might be ended, and that she might at least know whether or not she were going to see Jack—for a nightmare assailed her that it was just possible he might not be at Purnam after all. He did not know that they were coming; if he had, he might for that very reason be off up country. On the other hand, there was always the chance that he had left altogether. The very thought of such a disaster worried

[23] Hawse-hole: cylindrical hole cut through the bow of a ship through which the anchor cable may be passed.

Thira. She regretted now that she had not written and told him openly of the projected voyage and made a definite appointment to meet him. It would be too awful if, after coming all that way, her journey should be in vain! Submerging this fear at intervals came a wave of doubt as to how he would take her visit; what his attitude would be; whether he would be annoyed that she had pursued him—for, after all, she had to admit that it was flagrantly a case of pursuit, although, except that it might annoy Jack, she felt no regret at the thought.

When at last day dawned she felt a wreck, and had qualms as to her appearance under the pitiless glare of the sun. She could not possibly suggest going ashore before breakfast, so she lay listening in a half-conscious state to the noises on the waking ship.

The earliest riser was Bertie, for whom only one course of action, on that morning, was possible. There would be plenty of time for a trip ashore before breakfast. Permission for a boat was soon obtained from Captain Teed, and a few minutes later, unknown to the rest of the party, he was on his way to discover Jack. His ideas as to where to look were hazy, but he thought he could not go far wrong if he called at the Harbour Master's office.

On the quay he found a heterogenous assembly of various nationalities, chiefly seafaring men, and natives of all shades from dirty yellow to ebony black. He had no difficulty in discovering the office; his inquiries were answered volubly either in English or that universal tongue—compounded fragments in many languages—which serves as a means of communication in half the ports and harbours of the world. He obtained the desired information and then sought Jack's sanctum, only to learn that he was already out.

Along sundry quays he made his way until he came to the beginning of the new breakwater which was to connect the mainland to a small island, and to be extended beyond that as a protection to the shipping. Here the scene was full of life. Gangs of natives were busy loading and unloading trollies of stone and timber; overhead, immense cranes dangled their huge loads as if they were feather-weights. Bertie's eyes roved about in search of the familiar figure, confident of recognising it at any distance, and in a few minutes he perceived it, and smiled appreciatively. Far out at the end of the breakwater the gaunt frame of a large swing bridge, in course of construction, stood out like some straddling skeleton, blurred by supporting timbers. Near by swung an immense derrick, hoisting enormous girders into position. High up, on a little platform near its apex, stood Winthrop, clothed in white, unperturbed, contemplating the dizzy drop, apparently giving brief, expressive orders to the donkey-man and a gang below, who were fitting a girder into its place.

Bertie, arrived at the foot of the structure, discovered a ladder which would lead him aloft, and was about to climb when an abrupt challenge from a man on the staging stopped him. He explained the reason for his presence.

"Well, I don't think he'll want you up there," returned the first speaker, not too graciously. "What's your business?"

"Oh, several things. I'm from England; I don't think he would object if I went up. I'm one of his oldest friends," said Bertie, and added, as the man still hesitated: "If you are in any doubt about it, will you let Mr. Winthrop know that I am here? My name is Wilson, Bertie Wilson—that will be enough for him."

"Oh, that's probably all right. I am Mr. Winthrop's assistant; you must pardon me for stopping you. We get all sorts of queer people hindering with no good reason, and we have to be careful."

Becoming more genial, he showed the visitor a rough lift, and a moment later they were being whirled upward. Ivans, the assistant, stepped out and escorted Bertie to the narrow platform. Hearing voices, Jack turned round.

"Hello, Ivans, what have you come up for? And who the devil have you brought with you?" he exclaimed. "By Jove—Bertie!"

The two gripped hands.

Bertie stood for a moment looking Jack over.

"Well, old man, you look fit, though a bit thin and even harder than of old."

"Hang my looks, old chap! Tell me how on earth you got here—and, by the way, don't step off the edge. You might stop here longer than you like."

Bertie laughed.

"Well, I'm having a trip round the world, and naturally you and your land of exile had to be included."

"Good business, old man. You bet I'm awfully bucked to see you. But when did you arrive? Did you come on the P. & O., which put in here yesterday? If so, why didn't you look me up sooner?"

"Don't get ratty, my boy. I wasn't on the P. & O. boat; I came in that yacht," said Bertie, pointing to the *Siren.*

"The devil you did! Who's her owner—not you, I s'pose? She looks a nice boat."

"She *is* a nice boat, and the people on her are nice too."

"Who are they?"

"Guess. It isn't too difficult."

Jack looked at the yacht.

"I don't know her; and, what's more, I don't think I know anybody who owns a large yacht."

"Give it up?"

"Yes."

"It's Colquhoun's yacht, the *Siren*."

"Colquhoun's? Didn't know he had one."

"He hasn't had it for long; he bought it to take Thira for a long voyage. She has been off colour for months—ever since that accident at Kilmona. The party are mostly old friends of yours; besides Thira and Colquhoun, there are Mary Macintyre, Captain Seymour, and Kathleen Boston; you remember her. She was one of the Kilmona guests—came towards the end of your time."

"Yes, I remember her . . . is that all?"

There was a hope in Jack's heart that he might hear another name, but Bertie's next words destroyed it.

"There is Dr. Smith, the ship's doctor, brought specially to look after Thira, not a bad sort but a bit of a stick; and there's the captain, Teed—a real good chap. And there's me. That's the lot."

"But why did they come to this particular spot—right off the map?"

"Can't say, old man. We just seemed to drift here in the natural course of events. We started by doing the Eastern Mediterranean, then Egypt, then down the Red Sea and the African coast, and finally across here. And the devil's own time we had, too, the last bit of our journey. But that story can wait a bit."

"Some trip! Shouldn't have minded it myself. What about Thira? Has she been very bad?"

"I don't think there is really much the matter with her. She seems to be all right when she wants to be. She's all moods—sometimes peevish and snappy and at others just apathetic; sometimes her old self and full of spirits for a bit, but not for long together."

Jack seemed to ponder over this information. He cross-questioned Bertie as to the arrangements for the journey, and was scarcely surprised to learn that there were none. Bertie admitted that he had not the remotest idea of seeing Purnam; of course he had cast his vote for it when the suggestion was made, but it had seemed more a matter of chance than anything else.

Jack wondered. Had it all been mere chance? From what he could gather, Thira seemed to have had a great deal to do with shaping the course of their voyage.

"Well, it's a rum go!" he said. "The last time I heard from the Colquhouns was a letter from Thira, months ago, but she never said a word about being ill, or of any yachting trip; certainly not of coming out here. She wrote, before that, about London and her doings there. Of course I haven't known much about their movements since Kilmona."

"Ah—Kilmona. It was a great time, that. But what the dickens did you run away for in such a hurry?"

Jack looked a shade embarrassed.

"Perhaps I'll tell you later on. At any rate, this is not precisely the place for a yarn. Come down to my private den, old boy, and we can make ourselves comfortable and hunt up a drink."

They descended, after Jack had given a few instructions to his chief assistant, and made their way back to the office, where Bertie gave a brief outline of the outstanding incidents of the voyage. Jack, clearly, was preoccupied. He was genuinely pleased at the prospect of seeing so many old friends, life in this outpost of civilisation being not particularly social. But, on the other hand, he was not a little perturbed at the thought that this sudden descent must have been premeditated by someone. By whom? he wondered. Who could it have been but Thira? If not, why had she come to Purnam, where she knew he was stationed? He was not at all happy about it, and felt some anxiety as to the outcome of this unexpected visit.

During the conversation, though the venture and the members of the party were talked over fairly thoroughly, Bertie said nothing to betray his interest in Kathleen; Jack, however, made a pretty shrewd guess, from the little he said, as to the state of affairs. He made no comment, for he was not yet inclined to reciprocate, even with Bertie, on the theme of Janet, and therefore felt that it would be simpler not to ask for any revelations.

An hour had passed at Time's highest speed before Jack glanced at his watch, and stood up.

"Well, old boy," he said, "it's jolly to have you here, but I must get back. After all, you know, I am a paid servant now, and mustn't let pleasure interfere too much with duty."

His friend protested.

"Surely you can give yourself leave for once? The others will be most awfully hurt if you don't come off with me for breakfast on board now that they know you are here."

"No. I can't come out yet, Bertie, neither can I take leave without arranging beforehand. Of course, I can take it easily enough when I have fixed up things; but at the moment we are in the thick of a critical job on that span of the bridge. Once those main girders are in position I shall be free. What about lunch? I'll come aboard about midday, if you like. Mornings and evenings are our working day here; one can't do much towards noon without being grilled."

"Right," said Bertie. "I know you're an obstinate devil; so we'll leave it at that. I'll go back and report progress. Ta-ta, old man."

"Cheerio—and give my affectionate regards to the others, in varying degrees to suit the recipient," said Jack, laughing.

CHAPTER XXI

BERTIE had to stand a fire of cross-questioning from the rest of the party when they learnt how he had spent the early hours of the morning. Thira was evidently annoyed that Jack should have elected to stay and look after his work rather than hasten aboard, and though she tried to restrain her feelings there was a spice of petulance about her for the next hour or two.

A smartly turned out four-oared gig approached the yacht; sitting in the stern was Jack Winthrop. The neatly dressed native oarsmen showed the results of good training, and the boat itself was as spick and span as paint and varnish could make it.

In a few minutes it ran smoothly alongside, and a moment later Jack sprang up the ladder, to be received with a chorus of welcome from the group on deck.

There was no chance of individual speech amid the wealth of topics for discussion on both sides. News of things done and of friends left behind was exchanged, and Jack noticed that it was the ever tactful Mary who presently managed to introduce Janet's name and so tell him what he was secretly longing to know.

He had never been able to understand Janet's action, or to forgive her for it; nor, on the other hand, could he succeed in forcing himself to forget—it had been too ruthless a destruction of the joy and hope just born. Yet his heart was sick with longing to know something of the girl and her doings since that morning when she had so curtly cut him adrift. The experience had hardened him, and he was by no means the old easy-going Jack of the past; he was very much a man, and not one to be trifled with. Even these old friends perceived a change in him; he was pleasant enough, and his manners were as charming as of old, but beneath it all lay something stern, something that baffled them.

Seymour and Mary, privately comparing notes, admitted themselves puzzled. They had never been able to find the key to his sudden disappearance, or to decide whether Janet or Thira was responsible for it. From Jack's manner towards his hostess now not much could be gathered; he seemed quite at his ease, and it was impossible to guess what his sentiments towards her might be; nor did Thira's behaviour betray anything. She was lively and talkative, but not more so than she had often been. The natural excitement of meeting an old friend after a prolonged separation would account for her manner just as well as a state of nervousness or an attempt at hiding her real feelings.

She bantered Jack about his new attachment to his work, which had kept him from coming off sooner to the friends who had half circled the world to see him; he defended himself gaily, saying that an idle existence was now but a memory for him—in fact, that he could not imagine how he had ever endured such a parody of life. He did not speak of returning to England at present; when someone suggested it, he said he intended to stay until his job was finished—two or three years at least.

Thira's feelings almost defied analysis. Desperate at the thought that she would have to go back before long, she worried her brain for schemes to tempt him away, without avail. When lunch was over she manœuvred to get him alone. So far, her experience had been unsatisfactory; she could make no impression on the stony surface exposed to her attack. Nothing could have been more charming than Jack's behaviour to her; he was quite ready to discuss their previous joint experiences, even to the last episode of the disaster at Kilmona, but he ignored all points in their memories which might have touched on romance, and never gave her an opening to restart that phase of their friendship. To Thira it was like struggling with some apparently flimsy, almost intangible, but horribly strong veil, which resisted all attempts to penetrate it. Time was passing, and she knew that he must soon be going, and she could not in the least foresee when her next chance might come, or even if it would come at all, yet she could not think what line to take with him.

Suddenly the idea of trying to make use of poor Janet struck her. Very carefully she led the conversation up to the subject of her life in London, then casually brought in Janet's name.

Watching him keenly, she noted that Jack's attitude changed slightly; he seemed to thaw a little, though still reserved and quite unlike his old self. Then Thira took the plunge. Under the plea of an old friend's privilege, she asked him whether there was anything between himself and Janet.

For a moment she thought that the answer to her riddle was coming, for as she asked the question, she looked straight at him. For an instant a hard look flitted across his face, and he hesitated.

"Oh no! There is nothing in the way of a romantic attachment, if that is what you mean," he replied gravely.

"But you were more than ordinary good friends in those last few weeks at Kilmona; everyone thought that you two would make a match of it."

"Did they? Who was 'everyone'?"

"Oh, Mary and Captain Seymour and several others, including, I think, Bertie."

"Other people often seem to know one's business best. If you were to ask Miss Baxter she would tell you the same, I can assure you, and that she would never think of me in any other way than as the merest acquaintance."

Thira was puzzled, for she felt almost certain from his expression that there was more behind his words; yet if he said directly that there was nothing between them, she knew him well enough to know that it was true. But might his words not refer to the present day only? Had there been a romance which had ceased to exist? That was quite possible, though difficult to explain, unless the little fool had been jealous because Jack had taken herself, Thira, out riding that morning and had made a scene about it; if that were so she had played her cards very badly. It might be as well to put another spoke in her wheel.

"It seems, then, that we were all mistaken," pursued Thira lightly. "We were puzzled about it after you left, because she did not seem to miss you much; in fact, she hardly ever spoke of you, whereas with the rest it was always, 'Jack used to do this,' or 'Mr. Winthrop said that'—your exploits were always cropping up. But afterwards, in London, she would occasionally talk about you and ask questions."

"Did she? Probably it was only to show a polite interest in your friends," said Jack, as though it didn't matter much.

"Perhaps; but at the time I fancied that there must be more. You are right, though, or she would have wanted to come and at least see you."

"Did you ask her to join your party?"

"Yes; Richard even offered to pay all her expenses and make good her losses (you know she has to make her own living and keep her mother); but she refused."

"Did she know that you were coming here, and that I was here?"

Thira thought quickly. Could she, dare she, risk telling the half-lie that would be necessary to finish her work effectually? Suppose she were found out afterwards? . . . Well, it would be either too late then to upset her plans, or it would be of no consequence, because she would have failed. Anyhow, if she told him that Janet knew and declined to come, it would be a set-back and remove anything remaining in Jack's mind in Janets favour. She risked it.

"Oh yes; she knew that we should probably come to Purnam and that you were here; in fact, I wrote and told her so." She purposely omitted to add that she only wrote when there was no longer any possible chance for Janet to come.

"Then, you see," said Jack, laughing—but it was not a merry laugh—"that quite knocks the bottom out of all your romantic theories, and shows that even such wise people as you, Mary, and Seymour may sometimes make mistakes." And he turned the conversation to other topics.

Jack had never, from the moment of his dismissal, hoped that matters would change or that he might get back to a happy understanding with Janet; yet this latest knowledge that she had refused to join the yachting party, knowing him to be here, added a drop of bitterness to the resentment in his heart. But though it set Janet even farther from him, it did not help Thira; it made her chance more remote, for Jack was now hardened against any woman's blandishments for the future.

CHAPTER XXII

THOUGH they had started in the cool of the early morning on their journey up the river, the heat, as the sun mounted higher, became oppressive, and they landed on an island where the trees offered a welcome shade.

Winthrop had been persuaded to join the excursion, for after several days at Purnam they had not seen much of him. He had pleaded the stress of important work during the day and of plans and estimates to examine later, and on the few evenings he had come on board he had left after an hour or two.

Thira, more and more on edge, felt that time was slipping away with nothing accomplished. Even in her own inmost mind she could not have told exactly what it was that she wished to accomplish or what would be the consequences; all she knew was that she must somehow break down the barrier which Jack erected between them. She wilfully refused to analyse the position created if she were successful: she would not consider the effect on her husband. She did not know whether, if she could, she would leave him, throw up everything, and go off with Jack—if he would take her. It was that "if" which was upsetting her dreams.

She did not dislike Richard; she had a great esteem for him, and a half compassionate, half contemptuous affection; she did not under-value all that he had done for her and given her, but she felt that, in a sense, he had received value for his money, that in a way he had taken her at a disadvantage in marrying her before, in her inexperience, she could fairly know that her feeling towards him was not really love. Now, too late, love had come. Not, perhaps, the perfect love, ready to give all and asking nothing in return; for though she could if necessary give up a good deal for it, yet she asked much in exchange, and would not hesitate to sacrifice her lover's peace of mind, her husband's happiness, the esteem of her friends and guests, if only she might secure her desire. But could she secure it, and how was she to proceed? Unless she could make Jack respond, make him, too, feel that these sacrifices were not too great a price to pay for her love and herself, all her schemes would come to naught; and she must go back, defeated, discarded, to the old empty life without him. The very thought of it made her frantic; she could not, would not believe that it would come to that. Her present existence seemed unreal; it was like acting in a play; she took part in all that was going on about her, and appeared to show a proper and sufficient interest in the affairs of her guests, but all the time she felt these things did not matter, that they were no part of her own private inner life.

* * * * * *

Later in the day, when the shadows lengthened and it became possible to exhibit a little energy without the risk of sunstroke, the irrepressible Bertie produced some tackle and tried to organise a fishing competition. Undiscouraged by refusals, he at last induced Kathleen to come, whereupon it occurred to Dr. Smith that it might be interesting to see what sort of fish the river contained, and he announced his intention of joining them.

Bertie's face was a study, and Kathleen seemed none too enthusiastic at this addition to their party. Mary, as usual, came to the rescue.

"Tiresome people!" she exclaimed. "Why can't you take life easy and be idle?"

"This from you, Mary, the most energetic of the lot of us,"

protested Bertie, "is entirely uncalled for."

"Well, at any rate you shan't drag poor Kathleen off for miles. I will sacrifice myself for her sake, and come to keep you men in order." She lazily rose from cushioned comfort, exchanged an amused look with Bertie, and the little party wandered away along the shore.

They had been fishing for some time with quite a fair amount of sport. The astute Mary managed to annex the Doctor, and gradually led him farther from the others, until presently Kathleen and Bertie were by themselves.

Kathleen had refused to be bothered with a line, but after a time was persuaded to take the rod and try her hand. One or two small fish rewarded her, and she was getting quite keen, when suddenly there came a sharp pull. The reel began to scream as it flew out. In a second Bertie was beside her to help, and soon, in the excitement of the struggle, they were both holding the rod, his hands covering hers. At the end of a ten minutes' tussle a really fine capture lay at Kathleen's feet. Exhausted, she sank down on a rock to recover herself.

Bertie wondered whether to try for another fish, or sit by Kathleen. He sat down, mopping his brow.

"You managed that splendidly," he said.

"You did most of it," replied Kathleen. "I couldn't have landed it alone."

"Oh, you could; you are really quite clever at it. I believe you would make a first-class fisherman if you chose to try."

"I should want someone to teach me."

"Well, let me teach you."

"I should love you to teach me. You are so clever at all this sort of thing."

"Would you really . . . like me to?"

There was a look in Kathleen's face which thrilled him. She blushed.

"Of course I should."

"Why 'of course'? I might be rather disagreeable over it."

"I shouldn't be afraid of that," she answered, in a low voice.

"Miss Boston." His hand touched hers; she did not move, for by his tone she became suddenly away that the moment she had been waiting for, hoping for, had come. She looked up at him; her eyes were softly glowing. And Bertie knew, and spoke as a man should when a woman looks at him like that.

"Kathleen! Let me always teach you things, in return for what you have taught me . . . what love means. I love you. There is no one else in the world like you. You . . . you know, Kathleen . . . don't you?"

"Yes . . . I know, dear."

He drew her to him; she did not resist. And presently, as lovers will, they began to try to expound the wonder of their love.

"For ages I have wanted to ask you and haven't dared," said Bertie. "I was afraid you wouldn't care for me, and I might spoil everything and lose you altogether."

"Bertie, dear, I have been waiting, hoping that you would speak; I have wanted you quite as much as you have wanted me."

"What a fool I was for being afraid to venture! How long, dear?"

"How long have *you* wanted *me*?"

"Ever since you were half buried by the sand that day in Egypt. I think it was about then that I began to love you."

"Then perhaps that scarab has some good luck attached to it after all."

Exactly how long afterwards Mary came round the point within view of the fishers is uncertain, but the sight which met her eyes caused her to stop suddenly and turn back; by some means the Doctor was persuaded to turn back also and scramble across the island with her.

It was dusk before the lovers made any attempt to return to the boat, and when at long last they did so, derisive cheers and facetious remarks as to their number of fish greeted them.

"Oh," said Bertie coolly, "I have caught much more than that! I have caught the best and most beautiful girl in the world." He slipped his arm round Kathleen's waist, the proud lover to perfection.

"Oh, I am so glad!" cried Mary. "You two dear people! I have been waiting and hoping for this for ages!"

"*You* have been waiting and hoping? But why?" asked Bertie.

"You dear old ass—as if everyone but yourself couldn't see!"

"Well, we neither of us knew, so I'm hanged if I can understand your pretended wisdom."

"My dear boy, the crew knew, the servants knew, and we have all been expecting it for weeks and weeks and weeks."

"Pity you didn't tell us," said Bertie. "It would have saved us wasting a lot of valuable time, wouldn't it, Kathleen?"

"Perhaps it wasn't quite wasted," said Kathleen, blushing happily.

CHAPTER XXIII

A PARTY set out for the shore on the following morning, with the object of looking round the harbour works. Kathleen and Bertie had elected to remain behind on the yacht; Thira and Mary, with Dr. Smith as escort, went shopping in the town, so the inspecting party were reduced to Seymour, Teed, and Colquhoun.

Before going to Jack's office, Colquhoun stopped to recover his watch and chain, which he had left to be repaired. He had not worn them since the occasion of the accident with the sails, and the debated evil influence of the scarab had almost been forgotten; but the sight of it attached to the chain revived the subject. The three of them discussed it, and mentioned it to Jack when they reached his office.

After the customary hospitality of the Englishman abroad they set out on their tour of the works. Climbing into one of the empty trucks of a rope railway, they were speedily hauled to the top of the cliff. Arrived there, they started walking along the gallery which had been cut into its face.

Jack pointed out everything of interest, and it was something of a revelation to Seymour to hear him talking of tides and channels, draft of vessels, prevailing winds, water pressure, and engineering matters in general. It was evident that Jack was thoroughly master of his craft. The sailors were loth to leave the wharves and breakwater—the part of the undertaking with which they were most conversant, but after a time they moved on, and, following the road, rounded a bluff of the cliff, and for the time lost sight of the harbour.

Jack wanted to show them the quarries and his sand-pits, from which came the material for the breakwater and the quays, so they turned inland, passing through a narrow cutting which had been made, at first, to bring the stone down to the sea; ultimately it had been found simpler to cut another drive and take it direct to the breakwater by the rope railway.

Some few hundred yards farther on they again struck the contractors' line; here a busy scene fascinated them. Trucks of stone and sand were being hauled towards the sea by energetic little engines; empty trucks returning. They found Jack's assistant, Ivans, in one of the big quarries superintending the shaping of the stone, which was both cut and dressed before being sent down.

Blasting operations were in progress higher up, and they waited to see a big blast. They kept under cover until report of the charge had passed, then they hurried out in time to see a huge slice of the cliff split, heave, crumble, and come roaring down like an avalanche.

"It wouldn't do to be anywhere near that as it fell," remarked Colquhoun. "Just look how the smaller pieces fly about."

"Only last week," said Jack, "some of the men thought it would be less trouble to hide behind the rock instead of going to the pent-house, and two of the poor beggars got smashed by flying bits of stone. One died, the other is recovering. Queer how those things happen sometimes."

"Yes," agreed Seymour; " 'One shall be taken and the other left.' I have seen that happen often, in all sorts of circumstances, when there was no apparent reason why both men should not have been killed."

"Providence or Kismet has its puzzling ways at times," said Jack. "The more one learns and the longer one lives, the more one feels sure that there must be some power greater than ourselves, which controls and orders all these things."

For a moment no one spoke, then Seymour said:

"I think that it is the people who live in cities who are more afflicted with atheism, for they aren't brought into constant contact with nature. Everything comes to them ready-made and as a matter of course. Their food they have only got to buy; there are houses for them to live in, books and newspapers for them to read, tub orators for them to listen to, but nothing to see, or very little except humanity, and they are too much engrossed in their own affairs to study humanity. You don't often find a countryman an atheist. He nearly always has some sort of belief; and in all my years at sea I have never known a sailor who was an atheist. Even the biggest blackguards seem to have an undercurrent of some sort of faith and won't be at a loss for a prayer in a tight corner.

Colquhoun looked at his watch. "It's about time we were getting back, isn't it?" he asked.

"I suppose it is," said Jack. "It won't take us long from here. Would you like to go down on one of the trucks, or do you prefer walking?"

"May as well walk," said Seymour. They followed the railway back from the quarries, now and then stepping aside to avoid a train of trucks coming up or going down. After a while they came to the cutting through which the line ran down to the rope-way; it was about twenty feet wide by fifteen deep, and the banks were of shale, topped by a layer of earth and sand.

"You have left those banks pretty steep—almost perpendicular," remarked Seymour.

"Yes, the angle is a bit sharp, but the stuff is fairly solid; we have only had one or two slight landslides, and there is room enough for anything to fall without damaging the line."

They were walking four abreast along the track when a whistle behind warned them to let a train of loaded trucks past. They stepped quickly aside, the two seamen to the right, Colquhoun and Jack to the left, and a moment later the train separated them. It passed with a jar and a rattle, for the line was rough and the trucks were of the usual springless type. The last truck had just rumbled by when Teed shouted, "Look out!" and pointed to the bank on their left.

Jack looked up. In a flash he leapt towards Colquhoun, who was nearest to the bank, and tried to bring him back, but it was too late. A great bulging crack opened in the shale, and even as he grasped Colquhoun's arm the whole face of the cutting seemed to collapse, and with a dull, savage roar was upon them . . . .

As the clouds of dust floated clear, the two sailors saw Jack lying senseless on the ground. Of Colquhoun there was no sign.

For a moment they were almost stunned by the suddenness of the catastrophe; then, rushing forward, they tried to liberate Jack, who was half buried under the earth.

"Is he dead?" groaned Teed.

"No, I think not; but he's pretty badly cut on the side of his head."

They toiled at their heavy task.

"No hope for Colquhoun, poor chap," said Seymour sadly. "If he isn't smashed he must be suffocated. Run back to the quarries and get help and tools, old man . . . Wait—here comes the engine."

The engine came to a standstill close by, her driver having seen the accident and quickly reversed.

"Want men and shovels. I go fetch under-boss," he said. Climbing back into the cab, he drove off rapidly.

In less time than would have seemed possible the locomotive returned with several men. Ivans was the first to jump down.

"Great Scott! What has happened?"

"The bank fell in and caught them. The vibration of the train started it. Mr. Winthrop is only partly buried; poor Colquhoun is somewhere beneath all that."

Ivans was at work in a moment. Under his direction the men worked like demons. In a few minutes Jack was free, but he remained unconscious. They went on digging furiously, but carefully, for traces of Colquhoun, while Ivans made a hasty examination of Jack.

"Contusions and a nasty cut, but I think no bones are broken. He seems to have been missed by most of the heavy stuff; it was only the sand from the top which caught him; but he mustn't lie here. We must get him to the doctor."

The engine returned with more men and Ivans' assistant, so he and Teed were left in charge of the digging operations, while Seymour and Ivans, on an improvised stretcher, carried Jack away.

It was a sorrowful procession, and they knew that another sadder one must follow later. They laid him on his bed just as the doctor, summoned by messenger, arrived. A brief examination confirmed Ivans' diagnosis. No bones broken, but a mass of bruises and contusions beside the wound on the head. It would be useless, he said, to attempt to bring Jack round; far better let him sleep if possible, or at any rate let consciousness come back naturally. Seymour decided to stay with him while Ivans went back.

They had found Colquhoun, but it was some time before they could get him out. He was dead. Considering the manner of his death it was most extraordinary how few marks of violence there were; his face was undamaged, and its expression was perfectly peaceful. His neck must have been broken at once; his end had been sudden and painless, and he had escaped the horrors of slow suffocation which must otherwise have been his fate. Very reverently they bore their burden down to the sea to Jack Winthrop's house. It was agreed that Captain Seymour should break the news to Thira. Teed, for the time, would remain on shore.

CHAPTER XXIV

IT would have been difficult to guess what Thira's feelings really were. She had taken the terrible news wonderfully well, making no scene of distress, though it was evident that the shock had been very great in spite of Seymour's tact and kindness when, in words that came haltingly for the pain of it, he told her.

The whole ship's company were aghast at the tragedy. Though no one had specially loved Colquhoun, everyone had respected him, and such an end seemed so uncalled for, so unmerited, even crueller in his case than it might have been in some others. There was also intense sympathy for Winthrop, whose condition appeared to be dangerous. It had been a long time before he had recovered consciousness, longer still before he became able to understand what had happened; and then the knowledge of Colquhoun's death, for which he was inclined to blame himself, excited him feverishly. It was useless for the others to point out that such a catastrophe could not be foreseen; Jack would have it that it was his fault; for it was he who made the cutting too steep; it was he who had arranged the visit of the party; it was he who had brought them back through it. He acknowledged readily that it had been almost impossible to foresee a landslip, and that even yet he could not understand how it had happened; but that did not lessen his responsibility. He was very anxious to go and inspect the scene in order to arrive at some reason for the fall, but it was not safe yet for him to leave his bed. He could scarcely move his hands and arms, and the rest of his body not at all. Questioning Ivans closely about the whole affair, he could make nothing of it;

there had been no more slips, and the rest of the cutting seemed perfectly sound.

Jack fumed and fretted at his helplessness, but could do nothing. He was not even able to follow his old friend, when they laid him to rest in the little European cemetery. Almost all the crew, and every member of the ship's party, were present—except Thira. She would not come; she said she could not bear it. She had been to see her husband's body before it was put in the coffin, almost immediately on being told of his death, and had insisted on going to see Jack too, though at the time he was still unconscious. Later she had returned to the yacht in a dazed state of mind, and had not seemed able to grasp what it all meant.

Mary, Kathleen, and Bertie went to have a last look at their friend.

"Looks as if he had died in his sleep, or even as if he were asleep still," whispered Bertie, as they stood beside him.

"Yes. How calm his face is," Mary answered.

Kathleen said nothing, but she thought deeply. She had noticed at once that the scarab was still attached to Colquhoun's watch-chain, which was lying with other things on a table near the bed; it filled her with horror, and she wished that she could take it and throw it into the sea; but she could not bring herself to make any sort of a scene just then. She resolved, however, to approach Bertie on the subject later.

After the funeral, Mary went to see Jack, and was horrified at the change in him. It was difficult to believe that he was the same splendid man whom she had known; he seemed broken both in mind and body. She did her best to cheer him up, but with little success. Later, the others took turns at calling on him almost daily; Thira, who had not come ashore since the day of the accident, again being an exception. Jack was not sorry, for he felt than an interview with her would be more than he could bear. He did not attempt to visualise what the future might hold, for he could not yet tell whether he would recover or whether he was to be a cripple for life. He could not move his legs yet, and knew that it was a bad sign. What would life be like, he wondered, if he were to be always helpless like this, never again able to walk or get about? As with most men of action, he had few resources if the open-air life was denied to him. The doctor, from whom he demanded the truth, was grave and noncommittal; said that it might be only a case of bad bruising, and in time the trouble might pass after special treatment and rest. Jack, thus left to brood over uncertainties, found Bertie his best tonic, and was delighted when that genial spirit came and sat with him, ready to talk or be silent, according to his mood. Kathleen would sometimes come for a while, though it was an added trial for Jack to see these two together. He could not help noticing an exchange of glances, a touch, a brief caress, pass between them now and again, and he thought of another girl, of all that might have been. If Janet had not sent him away, there would have been no exile to Purnam; there would have been no *Siren* party; Colquhoun would have been alive; he himself would not have been hurt, and everything would have been different. Why had Janet turned him down? He wondered if he would ever find out; if he did, would it be any use? He felt he could never be anything but a handicap to any woman now that he was crippled. Was this misfortune a punishment? if so, for what? He had not been a religious man, but neither had he been a bad man. He had his own ideas of right and wrong, and as a rule had kept to what he considered to be the right—in short, he played the game.

Thoughts such as these, in a confused medley, flitted through his mind as he lay helpless. At such times a man is at the mercy of his active brain—the more active because of the body's idleness. He speculated upon life, upon the Universe, God, good and evil, and a thousand problems that have occupied philosophers through all the ages. And ever, after these restless imaginings, his wandering thoughts returned to Janet.

Thira came to see him after a while, but by then both of them had adjusted their ideas to the new circumstances. He felt utterly cold towards her; and she knew that for the present she must keep a restraining hand on herself. But the idea of giving him up was far from her. At the first news of Colquhoun's death and Jack's accident, she had almost rejoiced in the sense of freedom which it brought; then she had been horrified at her own baseness in an hour that should have filled her with sorrow. Yet she did not delude herself; she knew that she could not mourn for Richard, that he had not been the keystone of her life, an that if he had lived she would have been quite prepared to do him irreparable injury, if thereby she could gratify her own desires. In some half-comprehended way, however, he still restrained her; she felt that he must know everything now, even though apparently he had never had the shadow of a suspicion while he was alive. She was almost afraid of her dead husband, and had an uncanny idea that he was near her, watching her, reading her thoughts. It was this sensation which gave her pause, though even without it she would have considered appearances. There was no object in being rash when in a little while everything would come right, without any scandal or trouble. She felt sure that there was no other woman except herself for Jack; she did not believe that the affair with Janet had ever gone far enough to make a lasting impression on him. When they met, she showed herself just the charming Thira of old, very sympathetic, solicitous, but nothing more, giving no sign of anything deeper than just good fellowship; and this attitude relieved him from one cause of worry. It made everything much simpler.

*   *   *   *   *   *

Jack's recovery, with one reservation, was wonderful; but the reservation was important. The wound on his head had healed; his mind was clear and strong again; and he was able even to work. But he could not walk—his legs seemed entirely paralysed.

Dr. Smith, called in for a consultation, could only agree that it was a case for a specialist, and that Jack should be sent home as quickly as possible for expert advice. Thira at once invited him to return with them, and he accepted the opportunity, seeing no motive other than friendship. He was desperately anxious about his own future, and the thought of Thira's did not even cross his mind.

Very gladly, one glorious morning, did the group on the deck of the *Siren* watch the shores of Purnam dwindle in the haze. They had come there lighthearted, fearless of the future; happy to find its refuge after storm and stress; they left it saddened, thinking of the good fellow who was no longer one of their party. And Jack, supported by cushions in a wicker chair, watched the harbour fade from view—the harbour which had been his own work, and which now must be completed by other hands, other brains. He felt that he had his own private sadness, and, as the last glimpse of Purnam hovered like a faint cloud on the edge of invisibility, he sighed.

The spirit of adventure had passed. On board the yacht, all wished for home. To Kathleen and Bertie, England would mean a wedding; to the others, many different, recovered interests. To Thira it meant life itself, relief from her continual self-restraint, and freedom to reopen her campaign, which so far she must carry on with extreme discretion. She saw much of the invalid, and spent as much time as possible with him, looking after his comfort, assuring him of her certainty that he would completely recover. She could not, and would not, believe that he must always remain a helpless cripple. She wanted him well and strong; therefore he had to be made well and strong.

Jack watched her, and wondered. Has she really relinquished her claim upon him? Had the shock of Colquhoun's death caused a revolution in her feelings, or was it that now she was free, and it was no longer a case of forbidden fruit, the attraction had passed away? Or had she no further use for a man who had ceased to be active and manly—in the physical sense? It might be none of these things; but he was content with the result, let the cause be what it may.

CHAPTER XXV

THE trials of the Red Sea and the Suez Canal were past, and the *Siren* sped on through the comparative coolness of the Mediterranean. There had been a debate as to whether she should complete the journey by sea, or make for the Brindisi to connect with the overland route. Jack, because of his paralysis, would have preferred the quicker way, but shrank from the bustle and confusion of the long railway journey in his present condition; so the sea route was chosen.

On the yacht he felt that he gave but little trouble. The only person who had more than usual to do in looking after him was Tom, who took rather a pride in acting as nurse. Between the two men, so different in position, developed a quite definite friendship and understanding; Tom seemed to regard himself much more as Jack's man that Thira's, and spent most of his time in attending to his patient. Thira seemed pleased to have it so; she could see possibilities in it. She intended that Jack should stay in her own house, if he would consent when they arrived in London; therefore the more dependent he became on Tom, her servant, the easier it would be to bring this about. The only difficulties ahead rose from his own people, who would doubtless want him, even though it was many years since he had spent much time at home. If she could only keep Jack under her wing for a while, it would be odd if she failed to influence him. Knowing herself beautiful, she believe that she possessed the necessary charm to attract any man; and she would be rich. Upon that, however, she did not place so much value; for Jack was already well off, and later on, in all probability, would be comparatively wealthy. Her chief fear was that by some stroke of ill luck he might again come into contact with Janet. Failing in her disguised attempts to extract information on events at Kilmona, both from Jack himself and from the other members of the party, she was by no means satisfied.

Gradually she allowed her manner towards him to develop a softness, almost tenderness, without overstepping the boundary which might be thought proper between a hostess and invalid guest who were very old friends. She no longer seemed to plead for any return of sentiment, as she had once so obviously done, but appeared content to let him know that every little thing which she could do for him was a source of happiness and joy to her, which (so much she must be granted) it really was. Beyond that, she could wait.

Kathleen, sweet and thoughtful for others by nature, was especially so to him now, for in a mood of black depression Jack had unburdened himself to Bertie and told him the whole tragic story of his break with Janet. Bertie, full of sympathy, had asked permission to tell Kathleen, and now these two were determined to do all in their power to engineer a "happy ending." Hesitating for long to mention the subject to him herself, one morning as they sat on deck, she had spoken; and Jack, feeling her atmosphere of sympathy, went through the story from the beginning. Kathleen listened very quietly with scarcely a word of interruption, then delicately cross-examined him on various points, especially on the last twenty-four hours at Kilmona. Finally, she said, "There can be only one explanation, Jack, but I hardly dare to suggest it."

"For Heaven's sake," returned Jack, shifting uneasily in his chair, "if you can see anything which might give me a clue and help me to put things straight, don't let any scruples or any kindly consideration for my feelings prevent you. *I* can't account for Janet's sudden change."

"Well, I won't tell you now; I must think it all over carefully. But I promise that before we reach England you shall know what has just occurred to me, even if on second thoughts I disbelieve my own theory."

Jack begged her to say more, but she refused. Several times, when they had been alone, he had renewed his pleading, but without success. She questioned him on various details, but said that she was still considering her theory, and not yet ready to divulge it. When he wanted to know if she had told Bertie, she laughed.

"If I had," she said, "I might as well have told you straight out, for you would worm it out of the dear boy before he knew what you were doing; he is much too simple-minded for a conspirator. When I tell him, I shall probably send him to you to find the missing links in my chain."

* * * * * *

Jack and Bertie were sitting abaft the stern saloon, enjoying the fresh evening air.[24] The course was set for Gibraltar; Malta was fading behind in the mist; the shadows of night brooded over the horizon. Stars soon made the whole moonless sky a glittering glory. There was no wind; smoothly the yacht slipped through the water; a faint sea-music as she sheared aside the low swell, a quiet murmuring from her sides, a rhythmic pulsation, felt rather than heard, emphasised the silence.

"Wonderful night," said Jack. "Makes one feel small to look up at those stars and remember that they are suns—with a family of planets, very likely, much more important than our sun's little lot."

---

[24] Abaft: to the rear of.

Bertie grunted a sympathetic assent. It was a night to encourage confidences, even between Englishmen.

"I suppose," he said presently, leaning back and contemplating the brilliant constellations, "there's a purpose in it all, if we only knew."

"There must be, old man. I'm not much of a philosopher or theologian; these things are too big for me; but now and then, especially on a night like this, one has to wonder about them. I think the last time I spoke of such things was that night when Janet and I were out on the Atlantic, alone. We tried theorising a little, but didn't get much forrader, and afterwards . . . matters nearer home . . . well, we came to earth with rather a bump.[25] Much good it all did, too!"

"I want to ask you a few more questions about that business, old boy, of you don't mind."

Jack smiled, rather wryly.

"Fire away, then. But I've already told you about all I can. Has Kathleen fixed up her theory yet?"

"No; but she has asked me a whole lot about you and your past. Kathleen is terribly thorough, and as counsel in your case she neglects nothing and will examine each witness in turn. I fancy she had been having a go at Thira, unknown to that lady herself, for she has a subtle way of cross-examining. She knows everything that has ever happened to *me*, already; says people ought to know all about each other before they get married, in order to avoid misunderstandings. Fortunately I haven't got a particularly lurid past."

"Good boy," said Jack. "Lucky for you. I think she's about right—though it mightn't work with everybody. If there's nothing hidden, it's all serene—nobody can make trouble after. If I had

[25] Forrader: non-standard spelling of forwarder, meaning further ahead.

been able to spend more time with Janet I would have told her all about myself—although there was nothing very terrible in the way of skeletons in my cupboard to reveal; anyhow, nothing to make her give me up. But get on with your inquisition."

"Well . . . was there ever anything between, you and Thira?"

Jack glared.

"You mean did I . . . betray Colquhoun's trust?"

"Don't be an ass, Jack. I know you didn't. But was there ever—what shall I say?—a flirtation?"

"Thanks, old man . . . . Even if you had suspected me, I ought not to blame you, for appearances might have been misconstrued at one time. No—there was nothing of that sort."

"Then it was really only what we all took it for, simply a Platonic friendship?"

"That's it. Thira and I never touched on the deeper aspects—I mean character and sympathies and that sort of thing. We were just pals over sport and social amusements, nothing more."

"Not on your side, perhaps; on hers, other people were not so sure about it."

"What exactly do you mean by that? What did people imagine? and who were those people? If I am to be open with you, let's have it all, Bertie."

"Sure, old chap. It never occurred to me to think about it; I had known you so long. It was some of the others; they didn't take me into their confidence. But Kathleen has been questioning Mary, and she says that those first weeks at Kilmona they were in rather a stew at the way you were running about with Thira, and the way she always deferred to you and consulted you about everything—in fact, behaved as though the whole show was yours, herself included; and I am bound to say, looking back on it all now with my eyes opened, that it did seem a bit queer."

"Good Lord! What a confoundedly suspicious world it is! Any more revelations?"

"They took credit to themselves for keeping you apart on several occasions, but came down badly on the day of the accident, when you and Thira went off for that ride alone, and were away for so long."

"What! Do you mean to say they thought things weren't quite open and above-board about that ride?"

"Well, it seems that until you had actually started, no one knew that you had gone, or where you had gone."

"Well, I'm damned! Did any of these precious detectives say anything to Janet about their suspicions?"

"As far as Kathleen can find out they didn't; but Janet may have overheard something."

"I don't think so, for it doesn't fit in. She was as sweet as ever after we got Thira off to bed; even more so—because she was so relieved that I hadn't been hurt. She was almost glad it was Thira, in fact."

"Had she any doubts as to your relations with Thira, do you think?"

"She knew exactly what they were—knew everything that had happened between Thira and myself, with possibly one exception."

"Ah! What was that?"

For a minute Jack remained silent, gazing straight in front of him.

"Well, I hadn't meant to speak of it," he said at last. "But as you and Kathleen have been such bricks . . . it's just this. After her fall, Thira seemed somehow different. She showed me pretty plainly that she cared for me more than she should have done. I had fancied so for some time previously, so always avoided dangerous ground and gave her no opportunity for special intimacy; I wouldn't have had anything of that sort happen for worlds. Richard had always treated me with perfect confidence, and trusted me absolutely with Thira anywhere. But that day, after the accident, she as nearly offered herself to me as any woman could, without utter shamelessness."

"Tell me as much as you feel you can, old man; it will go no further than Kathleen, and you can trust her."

"Perfectly, old chap; all the same, I hate giving a woman away. I know she cared; I am afraid she does still, and though she doesn't move my heart a single beat faster, I can't help liking her; we have been friends so long, and she's been awfully decent on the boat and taken no end of trouble about my comfort."

Bertie's smile was a trifle incredulous.

"Anyone would pamper a handsome, eligible invalid. And it hasn't been all unselfishness, my boy."

"Perhaps not, but I can't help feeling rather a rotter talking about her like this."

"Well, you needn't, if you think it's more important to shield her than to solve the mystery about Janet; but you can't have it both ways. You must choose between Thira and Janet."

"Don't be an ass. You know perfectly well I don't want Thira."

"Perhaps not, but women are tricky——"

"O wise one!" interrupted Jack, laughing.

"—some women, anyway," continued Bertie, blushing; "and if you don't look out she will take you whether you wish it or not, before you are aware of it. She has a way with her, my son; and she's up to all the tricks in the noble art of man-catching."

Jack shook his head. "There's only one woman for me, and that's Janet."

"Then for Heaven's sake help us find out what's the matter

and finish your story of that last day."

Jack gave in, and, as far as he could remember, gave every detail of that ride and its sequel, while Bertie listened intently.

* * * * * *

The whole story was soon in Kathleen's possession; but not until their last day on board, as the *Siren* cut through the teasing little waves of the English Channel, did she tell Jack her conclusions.

"As far as I can make out, Jack," she began, "the whole business took place in twelve hours or less. Janet left you that evening as happy as a girl could be, to begin her spell of night-nursing. Thira had been restless, but had apparently settled down for a quiet sleep, and Mary left everything peaceful.

"Next morning, she was simply horrified at the change in Janet; she says she couldn't have believed that just one wakeful night could have made such a difference. The girl had simply gone to pieces, so she sent her off to bed at once, and gave orders that she was on no account to be disturbed. Perhaps you recollect that she didn't put in an appearance at all that morning.

"Later, when Mary saw her again, she had been crying; Mary put it down to her concern about Thira: and still thinks it was that, and says that it is a waste of affection, because Thira doesn't return it or appreciate it in the least. Mary tried to comfort her, and didn't see her again until you were having that terrific tussle with the mare, when she noticed the tense expression on her face, which changed the moment it was all over; she just looked stonily indifferent and walked away without a word.

"Then from Thira herself I got this bit of information. Soon after Janet came on duty she woke, and must have been rather bad, for Janet was devotion itself in ministering to her comfort for some hours; then she says she must have slept, for she dreamed a lot. She has a vague recollection of waking during the night to find Janet bending over her, quite a different Janet—a cold, hard-looking person with no sympathy or kindness in her face. Thira has never been sure whether it really was Janet or only part of her dreams, for in that confused night everything seemed fragmentary; and when she woke again Janet had gone, Mary was there, and the world seemed to be normal once more. The next night she was well enough not to need a nurse, and so she didn't see Janet again for some time, and when she did she seemed just as usual. Thira is sure that something must have happened between you two, though she doesn't know anything definite; but she says that after she got back to London, Janet often came to see her, and would talk about Kilmona, and especially about you, if she got the chance, and was evidently intensely surprised when she learned that you had gone away.

"That's about all I know, but I think it is enough to confirm my reasoning."

Jack had listened attentively, and now sat with a drawn look on his face, thinking deeply.

"And your theory?" he inquired at last.

"It isn't a very clear one, but it seems pretty obvious. My first impression, when I originally told you that I had a 'theory,' was that Thira, of set purpose, had told Janet about some episode between you and herself. I thought that possibly there might have been a flirtation, enough to support a story which could be used to upset poor Janet and set her against you. Of course, I know now that there was never any real foundation for my suspicions, but I also know that there was something between you and Thira, which, unless Janet knew the truth, might, if told to her by someone else, be liable to a completely different construction—in fact, the worst and ugliest construction. I don't believe, now, that Thira purposely told Janet anything about the incidents of that last day, but I think that in her fever she spoke of them, probably from her own point of view, which made them appear much worse than they really were, and exhibited you in pretty dark colours. Just think, Jack, what would be the effect on the mind of a girl like Janet."

Jack's face was grey with pain.

"If your theory is the right one, what must she have thought, poor girl! No wonder she was sickened; it would account for everything she said and did, and even if I had known what she was thinking, I doubt I could have convinced her that it wasn't true. If I get the chance, can I ever make her believe me again?"

"Poor dear!" murmured Kathleen. "I am grieved for Janet too; she must have suffered then, and probably still feels it keenly."

"It's too cruel," said Jack sadly. "And even if we did clear away the misunderstanding, how could I let her waste her years on a wreck like me? She is so full of life; it would be like shutting up a lark in a cage."

"I think you ought to give her the chance of deciding that; if the situation were reversed, and Janet was crippled, what about it?"

Jack appreciated the logic.

"I should want to be with her, near her, to look after her and take care of her."

"Naturally," approved Kathleen.

"Well, anyhow, it's all a dream. She sent me away, and I don't suppose she'll take me back."

"Jack, you've trusted me splendidly, but trust me a little longer; I'll find a way out if I can."

"I would trust you with anything, Kathleen. You're very near the angels, old girl."

CHAPTER XXVI

JACK Winthrop, from a wheeled chair at his window, contemplated Piccadilly and the Green Park gloomily. He had been back in London some weeks, and several specialists had told him little, and done less, to alleviate his trouble; the general opinion seemed to be that some slight displacement of the vertebræ, with a resultant pressure on the spinal cord, was the cause of his paralysis, but so far the seat of the mischief had not been exactly located.

His despondency was pardonable, with such a prospect—to be tied to a wheeled chair for the rest of his life. Sometimes he wondered whether it would be simpler to make an end of everything once and for all. He suffered no pain, but had to depend on others to an extent which irked him intolerably. He remained in London to be near the best advice and treatment, and to undergo a course of massage; but his progress, if there were any, was imperceptible.

It was a beautiful, sunny day, and, as he sat there, the picture before his eyes was full of motion—motion in which he could take no part. It increased his longing; even to be amid the life and activity outside was something, and he was on the point of ringing for his man and ordering his outdoor chair, when the servant announced "Mr. and Mrs. Wilson."

In walked Kathleen and Bertie.

They had been married within a month of their arrival in England, and had only returned from their honeymoon the day before; this visit was the first which they had made. It was a shock to them to find their old friend in a state of such depression, and to learn that his medical advisers held out poor hopes of recovery. They were not, however, the "poor-old-chap-how-sad-for-you" type; Bertie insisted that there must be some means of cure, giving instances of similar cases where the sufferers had completely recovered, and Kathleen, as ever, was sympathetic in the right way. Finding that he seemed apathetic to her suggestions, a sudden idea crossed her mind.

"Why not take tickets for Janet's show?" she said. "I hear it's awfully good, and that she is splendid."

For a moment Jack seemed startled. He looked at her, then turned his head again to the window.

"I don't think I could stand hearing her and seeing her . . . like that, now. I've never seen her since . . . "

"But you must see her again for the first time somewhere, somehow, and it should be easier, there, than to meet in the ordinary way."

"I don't know that there is any 'must' about it," returned Jack. "What would be the good?"

He glanced at his legs, stretched out helplessly on the chair.

"Look here, old chap," exclaimed Bertie, "don't you go off on that tack; you'll get well again all right by and by, so buck up and make up your mind to it."

"It's awfully good of you two to try to cheer me up, but these last few weeks have pretty well knocked all the pluck out of me; if anything could help, it would be the hope of winning Janet back, but . . . once she has made up her mind, she isn't easily turned aside. Quite likely she wouldn't even speak to me now."

"Jack!" Kathleen's voice was reproachful. "You don't know much about women, although you were such a spoilt darling. Women aren't like that. I'd bet anything that Janet must have repented over and over again since she sent you away."

Jack smiled grimly.

"I doubt it. You didn't see her face. It was like a stone mask."

"Well, all the same," insisted Kathleen. "I am right. The silly conventions don't allow women to recant without being asked, or I believe she'd have written to ask you to forgive her even without having matters explained to her; that is, of course, if she had been quite certain that you wanted her."

"Kathleen, you're an optimist."

"Well, I'm going to find out who's right, anyway. I know her pretty well, and I don't think she will have me thrown out; and if she does, it won't make matters any worse."

"You really mustn't do it, Kathleen."

"Why not? Has she heard about your accident?"

"I don't know. She may have; we have several mutual acquaintances, and news travels quickly."

"Well, if she does, and she hasn't even written to tell you how sorry she is, she is a little beast and not the decent girl I have always thought her."

"But how could she write? Didn't you say a minute or two ago that a woman can't make the first advances?"

They sat talking and arguing for some time longer, and the two visitors left with promises to come again soon, and come often until he was tired of them.

"Isn't he in an awful frame of mind!" said Bertie, as hey left the house. "What can we do to rouse him?"

"I'm going to talk to Janet," replied Kathleen. "I'm absolutely certain that when she knows the truth, and the state he is in, she will not only come to her senses but will go and see him—if he gives her half a chance."

"That is just what he won't do while he's crippled. That's Jack all over; obstinate as a pig; he will be full of notions of 'honour' and will shut himself up like an oyster, for fear of letting her see how much he cares and how much he wants her."

Kathleen remained convinced, however, of the rightness of her idea, and a day or two later carried out her intention of visiting Janet.

She was pleased to find her alone, and more than pleased at her reception. Janet was obviously glad to see her again, and was full of inquiries as to all that had happened. She knew of the wedding, but not any of the details, for she had not seen anyone who could tell her about it. She knew that Kathleen and Bertie were with the Colquhoun yachting party, and she had vaguely heard of misfortunes, but not much more than that Colquhoun had been killed in an accident and the trip cut short.

She had not seen Thira, though she had called to express her regrets and sympathy.

As briefly as possible Kathleen outlined the story of the voyage. Janet asked why they went to Purnam, and whether it was part of the original plan, and seemed surprised to her that there had been no set programme, but that they had just drifted in that direction in the course of their journey.

"That's rather odd," she remarked.

"Why? What makes you say that?"

"Well, you see, I received a letter from Thira soon after you left, saying she was sorry that I had refused Mr. Colquhoun's offer. By the bye, you heard that, I expect?"

"Yes, we heard all about it and your refusal."

"She also wrote that you were going to Purnam. That was long before you left Egypt."

"I am not much surprised—I always had a sort of suspicion

that our voyage didn't develop its direction unguided."

"But didn't any of you know where you were going?"

"No, it was all very cleverly done; it seemed to work out in the natural course of events and to be purely a matter of chance that we should arrive at Purnam."

"But perhaps it was chance."

"I don't think so, knowing what I do now."

"What do you know?" asked Janet, in a tense voice, though she was evidently trying to keep it under control.

"I know now that it must have been a 'put-up job,' as they say, and that Thira 'wangled' it so that she might get to Jack Winthrop; doubtless she didn't want people to know she was so flagrantly running after him."

"Was all the 'running after' on her side, do you think? Perhaps he had something to do with the arrangement."

"It was all on her side; I am perfectly clear about that, and when you have heard the rest, I think you will be too."

Kathleen proceeded with her tale, watching carefully to see what impression the various incidents made on Janet. She was soon in no doubt for Janet had given up trying to hide her feelings, and was oblivious of everything except Kathleen's recital.

When the accident, and Colquhoun's death, were told, she shivered.

"Oh, how terrible! Poor Thira!" she exclaimed, But when Kathleen went on to tell of Jack's injuries, she turned pale. Kathleen did not stop, but went straight on with her story.

"But of course he soon got better?" asked Janet.

"No, he didn't get better. We brought him home so crippled that he had to be carried and wheeled about; he couldn't move his legs."

"Where is he now? And what has happened to him since?"

"He is in London, but so far the specialists haven't been able to do anything for him. Bertie and I went to see him the other day; he is quite a broken man, and fears he may be helpless for life. He was such a fine fellow, so full of life and energy, and to see him like this is enough to make one cry. It's so frightfully pathetic."

Kathleen had as yet said nothing of Jack's confidences on the homeward voyage, nor had she let Janet know that she was fully aware of the Kilmona situation.

Janet was evidently painfully moved.

"Has Thira been to see him?" she asked.

"I don't know; but she would do him no good."

"I am not so sure. You say that she was very devoted to him after the catastrophe, and . . . you know that they were great friends at one time."

"Yes; but friendship doesn't always last. Sometimes it fades—and sometimes it goes too far."

Kathleen was getting down to her task.

"If Thira cares, and everything seems to prove that she does, I think he ought to let her help him to forget his troubles as far as possible."

"In what way? And why do you say he 'ought to let her help him'?"

"Because I happen to know something about those two which you don't, Kathleen."

"What do you know?" demanded Kathleen, almost angrily.

"I can't tell you exactly what it is, but I think that if Thira cares, Jack ought to marry her."

"You don't know much about Jack if you think he would ask any woman to marry him in his present state; besides, he doesn't care for Thira in that way, he never has."

"You think he has never cared for Thira as more than a friend? Never cared more than, as Mr. Colquhoun's friend, he should have done?"

"I don't think about it, I know. I know he would never have allowed himself to care dishonourably for his friend's wife. Jack Winthrop is about the straightest man I have ever met."

Kathleen spoke so heatedly that Janet was surprised.

"You think you know all about Jack," she retorted, "but you don't. He isn't the man you believe him to be."

"I don't like your insinuations, Janet. If I don't know all there is to be known about him, then Bertie does. They've knocked about together for years, and Bertie says there isn't a single thing about Jack's life which he need be ashamed of."

"That depends on what a man considers shameful."

"Now, look here, Janet; you and I have always been good friends, but I won't have you suggesting that Bertie, at any rate, would condone anything which was bad form or low down. You just tell me straight out what you mean."

Janet was very obstinate, and it took some shrewd cross-examination before Kathleen managed to extract the truth. Before she succeeded, she had to let her know that her affair with Jack at Kilmona, and its ending, was no secret. Janet tried evasions, but Kathleen pinned her down to the point until the whole story had been made clear.

Having managed to extract that, Kathleen then gave her own version of that last day of Jack's at Kilmona, as he had told it to her. At first, as Jack had prophesied, the girl simply disbelieved it, and Kathleen had hard work to show her that he could have no object in fabricating a story—since it was not until after Colquhoun's death that he spoke, when, had he wished, he could have married

Thira. It was not likely he would have taken the trouble to tell Bertie the story at all if it had not been true, for he had never dreamed that it would be repeated to Janet; and afterwards, when Kathleen had discussed matters with him and suggested that she should tell her, he had objected, and had said that even if she were told she would not believe it. So Kathleen went on, emphasising each point, until Janet gave way in misery and remorse. When Kathleen left her, she urged her to come back soon and bring all the news that she could.

Left to herself, Janet's thoughts wandered in a labyrinth. She realised her absurd—worse than absurd, her wicked error in refusing her lover any chance to clear himself. If only she had listened to his entreaties, or let him have some idea of what was at the bottom of the trouble, he might have been able to remove her suspicions, even though they were so horribly like certainties. If only . . . ! He need never have gone abroad; there would have been no yachting expedition, and no terrible accident. She felt responsible for the whole series of disasters, and it seemed to her that nothing she could do would make up for her fatal stupidity.

CHAPTER XXVII

JACK'S face was drawn with pain, and it would have been hard for anyone who had known him a couple of years before to have recognised him. All the virility which had been so marked had gone; weariness and despondency had taken its place.

He was feeling intensely miserable, particularly hopeless, this afternoon; there seemed to be nothing left in life worth living for. The shattering of his ambitions, the futility of his love, came near to wrecking his faith in everything and everybody. He tolerated the sympathy of his friends, and to some extent tried to repay them by apparent interest in what they had to say and their accounts of how the world went, but it was a poor substitute for what he called life.

He had heard from Bertie, on the previous day, of Kathleen's interview with Janet, and had gathered that after some dispute the correct version of the happenings at Kilmona had been accepted by her. Bertie, fancying himself as a diplomatist, thought that he had conveyed tactfully the impression that Janet was now heartily ashamed of herself and wished to be forgiven. Unfortunately, the impression produced was that she had reluctantly acknowledged that she was mistaken, but that she was fully justified in having given full credence to all she had heard.

Jack felt that there would never be any real reconciliation between himself and Janet again; there might be a sort of patched-up peace, should they happen to meet; though an encounter was hardly likely as things now were. He refused to see anyone except intimate friends, and even in his outings in his bath-chair he sought the semi-seclusion of such places as the Green Park or St. James's Park; Hyde Park or the Row never saw him.

This afternoon he was expecting Kathleen to tea, and was now waiting for her, the tea-table very daintily appointed in her honour.

He was not quite sure whether he was looking forward to seeing her and hearing her account of the interview with Janet; or whether he feared to rouse the pain and longing of old which had settled to a dull, ever-present ache. He was still wondering about it, when the door opened and the servant made an announcement. His back was turned; he did not catch the words, but he heard the door close and knew that someone was in the room.

"I'm glad you have come, Kathleen," he said. "I wasn't quite sure if I should be, but I am."

"Are you?" at the soft voice he started; his heart seemed to miss a beat. He turned his head and saw—Janet.

Half a lifetime seemed to pass in the pause that followed; yet it was but a few seconds before his brain adjusted itself to the shock.

"You!" he answered, at last.

Janet had counted on Kathleen's presence to tide over the first awkward minutes; it had been arranged that she should come at half-past four, and it was now getting on for five.

She felt horribly constrained and shy—almost dismayed. She had meant to gain forgiveness, reconciliation; to capture a lost love; but seeing Jack actually before her, her spirit quailed. In spite of Kathleen's words, the change in his appearance took her by surprise, for it betrayed also a change in the man himself. Here was a much harder, sterner man, almost a stranger, with a look in his face which she had never seen in the old days. She knew at once that she would have to start from the very beginning.

Both felt the situation electrical; neither could tell what the other was thinking or desiring. To Jack, although he was trembling at the sudden appearance of Janet, the whole affair held a sense of unreality; yet he was unutterably glad. She must have realised that she had done him an injustice, and it would be just her way to come and say so; he did not believe that she would acknowledge, even to herself, that she had acted wrongly; so it was rather fine of her to come like this.

Janet's mind, too, was bewildered. She had reflected upon the wrong she had done him, and known, judging only from her own feelings, how he must have suffered; and now she saw suffering such as she had not imagined. She could not believe that he would ever forgive her; to forget would be impossible.

But Jack, regaining self-control, spoke.

"Well!—this is kind of you to come and cheer a fellow up," he said, smiling; but he might have been speaking to an acquaintance made the day before yesterday, and of no particular importance. His tone made Janet shiver; froze on her lips all she had meant to say.

"I only heard yesterday about your accident," she answered hurriedly. "I hadn't any idea that you were hurt, or even that you were in London; if I had known I should have come sooner."

"Jolly of you to say so; but it seems to be the fashion. Several people I never thought much of before have looked me up, though I fear I made a poor return for their kindness, for I simply couldn't say much more than 'How d'you do' and 'Good-bye.' You'll soon be tired of me and sorry that you went out of your way to come."

It made Janet wince; it sounded like the talk of a man in a condemned cell. Her heart ached for him, and the tears were not far from her eyes, but she fought her feelings down before she answered.

"You mustn't talk like that about your friends."

"Ah . . . my friends!" said Jack, with peculiar emphasis. "Some of them do all they possibly can for me; but I haven't yet risen above the rebellious stage. I can't sing hymns and give thanks for my troubles—perhaps that frame of mind will come later."

"It hurts to see you like this," said Janet. Her voice broke, but she went on bravely. "Surely there must be some hope of recovery?"

"The doctors don't seem to think so; at any rate, they haven't done much for me up to now."

"I can't believe there is no hope! If I had to believe that, I think I should die—for it was all my fault."

Jack stared at her. "How on earth can you make that out?"

"If I hadn't sent you away, you would never have gone to that horrible place; then your accident wouldn't have happened. You would never have suffered like this if it hadn't been for me."

"My dear girl, you mustn't look at things in that light! To begin with, you were perfectly right; knowing what you did, or thought you did, you couldn't have done otherwise."

"Oh, but I never *ought* to have thought what I did! I can see it all now. How I could have been such a blind, unbelieving little beast as I was that day, I can't imagine."

"I don't see what else you could have done. Even now you have only my word to go on; and quite possibly—eh?—I am not speaking the truth."

"Don't! Don't make it worse for me. Of course I deserve to be hurt, but it isn't like you to take a petty revenge."

"I am not trying to hurt you, and I wasn't thinking of revenge; that is not my way even now, though I have altered considerably since . . . since then. I have gone far and learnt much these last few months."

"But surely you . . . you can forgive me . . . . Won't you try to, and let me be your friend again?"

"I ask nothing better than to be friends again, and no forgiveness is needed from me to you; if it were, it would be yours even without the asking."

Jack spoke quietly, slowly. Janet's heart beat fast when he began, but it sank when he said, "Nothing better than to be friends." What did he mean? The words seemed to raise a barrier between them. Yet, if he would really allow her to be his friend, she felt that in time she would overcome it.

They had arrived at an impasse for the moment, and the appearance of Kathleen, who came in full of apologies for being so late, relieved the tension. She omitted to mention that she had delayed deliberately in the hope that they might find the lost threads without her help. Janet's face told her at once that matters had not gone as she had hoped.

"You haven't even begun tea without me!" she exclaimed, after greeting them. "That adds to my shame—or did you forget all about it?"

"I'm afraid I am rather a bad host," said Jack. "You see, I haven't had much experience yet in entertaining ladies like this. I was so interested in what you were telling me that I forgot all about the tea."

Janet smiled a little wistfully. "I forgot too, so evidently we didn't want it."

"Well, I want some, anyhow," said Kathleen, picking up the teapot, "so you may as well join me."

Kathleen strove valiantly to keep the conversation general and non-committal, but it was hard work; and even when Captain Seymour called, shortly afterwards, there remained a sense of restraint, although he, not knowing what the others knew, was natural enough and chatted away cheerfully. He was very pleased to see Janet, and told her many details of the voyage and its adventures. She was especially interested in the account of their visit to the tomb of the Princess Ohora, and the suspicion attaching to the unlucky cylinder and its scarab, and for once, Kathleen thought, it brought luck, as it saved the situation and helped them all out.

CHAPTER XXVIII

TIME lagged heavily with Thira, though there was plenty to do if she had chosen to do it. She could not go much into society, being so recently widowed, but there were many people she could have visited quietly and who would have been delighted to come and see her had they been asked. She did not encourage anyone, however. She was in a curiously irritable frame of mind, took little interest in her immediate circle, her friends or neighbours, their doings or sayings. Since her return her life had held a sense of futility; she felt caged, puzzled. During the long voyage home she had founded the whole of her plans for the future on Jack Winthrop, for without him there was nothing left for her; and now she was without him, and could make nothing of him. Since his release from hospital she had visited him as often as she decently could at his rooms, but had altogether failed to establish the relationship she longed for, or even re-establish their old footing of friendship. That could never again be resumed; an undercurrent of self-consciousness must always exist, which had been entirely absent in the days when neither had any thought, desire, or fear beyond the happy, fleeting hour.

Thira understood now that she had overrated her own attractions. Jack had never thought of her in the way she imagined and hoped. She made no pretence to herself as to her own feelings, or what she had been prepared to do to secure his love; even in the days when every feeling of decency and honour ought to have given her pause. Now that there was no longer any impediment between them, other than his lack of response, she gave her desires free rein. She became determined to have her way. She was not convinced that he really did not secretly care for her; knowing how high was his sense of honour, she believed it more likely that he was refusing her advances simply because, as a cripple, he could not allow any woman to sacrifice herself for him; a ridiculous attitude, to her mind, but one, she knew, of which he would be quite capable.

Whatever Thira's faults, however far she had strayed, she was sincere in her love for Jack; but her love was not of that selfless degree which can renounce all, if by so doing the happiness of the beloved may be assured. She would have sacrificed anything for him, but not for his sake. It did not occur to her that he might be happier without her; she felt assured that if only he would surrender to her she could make his life a heaven on earth; and she would have endeavoured to do so. Believing that only a warped sense of honour held him back, because of his crippled condition, she decided that her first step must be to get him cured. In her opinion he was not crippled permanently.

There was a certain well-known quack who made a study of such cases, and Thira wanted Jack to submit himself to this man's treatment. If pity is akin to love, she argued, gratitude surely is nearer kin—and visions of Jack, well once more and so grateful to her that he would almost worship her, glowed in her mind. She was fairly certain that the old affair with Janet, if it had ever been worth fearing, was finished with; also, had there been any other woman in the field, she would have known of it somehow. That could hardly be, so hermit-like was Jack's existence.

She found him, when she next visited him, in his usual depressed frame of mind; the doctors had again failed in some variation of the treatment. It gave her an opportunity; she suggested a conference with her pseudo-physician, and Jack, ready to clutch at any new hope, however faint, agreed to send for the man at the earliest moment. Eventually Thira left him more cheerful than she had seen since his accident, and apparently his attitude towards herself had softened. Altogether, she felt a promising afternoon.

On her way home, she fell in with Captain Seymour, and carried him off to her house for tea; he had not seen her in such good form for many a day, and was agreeably surprised. He soon learnt the cause, for she made no secret of having been to see Jack, of her recommendation, and of her faith in the results. Seymour attributed everything to her admirable kindheartedness and the wish, common to them all, to see their old friend restored to full health. He expressed his approval of her ideas; expatiated on Jack's good fortune in having so many friends who were devoted to him; instanced Kathleen and Bertie, and then remarked how pleased he was that Miss Baxter had discovered Jack again and now went to cheer him up.

It was, one might say, an upper-cut to Thira. This girl, this possible rival, whom she had thought disposed of, on the scene again? What would be Jack's attitude to *her*? But the unconscious Seymour had not finished. Thira had to listen calmly while he "hoped that Janet would go often"; he was sure that "if anyone could cheer Jack up, it would be Janet." At Kilmona, he had felt almost certain that there was "some sort of understanding" between them, and it had always puzzled him why Jack left so suddenly; he supposed there must have been "some sort of lovers' quarrel," but he sincerely hoped that now they had "come together again" they would "make it up." He continued in this happy vein for some time, while Thira, fuming, called him idiot and driveler in thoughts that she ached to frame in savage words. She controlled herself, however, for it would never do to let this interfering intruder know her secret. She must answer him, so she decried the idea of anyone in Jack's condition proposing to a young girl, or even allowing her affections to become set on him.

Seymour replied that if the new cure came off that objection, at any rate, would be removed. Thira countered by saying that a cure, as yet, was far from certain, and that until it was, she felt that any such intrigue should be discouraged.

They argued about it awhile, the Captain innocent of guile. A glimpse of Thira's mind as he left would have astounded him. Alone, she raged; felt that to see Janet dead before her would have been a joy. Were all her schemes, all her hopes, all her dreams for the future to be endangered by this girl, whom she, in her folly, out of kindness, had taken to Kilmona? If only she had left things alone and let Jack treat her as he had at first, let him go on being as rude as he chose, all this would not have happened. But might-have-beens were useless; she must think it out, *do* something. She sat by the fire with her face between her hands and began running through all the possibilities.

Tom entered the room.

"I thought that I had better bring you these things, Madam."

"What are they? I don't want to be bothered just now."

"They are my late master's few pieces of jewellery and such-like."

"Well, why bring them here? And why now?"

"If you please, Madam, as I shall be leaving in the morning to enter Mr. Winthrop's service, I thought I ought to bring them to you personally."

Thira had quite forgotten that Tom was going so soon, and the mere fact that he was to leave to-morrow added to her disgust with the world.

"Put the things down and go away, and don't let anybody come near me until I ring! No one at all. Do you understand? I don't want to be bothered with fools' errands!" she snapped out venomously. Tom hurriedly placed the things on the table and fled, wondering what had happened.

Thira resumed her mental debate, but whipping her mind brought no solution of her problems. At last she rose to dress for her solitary dinner.

Passing the table where Tom had left Colquhoun's things, she glanced over them. Among them lay the unlucky scarab, and the sight of it brought old memories crowding. She was just going to pick it up when she remembered the suspicion with which Mary and Kathleen had always regarded it, so left it alone; but the thought of it obsessed her. Whilst she was being dressed she went over all the circumstances attaching to her possession of it, and the strange misfortunes associated with it. Perhaps, after all, there *was* something evil about the thing; she must get rid of it. But where, how? She could not give it to anyone; it might bring them bad luck too . . . *bad luck* . . .

Like a flash, the unspoken words illuminated a blank space in her mind. The scarab might help. Janet should have it.

CHAPTER XXIX

"HULLO, Jack! How are you to-day? Any improvement yet?" asked Bertie, as he shook hands.

He and Kathleen had come to hear the verdict of the celebrated unqualified practitioner, whose first examination of Jack had taken place on the previous day.

"Nothing doing yet, I'n afraid, old man."

"But what did he do to you or tell you?" asked Kathleen.

"He didn't do anything, except nearly drive me mad by running his long, bony fingers up and down my spine, and sticking them between my ribs."

"Hurt you much?"

"No; but tickled most infernally."

"But what did he *say*, damn you?" demanded Bertie.

"He gave me a rather fluky sporting chance. He says that he could probably cure me, but that, as matters are, he *might* kill me instead. To put me right he would have to try to shift something, but it might move the wrong way, and if so, well then—*finis*."

Bertie whistled, gazed at his friend, and mused. Kathleen looked distressed.

"That's a nice option to give a man. Have you . . . come to a decision? Seems a bit of a risk, old boy."

"Decided at once. If he succeeds—*if!*—I shall be able to stand again immediately, and probably even walk; though, naturally, I must expect to be a bit dicky about the legs after being a 'sitter' for so long. And he promises that there will be no after-effects of weakness—*if!* But I don't mind the 'if'—life isn't too pretty, seen from a bath-chair. He's going to explore my interior next week."

Excitement—sympathy—hope—a tremendous sense of adventure, filled the little room. Jack could talk of little else. If all went well, he said, he could never be sufficiently grateful to Thira for her suggestion, and sang the praises of her kindness, and her tact in not worrying him about it until he had made up his mind; she had not visited him since he saw the doctor, but he expected her soon.

"I am half-ashamed," he added, "at not being able to care for her in the way she would like—but I just can't."

"You certainly ought not to," said Kathleen decidedly. "You would be always regretting it; besides, why should you? Janet has more right to your consideration than Thira; though she may have refused you once, it was all a misunderstanding. She would give the world to set it right."

"Are you quite sure? Isn't it rather that she feels she once did me an injustice and wants to acknowledge it and be honest about it? She has had plenty of time to forget."

"Have you forgotten it?"

"Never; but that's different."

"Then why should Janet? I don't see where the difference comes in, but you may have a chance of finding out what she thinks before long. I shouldn't be surprised if she turned up to-day, for I told her that we were coming to hear the verdict, and she was awfully keen on knowing what had occurred."

They continued discussing the possibilities; both of his guests refused to entertain any doubts upon the success of the operation, though they admitted that it needed some pluck.

"No pluck," said Jack. "Anything's better than twenty or thirty years sitting down!" They were still arguing it out when Tom opened the door and announced "Miss Baxter."

Janet had been relieved, on arriving, to learn that Kathleen and Bertie were there. She was longing to hear the news, and hoped, after her previous experience, that their presence would make matters easier for her. The thought of being again alone with Jack was not exactly unpleasant, but embarrassing.

The story, retold, startled her with its possibility of danger, but she dared not protest.

"Do you think you ought to take such a risk?" she asked him quietly.

"Why not? What use am I now?"

"At any rate you are alive."

"You can't call this being alive. After all, it is for me to choose. If it comes off I shall owe an eternal debt of gratitude to Thira. She has been awfully good to me, and she must be a marvel of kind-heartedness, for I have been a bear to her."

Janet's heart sank. How far might not gratitude lead such a man? It might grow into something more. She could not deny Thira's kindness, having received much from her in the past, when Thira had nothing to gain by helping her; even this afternoon evidence had come that still some kindly feeling remained, in the shape of a note and a little present.

"Yes, Thira is kind-hearted," she answered. "She has been awfully decent to me in the past. I heard from her to-day—she wrote that she thought I might like to have something which she had collected during her yachting trip, and which Richard had worn for some time before his death. I brought it with me to show you in case it might interest you," she added. Opening her bag, she drew out a long thin chain, at the end of which hung the scarab.

"Damnation!" exclaimed Bertie.

"What is it?" asked Jack curiously.

"It's the haunted scarab! Throw it away!" cried Kathleen.

"*Haunted?*" Janet queried. She stood bewildered, the scarab swinging at the end of its chain.

"Yes. Throw it away at once! Drop it before you are hurt. We're not joking, Janet—really."

"How silly! Of course I shan't throw it away. It's much too pretty and quaint."

Kathleen almost snatched at the chain, she took it so hurriedly; Bertie attempted to take it from her, but she stepped quickly back. In so doing she fell over Jack's chair, upsetting herself and him. Jack, feeling himself going, caught automatically at the window curtains; but the strain brought down the curtains and the pole, with a crash, on top of them. The next moment they were all floundering in a heap on the floor.

Janet and Bertie stood astounded at the sudden mishap for a moment, then both sprang to the assistance of their friends. Kathleen was extricated easily, but Jack was not only enveloped in the curtains, but weighed down by the heavy rod, and partly under the overturned chair. At last they lifted him out, half stunned; either the rod or the wainscoting had caught his head as he fell, and blood was running down his face.

Janet was beside herself with anxiety, but Bertie kept cool as usual.

"Ring the bell, Kathleen, if you can get as far. We must have Tom and some hot water and a towel, if not a bandage," he said.

Kathleen, recovered, jumped up and ran to the bell.

Jack, still on the floor, gradually gaining his senses, took out his handkerchief and dabbed the trickle of blood.

"What the devil happened?" he asked.

"It was all my fault," cried Kathleen. "I fell against your chair and upset you, but I don't know what brought the curtain down. I am so awfully sorry! I am afraid I must have hurt you horribly."

"It's only a scratch," said Jack, "or a bruise. I remember I caught at the curtain to save myself, and, of course, down came the whole show. It was a funny upset altogether, and I don't yet understand how it happened, or what all the fuss was about."

Just then Tom arrived in answer to the bell. His mouth opened in astonishment at the sight of his master sitting on a heap of curtains, his face smeared with blood. The accident was briefly explained to him, and he was told to assist in getting Jack into his chair.

Bertie and Tom stooped to lift Jack, and had already raised him when he shouted. Thinking that they were hurting him, they stopped.

"Are we giving you a twinge, old man?" asked Bertie. "Are you more damaged than you thought?"

"No! It wasn't that . . . I say, old chap—I can feel my legs!"

For a minute Bertie did not grasp what he meant.

"Do you mean they're hurt?"

"No—I can *feel* them! Of course you don't get it; but I mean that I can feel that I have *got* legs! I haven't known they were there, except by looking, since the accident at Purnam."

"Do you mean that you can move them?"

"I don't know. Let me try! I can't the way you are holding me. Put me on a chair. Not my wheel chair, that other ordinary chair."

They did as he wished, and to his own almost delirious joy, and the delight of his friends, he found that he could move his feet and legs slightly in a natural way.

"I say!" he cried, "I believe that whack has done the trick without the help of Bob Sawyer's descendant.[26] Look here, you two, just catch hold of me and lift me on to my feet, so that I can try if the rest of me will move too."

They raised him carefully. Very slowly and heavily he moved first the right foot and then the left; and then, supported by an arm on each side, managed to take a step or two forward.

"Good heavens! It's done it!" he cried.

"Oh, thank God! Thank God!" cried Janet, with tears of joy running down her face, not caring in the least what the others thought.

"Kathleen," said Jack, "I shall bless you for the remainder of my days for having knocked me over and given me just the bump I needed."

"Dear boy, I'm so glad." Kathleen was ready to cry for sheer joy at seeing Jack on his feet again.

"It's a rum go, but I think that you ought to see the doctor, after all," said Bertie.

"What for, when the job's done?"

"So that he can see if you are really quite cured, or whether you must still be very careful until you are perfectly right. Don't you think so, Kathleen?"

"Perhaps it would be as well. Do you think we could get him now? It's a bit late, but those chaps often stick to work at all hours. We could try. Shall we?"

"Oh, please do," said Janet, who had been very quiet but who was now radiant. She was not thinking of herself, or of what this change might mean for her; she was simply overcome with

---

[26] Bob Sawyer is a dissipated medical student in *The Pickwick Papers* by Charles Dickens.

happiness at seeing him better. His whole aspect had changed even in those few minutes; he looked on the way to regain his hold on life.

"Well—what about the telephone?" said Jack.

"Just tidy up those curtains as much as you can, Tom," he added, "and then send out for someone to come and put them up again; the room looks horribly bare with them down."

"Yes, sir." Tom stooped to gather them together, and picked something up. Bertie, watching him, saw what it was.

"Put that down quickly!" he almost shouted, and Tom, looking rather amazed at receiving so peremptory an order, placed the scarab on a table.

"Beg pardon, sir, but I was wondering how that thing came here."

"Miss Baxter brought it, if you want to know."

"Beg pardon, sir, but it came as a sort of surprise. I know as how I ought not to have asked, but the last time I saw it, it was in Mrs. Colquhoun's drawing-room, and I was a little took aback to find it here. You'll excuse me, sir, but it does seem a bit queer that whatever that thing happens to be about something always goes wrong. I venture to think that it would be best put away."

"We are agreed on that, Tom," said Kathleen.

"Yes, ma'am. I couldn't help overhearing what you used to say about it sometimes on board the *Siren* to Mrs. Colquhoun; but she wouldn't take no notice, and we all know what came of it. If I might make so bold as to say so, Miss, I don't think you would be wise to have it about you," he said, turning to Janet.

"Well, if it brought bad luck before, it has brought good luck this time, hasn't it? And really I don't quite see what I am to do. I can't very well send it back to Thira, can I?" she asked, turning to the others.

"She ought never to have sent it to you, knowing what she did about it," said Bertie.

"Perhaps I had better burn it," said Janet, and moved to pick it up.

"Don't you touch it!" snapped Jack from his chair.

Janet stopped short, surprised at the tone of his voice, but with her hand still outstretched.

"You aren't to touch the thing," said Jack again.

"But why not? It's mine."

"No, it isn't," said Kathleen. "It really belongs to Professor Tremaine. He only lent it to me; he said he might want it back again, to finish his investigations; all things considered, I think it had better go back to him at once."

"I think it had better remain where it is," said Jack, "for from all accounts it doesn't seem to have any evil effects as long as it is left alone."

And so it was agreed that it should remain with Jack for the present, and the party dispersed, Bertie alone waiting to hear the doctor's verdict and promising to hurry back with the news.

CHAPTER XXX

THE doctor, intensely interested in Jack's account of his accident and its results, made a very close and careful examination. He said that the fall, or the blow, had done everything which he himself would have tried to do, and had removed the cause of all the trouble, and that if Jack would go gently for some time, in order to give his nerves and muscles a chance of recovering their form, a few months would see him completely recovered.

Fortunately there is no need to describe Jack's feelings. His whole outlook had suddenly been changed and restored to its old values; in fact, it was life again, instead of mere existence, and no ordinary trouble, he thought, would ever have power to depress him after such an experience. But . . . the manner of the cure! It was simply bewildering; all the circumstances were so queer. Odd indeed, for one thing, that Janet should have brought the scarab to his room, and that Kathleen, by just tripping over his chair and upsetting him, should evolve so much good out of a seeming evil.

He was in his sitting-room again, having—magnificent achievement!—walked there unaided, his legs being still shaky and his gait decidedly unsteady; nevertheless, he could walk, thank God! Musing over it all, he began thinking of the scarab and its history, and of the misfortunes which had befallen everyone who had owned or worn it. It seemed scarcely credible that the inert curio could possess evil powers; yet there could be no doubt that misfortune dogged those who had been associated with it recently. Certainly the others seemed quite convinced of its "black magic"; but, if that were so, why had Thira sent it to Janet?

As he pondered, the reason formed slowly in his brain—a reason he was reluctant to accept. Yet it looked suspicious. Could she have sent it to Janet so that its ill-luck might in some manner fall upon her? He hated the thought, but it would not be set aside; the more he considered it, the more damning the evidence became against Thira. There seemed to be no other ground for her selection of just that gift; and why, in any case, should she have sent a present to Janet just now at all, unless . . . ? He rang the bell for Tom.

Tom, perplexed, went creditably through a very thorough examination on the whole history of the scarab, as far as he knew it, since it had come into Kathleen's possession; on all the details of the voyage of the *Siren*, and everything else which by any possibility could bear on the subject. Finally he was sent for a small cardboard box, string, paper, and sealing-wax.

Jack had made up his mind what to do.

He packed up the mystery and sent it by post to Thira, with a note saying that Miss Baxter had left it behind her, having had an accident with it; also, having learnt from Kathleen and Bertie the suspicions of danger to any owner of it, he expressed some surprise that Thira, knowing its history, should have selected it as a present.

That was all, but it was enough.

*   *   *   *   *   *

"DEAR JACK,—I received your letter and the scarab. It was not a nice letter, and I don't know what you meant, and I don't think I deserved it from you. After all the years we have been such good friends, I should not have expected you to insinuate that, knowing the scarab carried bad luck, I sent it to Janet for some occult reason which you omit to explain; neither can I see why you should imagine I wished her bad luck. Certainly you do not actually say as much, but, reading between the lines, I can put no other construction on your words. Well at any rate, I don't believe in the theory, and am going to wear it always, night and day, so we shall see how much truth there is in it. I am very glad to hear that you are better, and shall hope to see you again soon and find you in a sweeter temper.—Yours ever, THIRA."

So wrote Thira on receipt of Jack's letter. The return of the scarab had come as a shock; she felt her castles falling, and saw Jack slipping from her. That this latest disaster was partly of her own making only incensed her more deeply, for Jack's meaning was quite clear, and she felt that unless she could remove all suspicion that she intended evil to Janet, he would never believe in her again and there would be an end to her hopes. Apart from this, hope lingered, for now that Jack was getting well she thought she stood a better chance than before.

She only partially believed in the scarab's influence, and if, by wearing it, she could prove to Jack that his suspicions had been unfounded and unworthy, she felt that he would be ashamed, and might give her the opportunity she desired so feverishly. The game was worth the candle, so she sent her letter, and waited.

CHAPTER XXXI

NOW that he was restored to health, Jack had fully made up his mind that he would try to undo the mischief which had broken the bond between himself and Janet. The right course, he realised, was to go to her, and gladly he went. Waiting in her drawing-room, he was strangely excited. How would it end? What would she think? What would she say? He must win her back . . . . The door opened, and she was there.

Each had prepared many speeches for this anticipated moment; but fate, impatient, took the lovers in hand at once; even the weather-talk was omitted.

For a moment, and only a moment, Janet stood there with shining eyes. Then she was in Jack's arms, and everything was forgotten. In that kiss all her waiting, hoping, longing, broke up and melted away; she was as one who comes home again after long years of exile.

"Thank God!" whispered Jack. "I have got my little girl back."

"Jack! Dear, dear Jack! However could I let you go?"

"That's all over, darling! We have found each other. Nothing else matters."

Nothing else, she knew, mattered; enough for her to cling to him, to feel his strong arms round her. Enough for him to know all barriers were down at last.

He swayed a little; for a moment he thought he would fall—his strength was slow in returning.

Janet, realising this, ran to get a chair.

"How selfish of me to let you stand! Come, dearest, let's sit down and be comfy."

Together, as lovers will, they confessed and forgave; and then came the more sober talk which was needed to explain the unillumined patches in the story of those lost months. Jack asked Janet why she had refused Thira's invitation for their yachting expedition, and she explained that she had not the remotest idea that Purnam was on their itinerary; not until long after the *Siren* had sailed did a letter come from Thira, saying that she meant to go there and expected to see Jack. Janet described her trouble of mind when she had learnt this; how she had raved at having thrown away the chance of at least seeing him, although, on the other hand, she had at times felt that it would have been misery to see him with Thira, knowing what she did—or rather thought she did.

Jack then told her all about his relations with Thira, and just how far they had gone; his astonishment when the yacht arrived at Purnam, with Thira on board; told her of the accident, of Thira's kindness to him on their homeward voyage, and of the beast he had felt for not being able to reciprocate in the way he knew she desired, even though he doubted whether there were the ghost of a chance of her, Janet, relenting.

It was rather a sad story that he unfolded, and there were tears in Janet's eyes as she listened.

Among other matters, they discussed the scarab and its attributes. Neither of them put their suspicion into words as to why Thira had sent it to Janet, but it was vividly present in their minds, and there seemed no room for any doubt.

At long last Jack tore himself away, with instructions and promises to come again at the earliest possible moment the next day.

"I shan't sleep for excitement," said Janet, as he left her.

"I shall sleep better than I have for months," said Jack. "And my dreams——"

"Your dreams . . . you shall tell me to-morrow, dear."

CHAPTER XXXII

KATHLEEN and Bertie rejoiced at the good news, so successful an end to their scheming. They had been the first to hear it, for both Janet and Jack had rung them up immediately to convey informal thanks to the conspirators.

Captain Seymour and Mary were not far behind with congratulations. They happened—it was not an uncommon occurrence—to be together when they heard of it; of course both said that they had foreseen it all along, in fact they had known that things must end in an engagement even so far back as the days of Kilmona.

But while congratulations flooded in, it was noticeable that Thira held aloof. Mary had rung her up to tell her the news, but her reception of it was not exactly demonstrative; and the answer "Not at home" had greeted Seymour's call shortly afterwards. No one had seen her or been able to ascertain what she really thought about it.

Kathleen and Bertie, to celebrate the occasion, determined to invite all the members of the Kilmona party to dine, without letting their individual guests know that the others would be there. Thira, however, sent a refusal, giving as a reason that she was not yet dining out.

It was a merry company which gathered at Kathleen's table, and she was a very proud young hostess, for it was almost her first big party in her own house. The old joyous spirit of Kilmona days at their best seemed to preside, and chaff and banter flew furiously. Mary's liveliness was noticeable, and Seymour, in good form, was full of genial humour.

The ladies had retired from the table, and the men were about to follow, when a servant brought in the evening paper. Bertie was setting it aside, when a question as to an event of the day made him open it. The others noticed his glance become fixed, his hands grip the paper rigidly.

"What is it, Bertie?" asked Seymour.

"Read it," he said, passing the sheet across, and indicating a certain headline.

Captain Seymour took the paper.

"How awful," he said, in a low voice. "It's about Thira, you fellows. She's . . . we shan't see her again . . . . Shall I read it?"

They assented, anxiously listening as he began:

"TRAGIC DEATH OF A WELL-KNOWN SOCIETY LADY

"The death of Mrs. Colquhoun, the widow of the late Mr. Richard Colquhoun, who himself met his death in a sudden and tragic manner a few months ago, is reported this morning.

"The circumstances of the case are as follows:

"The servants in the Colquhoun household were awakened in the early hours of the morning by a strong smell of burning. A search of the house soon made it evident that the source of it was Mrs. Colquhoun's bedroom, the door of which was locked. No response being obtainable in answer to continuous knocking, assistance was obtained from the fire brigade and the door was forced.

"The room was found to be full of thick acrid smoke, and it was only with the aid of their masks that the firemen were able to penetrate into it. They discovered that the bed had been on fire, and was still smouldering. Quickly extinguishing it, they then discovered that the curtains had slipped and partly fallen on a small night-lamp which it had always been the lady's custom to keep burning beside her bed; being of heavy woollen material, they had not blazed up, but had merely smouldered slowly, and were even at the time only partly consumed, the fire not having reached the bed-linen.

"On the removal of the superincumbent mass, the unfortunate lady was found to be dead. A doctor, hurriedly summoned, pronounced life to be extinct. There were no marks of burning on the body, neither was there any disfigurement or other visible damage. The cause of death appears to have been suffocation, whether by the curtains or by the smoke has not yet transpired, but will doubtless be cleared up at the inquest, which must, of course, be held."

There was a dead silence in the room when Seymour finished, broken in a few seconds by low-toned expressions of horror. The shocking story, at once conveyed to the ladies, put an end to the evening's merriment, and after a desultory discussion of it the party broke up. To several of them it had been a nerve-shattering piece of news, and to all a matter of personal concern, for Thira had been a general favourite among her friends.

Jack and Janet remained behind, purposely detained by Kathleen.

"I want to ask you all something," she said.

They gathered round and gave her their attention, for her voice was grave.

"Do you think it had anything to do with the scarab? You sent it back to Thira, didn't you, Jack?"

"Yes, I did, and she took it rather badly. She wrote that I had practically accused her of sending it to Janet by way of trying to bring misfortune upon her, and said that to prove how little value she attached to the suspicion of its evil influence, she intended always to wear it, to show me how much I had misjudged her. I didn't believe that she meant it, but it is quite possible that she carried out her idea."

"What madness if she did," cried Janet, aghast.

"Yes," said Kathleen. "It was sheer perversity, for she had seen all that happened before to other people, and had once tried it herself; you remember when the topsail fell on her?"

"I fancy she was a bit mad lately," said Bertie. "At any rate, that is the kindest way of looking at it."

They left it at that, and Jack took Janet home. In the cab she asked a question.

"Jack, do you think she was trying to get killed?"

"No, darling. She wasn't that sort."

"Then why did she wear the scarab?"

"Do you think that we ought to try to arrive at her secrets now? The old saying still stands good, 'De mortuis nil nisi bonum'; oughtn't we to leave it alone?"[27]

---

[27] Of the dead speak nothing but good.

CHAPTER XXXIII

SOME months later, Jack and Janet were sitting at breakfast in their pretty morning-room, opening their letters.

They had been quietly married within a few weeks of Thira Colquhoun's death, and they had settled down to happy married life in their country home. Jack had recovered his strength, and both of them loved the country, where crowds and social "crushes" were unknown.

"This one is from our old friend, Captain Seymour," said Jack. "He wants us to go up to London and stay with him for a couple of nights; says he has something very interesting to show us, and is asking some friends to meet us. Shall we go?"

"I suppose that we ought to; but I'm not a bit keen. London doesn't attract me."

Jack laughed.

"You're a real home bird! Well—shall I say 'Yes' or 'No'?"

"You had better accept. I shouldn't like to hurt his feelings, for he's rather a dear. When are we to go?"

"He says next Thursday; to-day is Friday, so we have time to think about it."

They were very curious at the hint in Seymour's letter, but soon gave up guessing, and were not sorry at the opportunity of again seeing the old sailor who had shown them so much kindness in the past.

He received them very warmly at his house in Chester Square, but refused any information until the evening; nor would he say whom they were to meet.

It was a very pleasant surprise, when they assembled for dinner, to find the guests were Kathleen and Bertie, Mary Macintyre, Captain Teed, and Dr. Smith—in fact, the whole of the survivors of the *Siren's* party.

Janet had never met Dr. Smith or Captain Teed before, but she had heard so much about them that they seemed friends at once. She was immediately on good terms with Teed, though it was not so easy to feel at home with Dr. Smith, with his rather formal manner. She soon found out that the others knew no more than herself about the reason of the gathering, and Seymour steadfastly declined to be drawn.

Not until coffee had been served in the drawing-room did their host disclose his secret. He opened with a little set speech.

"My dear friends," he began, "I have asked you here this evening in order that we may be together in the conclusion, as far as we shall ever be able to arrive at the conclusion, of a mystery with which all but two of those present became associated at the same time, and with which the excepted two have since become associated most closely and curiously.

"It will be within the recollection of all but those two that after the visit to the tombs which we made with Professor Tremaine, the Professor promised us that if he solved the mystery of the death of that unfortunate lady, Princess Ohora, he would let us know.

"You also remember that, after we had left Egypt and were on our way down the Red Sea, it was discovered that the small ivory cylinder which Tremaine had given to Miss Boston, now Mrs. Wilson, was not what it appeared to be, but was really the covering of a parchment, or rather of a papyrus.

"You will remember that this document, having been removed from the broken cylinder, was carefully and cleverly restored and placed under glass by Captain Teed; also that the cylinder contained an Egyptian scarab, in a gold setting, the seal on which was similar to that on the document.

"The series of accidents which seemed to follow the possession of that cylinder will still be vividly present in your memories, and I need scarcely refer to them; you will recollect, however, that in response to Mrs. Wilson's urgent entreaties, it was decided to return the cylinder and its contents to Professor Tremaine; and that they were so returned from Aden.

"Unfortunately the scarab did not accompany the cylinder and papyrus, but was retained by Mrs. Colquhoun. I say unfortunately, because events which followed, and revelations which I am now in the position to make to you, taken together, can leave no doubt that the retention of that scarab was responsible for the deaths of two of the company, and of much sorrow to us all; although there were certain after effects which must not be classed as misfortunes." Here Seymour looked across to Janet.

"Within the last few days a letter had reached me which I am about to read to you; it is from our very charming friend, Professor Tremaine. He writes as follows:

" 'MY DEAR CAPTAIN SEYMOUR,—You will remember, perhaps, that when we parted in Egypt, I promised to let you know if ever I should be able to unmask the mystery of those tombs which we explored together with out friends. Alas, that two of those friends are no more! The unfortunate news has come to me that both Madame and Monsieur Colquhoun have come to death, and both in a dreadful manner. That being so, I had to think to whom I might communicate my discoveries, and as your address was that I could most easily obtain, I am taking this liberty to send to you a brief account, or a history, which I have succeeded to draw from the papyrus that you so kindly sent me, and others which, as a result, were also found; together with aid from the inscriptions on the wall of the larger chamber, which you saw when you were visiting the tombs.

" 'The translation is very crude and by no means finished, but I trust that not the less you may find interest, as also my other dear remaining friends, if you are able to be in communication with them.

" 'With my most profound expression of regard, I have the honour to remain,

" 'HUGO MARIE TREMAINE.' "

Seymour then read the document here reproduced:

THE STORY OF THE PRINCESS OHORA

In the fifth year of the most mighty King Amenhotep, Ruler of Upper and Lower Egypt, Lord of the World, and most sacred Monarch of all people, it came to pass that a certain woman of the temples found favour in the King's sight, and that it pleased him to take her to himself to wife.

Now this Princess, being a priestess of the Temple, had much knowledge which was not given to the people. She had, in fact, knowledge which was not before given even unto the King himself. She was also learned in many arts which were only usual to the priesthood and not known to others.

The priests were therefore afraid, and there was much outcry among them that the King should do this thing, but the King laughed in his beard, saying, "What! Shall I, the King, be ruled by priests? Am I not greater far than all, yea, even than the priests, for am I not High Priest by reason of my kingship? Am I not the road of my people to the fields of heaven? Get ye hence and trouble me not, lest evil befall you."

So the priests fled from the King's presence; yet in going did they murmur that it was an evil thing which the King did, and that evil would come of it.

Now the woman being come into the King's household and the King's bed, became to the King of exceeding great value; he made great gifts to her; of whatsoever she asked of him, that he gave to her; for he loved her with a great love, such as he had given to no other woman of his palace.

Now it came to pass that the woman, being taken to the King's heart, became bold to make clear to the King certain matters pertaining to the ways of the priests and their doings within the sacred houses.

The King was greatly angered when he learned of these things, understanding wherefore those priests had resisted his taking of the woman to himself; and the King, having great wisdom, read the riddle, that they had so acted for fear lest he might learn from the woman of their evil doings, and that punishment might fall upon them.

Then the King called together a great assembly of the chiefs of the people, and he stood before them in all his glory with his standard-bearers and swordsmen round him, and the great men of his council, and the governors of the provinces and a great assembly of soldiers; and thus spoke the King unto them, telling them of those things which had come to his knowledge, saying:

"Shall we abide this thing in our midst? That the houses of our gods, the sacred virgins, our daughters and our young sisters, shall be for the pleasure of these vile men? Shall we not rather cast them out utterly, so that the houses of the gods may be cleansed and re-established; and sacrifice be made of great repentance and purification?"

Then the people cred out with one voice:

"Let an end be made of this abomination."

Thereupon the King spake unto his Captains and soldiers, saying:

"Hearken unto the voice of the people, to the voice of the Councillors, to the voice of the wise men. Go forth in my name. Take the priests from the temples which I tell unto you; bring them forth and let them be destroyed, as a peace-offering to the gods; that the land may be clean and peace be again among us."

Then went forth the Captains and the soldiers, and they entered into the temples and gathered the priests together and brought them forth and slew a great multitude of them; and the people rejoiced at the doing, for the priests had wrought evilly with the people, compelling them to give whatsoever they had lusted after, and this they had done falsely in the name of their gods; and no man had dared to complain, for fear worse must befall him.

But some of the priests, being forewarned, or being at a distance, escaped and fled to remote places, and hid themselves.

Thereafter the King made new priests and a new religion, and there was peace and happiness in the land.

Now the King was much honoured; also the Princess Ohora was revered of all the people for that she had brought this matter to pass; and the King, seeing how she was beloved of the people, and himself having great love for her, made her his Queen; the Queen of all Egypt, the Upper and the Lower, so that her word was first in the land after that of the King.

Now the Queen sent out spies to find out those priests who had fled and escaped destruction. Many were taken and put to death, but some were yet left, and those that remained hated the

Queen Ohora with a deadly hatred, and plotted how they might be revenged upon her.

And it came to pass that the King made a journey throughout his kingdom, that he might himself see what was the state of his people. Chiefly he journeyed in the royal ship, and his beloved Queen journeyed with him, also a great concourse of courtiers, councillors, guards, and servants.

Now on a certain day it pleased the King to visit the tombs of his fathers that he might make sacrifice for them, as was meet, and as was the custom from time to time. Therefore the King got down from his ship and was carried in his palanquin across the green lands to the outer desert and the place of the tombs; much of his people went with him and the Queen also went, being weary of the ship and desiring to see the country, and the tombs, and the temples. Now the day being hot and her lord being occupied with his pious devotions within the tombs, the Queen gave orders to erect her tent near by one of the smaller temples, amidst a grove of trees. There she rested for a while, her ladies waiting on her and music being made for her.

Then was the Queen desirous to go up into the temple, and took her most favoured lady and a few guards, and went thither. At the gates she bade her guards stand and await her; she herself entering the temple with only her lady.

Now after some while the King, having finished with the making of sacrifice, returned to the tents seeking the Queen, but she was not yet there. The messengers flew to report to her the coming of the King, but they came again, saying that the Queen was still in the temple and that the guards dare not enter since she had bade them stay without. Then the King, being much vexed, went himself to seek her, and being entered into the temple found none within; very wroth, the King came forth and spake furiously to the guard, saying:

"The Queen is not within, and yet ye linger; surely ye must have slept when she passed out."

Then were the guards full of fear, but they made bold to answer:

"O Lord and King, neither sleep nor slumber has been with us. Here, where the Queen commanded, have we stood, since she entered within, and none has passed in or out."

Then the King caused search to be made whether there might be any other entrance, but none was found; neither was the Queen found nor the lady who had gone in with her. Then a great fear fell upon the King lest evil might have befallen her, and he caused the whole company to search for her round about; and the guards who had been at the door, he had bound.

Then sought they in all places, but found not.

And a madness possessed the King, and he caused those guards to be brought before him, and questioned them; but they could tell nothing, having seen nothing. Therefore the King had them beaten with rods, but yet they could tell him nothing; so he beat them yet more, until some died; but, learning nothing, he desisted from his rage.

Then he caused to be sent down to the ships to bring engineers and more men. Very quickly came the engineers, and the King commanded them that they should pull down that temple, stone by stone, and that none of the whole company should go hence until that was accomplished. He caused guards to be set round about in two circles, at one hundred paces and at three hundred paces from the temple, and he placed officers in command that no one should pass, either to come in or to go out, save with his seal. Then the King withdrew into his tend full of grief.

Therefore the engineers fell upon the temple and tore it down, and now, behold it was revealed that there were secret chambers and a secret stairway going down. Then was word sent to the King, and he came hurriedly and commanded that soldiers should go down to see what they might find. Then the soldiers went down and they brought back the body of that lady who went with the Queen; it was found in a chamber below, but of the Queen found they no trace.

Then the King went himself down into the earth with his chief men; and he, having come into a large place, no other way was seen, in or out, save only that by which he had come in. So the King commanded to break down the walls and to tear up the floor and to finish pulling down the temple. So the engineers toiled further; and behold yet again, in the wall of the chamber, was found a hidden way, but this way went out into the desert, behind certain hills, where the ground was stony, and there ended.

So the King caused fresh search to be made, and every temple like unto that whence the Queen had been lost, he broke down. He caused vigilant search to be made for those remaining priests of the old faith; and wheresoever one was taken he caused him to be tortured, to draw from him all that he might know. For of his own mind, the King was assured that it was the work of the priests which had taken his Queen from him.

Many priests died, but told nothing. Then on a day came the officers of the King, saying:

"O Lord and King, we have made a man speak, and this is the manner of his speech: 'Behold, the priests made a plot to take the Queen alive and carry her off to use her against thee, O King. They put spies in thy household who should tell them whither she went, so that they might get at her.' The names of the spies we have also. They were all of the Queen's household among her women."

Then was the King more furious than ever before, and he cried out:

"Is this man yet dead?"

And they answered him:

"Nay, O Lord and King, he is not yet dead."

Then went the King unto the torture-chamber, and had even more grievous pains put upon that man, so that he might reveal the place to which the Queen had been taken; notwithstanding that the man cried out that he knew not, not being of the inner council; and continued to cry out until he died.

Thereafter the King caused those others, the spies to be sought out, and he dealt terribly with them; in such ways that none had ever thought of before, so that their lamentations were fearful to hear. All that they could they told, hoping to save themselves, but whither the Queen had been taken they told not, for that they knew not. So these also died and yet the Queen was not found. Long time the King continued to search, but found not, though thousands of people sought and many priests were taken and after torture died, and many temples were destroyed in the searching.

Never again in the life of the King was any trace of the Queen Ohora found. So the King came to his time; and he too died, and was buried with his fathers in the tombs of the Kings.

CHAPTER XXXIV

NOTE BY PROFESSOR TREMAINE

HERE we come to the end of the story of Ohora and Amenhotep as depicted by the frescoes. But it was fated that the mystery should be solved through other channels—from those little ivory cylinders which so puzzled us, and which we at first thought to be of not much value. It was not very long after you had visited us, that news came to me that certain Arabs had been overwhelmed in a sand-storm and utterly destroyed. We went to see if anything could be done, but there was nothing to do except to bury them properly. It was, however, most curious that they should turn out to be our tomb robbers. From their baggage was recovered all those things which they had stolen from the tombs.

Now, therefore, we had in our hands all the clues, except that which we learned only later from you; the secret of the hollow cylinders. At last, when we had that also, we were able to place the whole story together. It must be put in more simple language than the story of the King, for it is not of the connected style of the hieroglyphics as that is.

THE STORY OF THE PRIESTS AND THE QUEEN OHORA

The priests of Amon, having been driven from their temples by the King, on account of their evil ways, sought sanctuary in obscure places in the outlying corners of the land, among the rocks and hills and in the more distant oases.

But even thus they were not safe, for, urged on by the Queen Ohora, the soldiers of the King sought out many and destroyed them; so that each month which passed saw them more reduced in numbers, and it seemed that, after a time, not one would be left alive.

Then those that yet remained took counsel together how they might escape. To leave the country was impossible, for on two sides was the sea, and on the others the desert and the wild peoples of the south. To attempt the desert meant probably death by thirst; to go south, captivity and death at the hands of the savages. Therefore they agreed that they must by some means contrive to put an end to the Queen Ohora, to whom they attributed all their troubles, and without whom they believed that their persecution would cease.

Even yet among the people they had their friends and supporters, so that it was not difficult for them to obtain spies who would keep them informed as to what was in progress. Even in the royal household they managed to introduce their emissaries; but they could do no more at the beginning, for fear was abroad, and none dare raise his hand against the Queen for terror of what might befall at the King's behest.

Almost the priests and their party were in despair when news came of a proposed Royal progress throughout the land. At this the wretched men took heart, for during the journeyings of the Court into far districts, it seemed likely that by some means they would be able to accomplish their evil designs. So they redoubled their spies and sent their people among the King's servants, and arranged for messengers to bring them news of what was forward. So it fell out that they knew exactly where the King would go, and what he intended to do from day to day.

When the news came that he was to go to the tombs of his fathers to make sacrifice, they rejoiced, for they felt that their chance was come. Some of them actually ventured in disguise into the royal household; others, more fanatical than the rest, prepared to slay the Queen with their own hands, if necessary, even at the sacrifice of their lives, should opportunity offer.

Now, among the Queen's women were several spies, and these, learning that the Queen intended to visit the small temple near the tombs, in the cool of the evening, managed to send word to her foes of this matter. Then the priests who were concealed among the servants found their way to that temple and hid themselves.

This temple at that time had no priests in charge; it being of the forbidden faith, and therefore deserted.

Having their task thus made the more easy, the priests hid in the temple and so placed themselves that, should the guards come within, they could fall upon them from behind and slay them suddenly by stealth, thus taking the Queen alive. This they would do by throwing a cloth over her head and binding her.

It fell out that the Queen came without her guard, and with only one lady-in-waiting, so that the attack was simple, and both women were taken in cloths. Then they were quickly bound and carried down to a secret chamber which was well known to some of the priests. Here the lady-in-waiting, being only an encumbrance and of no value for their purpose, was quickly strangled, while the Queen herself was borne away through a secret passage, and so into the desert out of sight of all her people.

Near the exit to this passage was the entrance to yet another secret way which led down into the lower chambers of the tombs, so concealed that none but those acquainted with the secret could find it. Into this passage the priests carried the Queen, and so down to the vaults beneath.

Here it would seem they kept her a prisoner for a long time, themselves not venturing forth until the hue and cry had died down. Exactly how long this phase lasted, or what happened in the interval, is unknown; but after a time it would seem that the priests tried to bargain with their unhappy captive; her life was to be spared in exchange for help in restoring them to their former offices. In this they were unsuccessful. The Queen seems to have scorned their offers and, even in the dire danger, to have treated them with scathing contempt. But those priests were not to be lightly turned aside from their purpose, and failing persuasion, they tried various forms of torture.

All of these things they duly recorded; why, it is rather difficult to understand, unless it were that in case of success they might obtain due credit from their colleagues. It was certainly a dangerous thing for them to have done.

They attempted to force the Queen to sign certain papers, but this she refused to do, even though they starved her until the verge of death. All that they obtained from her was the calling down on themselves of the most frightful curses; which filled them with fear.

Finally they threatened her with the awful death of slow suffocation by the waxed cloth, unless she would do as they desired. It would seem that she remained obdurate and they became desperate, and decided to make an end of her; thus, at least, they would put it out of her power to do them further harm.

Therefore having inflicted upon her every possible indignity, they made ready to finish her. She was already very near death; the vile creatures jeered and scoffed at the poor helpless woman, thinking that she could do them no harm. Death would be welcome to her as a release; but in her last moments she rallied sufficiently to lay upon them the most awful curses, foretelling how but few of them should ever leave those tombs alive, and that those who did should be taken by the King and should die in horrible agonies.

She cursed them and everything pertaining to them; having herself been a priestess, she knew their weakness. She cursed the place where they had laid her; everything that they touched or should hereafter touch; anyone that should again lay hands on hers or anything of hers so long as she might yet be alive; or afterwards, so long as her body should lie there.

At last, to silence her awful tongue, some of the bolder among them seized her and wound the waxed cloth, previously prepared, tightly round her face and head, so silencing her for ever.

That done, they seem to have recovered from their dread of her, and to have remembered that as a priestess she must at least be decently buried—or perhaps it was really their superstitious fear of the unburied dead which compelled their action. At any rate, they proceeded with the embalming and entombing of her poor outraged body. Whilst some of them did this, others were dispatched to carry the news to their friends outside; others, again, must have written the records of the happenings; for they were all set down, though in such a manner as to make their action appear as virtuous retributive justice, instead of the brutal murder which it actually was.

The remains were placed in a stone coffin, together with all that belonged to her in the shape of dress and jewellery; they dared keep nothing of hers for fear of the curses which she had attached to these things.

They enclosed a copy of the records which they had made in small ivory cylinders and placed them in the coffin beside her. Thereafter, they must have sealed down the stone lid, probably to make any wandering of her spiritual body impossible; and thus left her where she lay, to lie there through the centuries undisturbed.

Now among those curses which she had uttered, were these:

That if anyone dishonoured or removed her body from the sepulchre they should die the death in some sudden and awful form. That if her grave were left unnamed and unknown, those responsible should never see the light of day. Also, she laid her most frightful curse on anyone who might hereafter use her seal or take possession of it. She would doubtless fear the priests using that seal for their own evil ends; so she foretold that any one who took her seal should die by the same death as that by which she had died; namely, by suffocation upon them suddenly and without their knowing how or whence it came. That anyone even handling that seal should run the risk of death, but might escape by surrendering it. She swore that she would not rest in her grave until all that she foretold had come to pass.

* * * * * *

How are we to account for the mysterious happenings for which we cannot find any explanation? Every day many things happen round us, and even to us, which we could not explain if we were asked to do so, and yet we accept them as a matter of course; why then question those other things which are outside and beyond our finite understanding?

Now it has fallen to me, Hugo Marie Tremaine, after many thousands of years, to record these facts and to certify to the verification of some at least of those weird and terrible prophecies.

Even before we had finished piecing together the fragments of this story, in the course of our researches we found something which, later on, we could not fail to associate with these prophecies.

We discovered that the well by which we had entered that chamber was not the sole way by which entrance could be made. One day, examining the walls, we observed what seemed to be a very close joint or a line left by the chisels of the builders, and not far from that we found yet another. This aroused our curiosity. Hitherto we had been of the opinion that the whole chamber had been hewn out of the living rock, and that there was no way in or out save by the well.

Further investigation was rewarded by the discovery that there was a huge single slab of stone which, when pressure was applied, revolved on a central pivot, giving access to a passage through the rock. This way led up a long slope to another room of a similar sort; from there, another passage led towards the face of the cliffs, but at a different angle from that through which we had made our entry at the beginning of our discoveries. We were able to follow this new road for some distance, but then it was blocked by a fall of the roof.

This seemed a natural fall, and was composed of loose stones, some quite small, others so large that we had to resort to blasting before we could remove them. Beyond this fall was a clear space of some length, and then again there had been another collapse of the roof. So far as we were able to judge, the rest of the roof was perfectly sound; even our blasting seemed to have had no effect on it.

In the space between those two falls of the roof, we found the skeletons of a number of men, together with a few articles of metal, such as bronze knives and ornaments.

Now how had those men come to be there? It was self-evident that they had been trapped by the falls of the roof; but it appeared strange that two such falls should have occurred at the moment when those people happened to be between.

The obvious conjecture must be that those bones represented the remains of the murderers, attempting to leave the scene of their foul deeds.

Thus one prophecy at least was fulfilled.

Later, another curious thing came to pass:

We had never further disturbed that poor one in her coffin. Somehow it went against the feelings to do so; also, it was perhaps because, at the first, we could not have brought her out of the tombs in her coffin through that very narrow crooked passage which you will remember; to have attempted to move her without the coffin appeared to be impossible, for the remains were so frail that to have tried to lift and carry them would have resulted in breaking the poor body into fragments. So we had left her to lie there as she was when we found her.

It was only after we had cleared the new way and opened a fresh way out, which was straight and easy, that we really thought again of removing her. We went to look to see how best it should be done, but, having decided as to that, we wished to look upon her once more as she lay there, and as we had at first seen her on finding her. We gently lifted the stone lid of the coffin.

There was no body. Nothing but a thin layer of greyish powder.

Was it merely that nature had finished her work, and that the action of the air had completed the decay of ages, and that the poor, weary bones had fallen to dust, and with them their wrappings?

Or was it perhaps that, her prophecies all fulfilled, she was at last free and at peace; and so went hence?

www.ingramcontent.com/pod-product-compliance
Lightning Source LLC
Chambersburg PA
CBHW020933310726
48980CB00007B/756/J
* 9 7 8 1 9 1 7 1 1 3 0 6 9 *